Baby Dear

Linda Huber

For my Huber and Keller families in Switzerland

Prologue

The baby was still crying on the sofa, blood smeared down the front of her pink cardigan. He was sorry about that, poor baby – she must feel terrible with all that gunge on her chest. But at least the wails were dying down; it was more like whimpering now. He stared at her for a moment – not touching, in case he set the howls off again – just looking. How perfect she was.

It was time. Thank God he still had the gun. He stood in the living room doorway where no one would see him from outside. The metal was cool in his hand; he took a deep, shaky breath and then another. Could he do this? Should he? Yes, of course he should, in fact he must, because it was the only way to end this hell. How good it would feel to be rid of the pain and confusion – when was the last time he'd felt like a normal human being, the last time he'd been happy? Weeks, if not months, and that was no way to live.

He gripped the gun, his hand shaking, and stared at the baby. Had all that blood really come from such a small human being? But it wasn't his blood either and oh, no, her thin little voice was yowling again, so maybe she was in pain. Quick, quick. It was the best way out for them both. They'd be together forever in heaven, and that would never happen in real life now.

Even as a boy he'd been a good shot, one of those kids who always won the big cuddly toys you got at fairgrounds for shooting plastic discs off the wall. This would be much easier, but could he do it? End a life?

His girl…

He should do this quickly and put them both out of their misery. Eyes fixed on the baby, he raised the gun.

Chapter One

Caro

Caroline Horne shifted on her chair, the hard plastic hot beneath her legs. What was it with waiting rooms? She'd been okay about the appointment before she got here, but now butterflies the size of squirrels were crashing around in her tummy, and Jeff was hyperventilating beside her. This was their long-awaited consultation after the first round of fertility tests, and the outcome was the most important thing in Caro's life. She wanted a baby to love. End of. Pushing unsteady fingers through brown curls, she exhaled through pursed lips. *How much longer?*

'Mr and Mrs Horne? You can come through now. Dr Bingham will be with you in a moment.'

A nurse led them into the consulting room and Caro perched on another uncomfortable chair, fighting to keep her hands steady. She clasped them firmly round her handbag and glanced at Jeff. He was trying to look at ease, leaning back in his chair with his legs stretched out, but she could see his fingers shaking, and the hair above his brow was dark red with sweat.

Dr Bingham strode in, all distinguished grey hair and 'Good to see you two again'. He took his place on the comfortable chair behind the desk, and clicked around on the computer.

'Have you got the results?' It was out before Caro had time to think. But there was no reason she shouldn't ask; doctors weren't gods in white coats nowadays, and he knew as well as Jeff did how she felt about this baby – the one who didn't exist yet.

As Dr Bingham leaned across the desk and clasped his hands, panic seared through Caro. This wasn't going to be good news;

1

she could tell. She reached across and gripped Jeff's hand, and he squeezed back.

Dr Bingham's voice oozed warmth and sympathy. 'We have and I'm sorry, but there's a problem.'

Caro closed her eyes. No, no. Every other woman she knew could have babies. Why couldn't she?

'Mr Horne – Jeff, I'm afraid the problem lies with you.'

Caro's eyes shot open – what was he saying? A guttural croak rasped from Jeff's throat as he snatched his hand away, feet jerking back under his chair.

'What problem?' Again, it was Caro who asked. Her hands were slippery on her bag. This couldn't be happening. The nurse was giving Jeff a glass of water, and his teeth were chattering against it.

Dr Bingham began to explain. It was one of those things, he said, not anyone's fault, though Caro could tell this was something he said to all the worried couples in a situation like this. It was better if it wasn't anyone's fault.

She couldn't help herself; she began to cry, and the doctor pushed an almost-empty box of tissues towards her. Jeff tried to take her hand, but she needed both of hers to blow her nose and wipe her eyes. The doctor went on to say Jeff's sperm count was low. Very low. All but non-existent, in fact. A horrible wave of nausea hit Caro, and Jeff slumped in his chair, his cheeks turning mottled red and white. Dr Bingham went on with his explanation, sympathy written all over his face, though of course it was an act. Doctors didn't get personally involved.

Caro sat there, stiff and unmoving as a white-hot thread of horror gripped her heart and spread like fire to every corner of her being. 'So – can I still have a baby?' It came out in a squeak.

If they wanted a child that was biologically theirs, explained Dr Bingham, the only option was IVF. In-vitro fertilisation. Jeff's almost non-existent sperm could be injected into Caro's eggs to see if a baby would start. If it did, it would be replanted into Caro's womb to grow. But Jeff's sperm was apparently of such poor quality that even this was unlikely.

Caro stared at the doctor, unable to speak. So. There would be no baby for her and Jeff. No pram-pushing in the park, no school run, no happy family. No everything she'd ever wanted, everything she'd been planning for the past two and a bit years.

Dr Bingham came around the desk and sat on the edge right in front of them. 'There are other options. Artificial insemination, or…'

Jeff leapt up. 'No – way,' he said, and Caro flinched at the despair in his voice. 'I do – not – want – another man's child growing in my wife.'

He fled from the room, and Caro blinked at the doctor. Exactly three minutes later she was running after Jeff, clutching a handful of leaflets on everything from IVF to adoption.

And her whole world was a different place.

Chapter Two

Sharon

Sharon Morrison rolled her feet to the floor, then heaved herself up from the sofa, one arm round her enormous belly. She stood for a moment to get her balance and caught sight of her reflection in the glass door of the drinks cabinet. How on earth had her life come to this?

It was crass. She spent half the time panting and puffing because the baby was taking up so much room she couldn't breathe properly, and she could hardly move because she'd put on sixteen kilos and waddled now instead of walking. With her long blonde hair and pink-and-white complexion, she looked like Miss Piggy on an off-day.

Blinking back tears, Sharon trailed into the kitchen to put the kettle on. Afternoon tea for one, and it would be dinner for one too. Craig had gone to Glasgow for an Opticians Association dinner, and normally she'd have gone with him, wearing a lovely evening dress and feeling glamorous beside her tall Mr Darcy-lookalike husband. Glamorous! That was a bad joke these days, when she barely managed half-an-hour without rushing to the loo. Posh dinners and networking with Craig's colleagues was beyond her, so he'd gone without her – but that was typical of their marriage nowadays.

She stood massaging her bump and was rewarded by the usual gut-wrenching sensation as the baby moved beneath her hands. It was a girl; they'd known that since the 20-week scan. In spite of herself Sharon smiled, then pressed her lips together as two tears escaped and trickled down to her chin. They hadn't planned this baby. They'd been busy working their way up their respective career ladders and collecting furniture for the flat, one of five luxury apartments in the centre of Bridgehead. They had the best one, right on top with a roof terrace overlooking the river. On a clear day, you could see Edinburgh and the Forth Bridges. Life had been exactly as Sharon wanted it – fun, interesting and heaven knows she was married to the man of her dreams.

Then around the middle of October she'd been sick two mornings in a row. The first time she blamed the sushi she'd had at a party the night before, though Craig was fine and he'd eaten sushi too. But the following morning she was sick again and somehow, she felt different. A niggling suspicion was worming its way into her head. That tummy bug she'd had a few weeks ago… Sharon bought a pregnancy test on the way to work and locked herself in the loo as soon as she got there. Positive. The doctor confirmed that even one day of the runs could be – and obviously had been – enough to stop her pill working.

So, there she was, pregnant and scared and resentful, knowing Craig would be scared and resentful too, and he was. Oh, they'd talked about a baby one day – in five or six years, maybe. But not yet. The baby had stolen five years of her life. Why had she kept it? Her good Catholic upbringing could take the blame for that.

The kettle boiled and Sharon poured water over a Lady Grey teabag in the Clarice Cliff mug Craig had given her last Christmas. A comfort drink in an expensive mug. Had Craig arrived in Glasgow yet? In the pre-pregnancy days, they'd texted each other about things like that, but this baby had put an end to even light-hearted communication, never mind the deep stuff. It was dire. Sharon had no idea how Craig felt about approaching fatherhood, or the sudden terrible change in their relationship. He'd never been big on heart-to-hearts, and now he was ignoring the pregnancy as hard as he could. What if he couldn't live with a baby? What if she couldn't? What if he left her?

Sharon pushed the mug away. If she stayed here any longer she would go bananas. The sun was shining – she would walk through the park to the library.

Pulling her jacket round her bump, she left the flat. It wasn't going to be a fascinating outing. But at least it was a distraction from being four weeks away from giving birth and still not sure if you wanted to be a mother.

Julie

Ten to three, her shift was nearly over. Julie Mayhew wheeled the 'Returns' trolley over to the 'B' section in Bridgehead Public Library and began to insert the books into the shelves. Dan Brown had done well this week; he always did in the holiday season. So had Agatha Christie, thanks to the recent series of Poirot films on TV, and Miss Marple had profited by association.

Julie glanced outside as she moved across to 'D'. A woman was making her way up the driveway, hands clasped under an enormous belly. The poor soul looked as if she could barely put one foot in front of the other; she had flopped down on the bench under the ash tree now. Julie winced in sympathy. It could have been her a few months ago, hugely pregnant and permanently exhausted. This woman was about her age, but the resemblance between them ended there, if that posh maternity outfit was anything to go by.

Julie glanced down at her own clothes and grinned. Who cared that she was wearing chain store trousers and a blouse from Mirabelle's pre-summer sale? Her figure was back to normal at last.

'Off you go now, Julie. I'll finish these.'

Dee-Cee Taylor, the head librarian, took over the trolley, and Julie escaped.

Her steps slowed as she drew level with the woman on the bench. 'Are you okay? I work here – would you like to come in for a cup of tea?'

The words were out before she'd engaged her brain and Julie had to force herself not to glance at her watch. If she took this woman inside for tea there would be no time to do the shopping before collecting Sam from After School Club and Amy from the child minder's, which would mean dragging a tired four-year-old and a baby round the supermarket. Not a great end to the working day.

The woman heaved herself up. 'I'd kill for a cup of anything wet. It was further than I thought, coming here. And my legs don't seem to hold me up as well these days.'

The words were cynical, but gratitude flitted across the other woman's face before being replaced by a wry expression.

'Been there and got two t-shirts,' said Julie, linking arms. Time to do her good deed for the day.

It was difficult to keep the humorous tone in her voice when she heard the woman's story, though. It was so different to her own. This Sharon had both money and a husband, and although she admitted she'd planned to start a family 'someday', neither she nor her husband seemed to be looking forward to their baby.

Julie was silent for a moment. Even during the worst time, just after Matt left, she had never stopped wanting her children. In fact, being Sam's mum and looking forward to Amy's birth were the two things that had kept her going.

'You think I'm a selfish cow,' said Sharon, and Julie could hear the flatness in her voice.

'I think you're a scared selfish cow,' she said frankly, leaning back in her chair. 'Are you worried your husband might leave you? Or have an affair? I've got both those t-shirts too – but it doesn't take a pregnancy for it to happen.'

Sharon rubbed her hands over her face. 'Some t-shirt collection you've got. I suppose I am looking forward to the baby. In a way. But – nothing's going to be the same again, is it? I don't know anyone else with a baby, and I don't know what Craig thinks about it all either.'

Julie stood up. 'Look, I have to collect my kids. Why don't we go somewhere for lunch on Wednesday? I finish work at twelve. You'd meet my little one and we'd have more time to talk.

And I could introduce you to a couple of friends with babies. One of them's due in four weeks so you might even end up in the labour ward together.'

'Great. We can yell a duet across the corridor.'

They made arrangements, then Julie raced towards the town centre. At least Sharon had a sense of humour. It sounded like she'd need it.

Jeff

The supermarket was going to be mobbed. Four o'clock on Monday afternoon wasn't a good time to go shopping, he thought, staring glumly at his list. He and Caro did the weekly shop on Thursdays, but of course last week Jeff hadn't known he was going to need ingredients for a special meal.

He stood at the kitchen window and watched as the Cameron's Ford lurched into the carport next door. Gina helped her two oldest kids from the car and then unloaded the baby, and hot tears sprang into Jeff's eyes. How lucky they were. Gina would have been to the park with the other mums, and they'd have talked about heaven knows what and played with the kids, maybe had a coffee somewhere. How Caro would have loved to be a part of all this, no, how she *would* love it – because it wasn't completely impossible, was it? Surely, they might still become parents someday?

Dream on, said a sarcastic little voice in his head.

Jeff turned back to the immaculate kitchen and slid a cup into the espresso machine. Dr Bingham's words last week had echoed round and round his head ever since, and he hadn't been able to stop them. It had been the worst afternoon of his life – talk about Black Friday. What were they going to do?

Jeff lifted his cup and wandered through to the living room, picturing his wife with a baby. Cradling it and singing – happy, smiling, loving, like she'd always wanted. What if she left him? Another man would be able to give her a baby.

For the nth time since Friday, a wave of nausea rolled through him, and Jeff massaged his stomach, taking shallow breaths. He had a lovely wife he was crazy about, and a beautiful home. It was enough for him, but Caro wanted nothing more than to be a mother. They'd been married for just over two years and trying for a baby almost since the beginning.

A sob caught in Jeff's throat. He and Caro were happy together. He could give her everything else she wanted – she wouldn't want to split up over this, would she? The weekend had passed in a daze; they'd barely talked about the implications of his infertility, mainly because he'd escaped to work for most of the time. He couldn't face Caro's eyes and it was all too raw, too painful. But they had to talk.

Which was why he was planning a special meal for tonight. Good food, a glass or two of wine, and they could have a long chat and put things right.

Jeff drained his cup, checked his wallet and went out to the hallway for the car key. It was good luck he wasn't working this evening. He usually did on Mondays, but Davie had phoned that morning and asked him to change shifts in Cybersonics, the internet café they ran together, so a special meal for Caro would be no problem. He was going to make chicken curry – it was her favourite and they had a brilliant recipe. The list of ingredients was long, but the supermarket would have everything.

A sob caught in his throat. How very much simpler life would be if he could buy a baby too.

Caro

Caro pushed rice and curry sauce round her plate, forcing herself to swallow the odd mouthful and trying to avoid Jeff's eyes. For once, a lovely meal cooked by her husband wasn't making her feel cherished. As if a plate of curry would solve anything. Jeff's behaviour over the weekend had been the pits and although she could imagine how gutted he must be, ignoring the problem wasn't the way to go. On Friday afternoon she'd been desperate to talk about this baby they were so unlikely to have, but Jeff had blocked her every time she'd started. Then he'd vanished out to work and she'd barely seen him since.

'Another chapatti, love? They're the good ones.'

Caro glanced up and then down again. His expression was so hopeful – it was pathetic. This was so not what she'd signed up for. Hot resentment fizzed inside her, and she could feel her face closing. She probably looked like a teenager in a strop and she didn't want that, she wanted to behave like a grown-up. But that was impossible with Jeff gazing at her like a hungry dog trying to ingratiate itself with its owner.

He had obviously planned this meal so that they could talk, have a heart-to-heart like they'd done when they decided to go for tests in the first place. So why was he yakking on about bloody chapattis? But then, she wasn't talking either.

'I'll halve one with you,' said Jeff brightly, tearing a chapatti in two and putting one piece by Caro's plate. 'Come on, love. It's your favourite and I made it specially. I – I want us to talk, Caro.'

She made herself look into his spaniel eyes, weariness washing through her. He had put on a clean shirt for their meal and she was a mess. She'd barely slept all weekend and she hadn't done her face again after work. But what did any of that matter? Caro laid her fork down. Food was the last thing she could face right now.

'Oh Jeff,' she said, hearing the depression in her voice. 'I'd have talked all you wanted on Friday, but now... What can we possibly say that'll change anything?'

He began to tremble, and she saw the sweat shining on his brow. 'Caro, love, I want us to get through this and be happy together. Of course I want a baby too, but – surely we are more important? Our marriage?'

Theoretically, he was right, but it was exactly what Caro didn't want to hear, because it wasn't true for her. A baby was an absolute necessity if she was going to be happy. It was actually the biggest reason she'd married Jeff.

'Our family is the most important thing,' she said heavily. 'You and me – and our baby. But it doesn't look like there's going to be a baby, does it?'

He was silent, cowed in his chair.

Caro fiddled with her fork, then took a deep breath. She would say exactly what she was thinking. 'I went on the internet and found out more about IVF,' she said, looking straight at him.

He mopped his brow with the Easter chick serviette left over from the last dinner party, when someone had teased them about being 'dinks' and Caro had laughed and said they wouldn't have a double income forever. Everything was rosy then; she'd been happy and hopeful about the upcoming tests, because doctors could do everything, couldn't they?

She'd found out different now. 'Jeff, it sounds horrific. They bombard you with hormones to stimulate your egg production. I could end up bloated, with a permanent headache and mood swings worse than you get in the menopause. And there's no guarantee of success, it's actually a lot more likely to fail. You heard what Dr Bingham said. I just don't know if I could take it… But if I don't, there won't be a baby, end of, and if I do there most likely wouldn't be a baby either. The whole thing sucks.'

His Adam's apple moved up and down and for a moment she felt sorry for him. This wasn't his fault. He was so infatuated with her, had been from the day they met, at a barn dance Caro's workmates dragged her to. Jeff was a lovely guy, nine years older and more sophisticated – not to mention rich – and Caro had allowed herself to be swept off her feet. The following week she'd come back here with him, seen the house, and realised this was the relationship she'd been waiting for. Except now she knew it wasn't.

If he would only accept that this terrible thing was happening to them, then maybe they could find a way round the problem. She'd have nothing against artificial insemination. But he was trying to play it down, and that was very hard to take. His next words only confirmed this.

'Well, love, maybe we can look into adoption? Or – or foster care, or something? We won't give up, will we?'

Something inside Caro snapped. She leapt to her feet and with one swift movement swept plate, glass and cutlery from the table. 'Don't you understand? Don't you even care? You don't, do you? You know we wouldn't get a new baby to adopt, they're toddlers at best and usually a lot older – and I'm not going to foster a baby and then have it taken away again. I really, really wanted my own tiny baby to love right from the moment it's born, Jeff. I wanted to be *pregnant* and that's not going to happen. I feel like someone I love has died.'

She left Jeff amidst the wreckage of his dinner table and took refuge in the bathroom, listening to him clearing up downstairs. Still fuming, Caro ran a bath, and when it was full she lay back in the hot suds and closed her eyes. She shouldn't have chucked all that stuff on the floor, but it was so frustrating. It didn't seem to matter to Jeff that they couldn't have a baby. Or at least, it mattered in a different way.

Caro slid under the water. A bath was a good idea, she thought dully. Warmth comforted, and heaven knows she needed comfort. Her life was in tatters.

Sitting up again, she took the loofah and started to massage round her shoulders. This was the time of year for short sleeves and skinny tops. Caro gazed miserably at her slim, perfect body. Oh, to be a big fat pregnant mum with stretch marks and varicose veins, and a bump with a baby that kicked and made ripples in the bathwater, like Louise's had. Louise had been pregnant last year and she hadn't talked about anything else. And Caro had to sit in the same office all through the pregnancy, listening to the details… Why not me, why not me, her soul shrieked every day. I've been trying all this time, what's wrong with me?

Now she knew there was nothing wrong with her. What on earth were they supposed to tell people? A low sperm count was such an embarrassing thing to have to admit to.

The water was barely lukewarm now and Caro reached to pull out the plug. Tears mingling with bathwater on her face, she stepped onto the mat and wrapped herself in a towel. If she stayed, she would be drying off this same horrible skinny no-baby and not-a-mum body for the rest of her life. If she left Jeff, she could kiss goodbye to the lifestyle she'd become used to. Where was the way forward there?

All Jeff wanted was for them to grow old together and weather life's storms. Well, this was one of life's storms. But right now, Caro wasn't at all sure she could weather it.

Chapter Three

Sharon

S haron drained her mug and clunked it down on the coffee table. She had a whole day ahead of her and nothing to fill the hours until it was time to be a proper little housewife and make dinner for Craig coming home. No classes with students making funny mistakes, no banter amongst the other English teachers in the staff room and no-one saying, 'Hey, you must read this, it's brilliant.' Just her and the bump. Full stop.

At least she had tomorrow's lunch with Julie to look forward to. Today she would – yes, she would go into town and buy some lovely smelly stuff, then come home and pamper herself. She should make the most of the peace and quiet, because before long she'd be changing nappies and shushing a screaming baby.

Sharon pressed her lips together. Pampering herself was well and good, but she couldn't pamper away the fears, could she? They – and the baby – kept her awake at night. What if she hated being a parent? What if Craig hated it? And the big, huge, heavy one – what if she took one look at the baby and thought – oh my God, no?

Get a grip, woman, she told herself. Look on the bright side. Four more weeks and then at least you'll be able to leave the baby in a different room now and then. Sharon pulled her cardigan over the bump, knowing she was whistling in the dark.

An hour later she was walking along the High Street – who was she kidding, she was waddling better than Donald Duck. Sharon glared at her reflection in the shoe shop window, then turned into the largest department store in town and made her way to the cosmetics section.

A sales assistant rushed to help her. 'Body lotion? Right.' She produced two sample bottles and set them on the counter. 'Try these, they're nice and light and flowery. Here, sit down, take your time.'

Sharon allowed herself to be creamed and advised and eventually persuaded into buying several bottles and jars, and left the shop feeling much more positive. She would window-shop down the High Street now, then go home along the river pathway and after lunch she would put a lounger on the terrace, do her nails, and blob. Shopping was tiring.

She stopped for a moment to look at a jeweller's display, then moved on more slowly, dismayed to find her legs trembling. This whole pregnancy thing was so crappy; her body didn't belong to her any more. A wave of giddiness hit her and she put out a hand and steadied herself on the nearest shop window. The feeling got worse, though, and black spots appeared before Sharon's eyes. She dropped her bag and leaned her head on the window, conscious that her heart was pounding and sweat had broken out on her face.

'Are you okay? Can I help?'

'Take her other side, Phil. In you come, love.'

Men's voices were speaking, and Sharon felt strong hands grip her arms. She was walked indoors and lowered onto a hard chair. The dizziness receded as she leaned her head on a counter, breathing deeply as doubts swirled mockingly round her head. *Why am I doing this? – I'll never make it as a mother. I don't want to, either.* Tears, never far away, rushed into her eyes and she wiped them away with a cold hand. A man was staring at her, his face shocked. Hell – had she spoken aloud?

'Here you are.' A younger man brought her a glass of water and Sharon took a sip, sitting straighter on her chair. That was better, thank goodness she hadn't passed right out. She looked round. This was Bridgehead's one and only internet café. The two men were standing on either side of her chair, gazing at her with almost comically concerned expressions. The older one was clutching a mobile, his thumb hovering over the '9' button.

'Should I call an ambulance?'

15

Sharon shook her head. 'No need for that. It's just this—' She choked the words 'bloody pregnancy' back. '—just what being pregnant does to you. It's the pits, but I'll live to see another day. I guess.' She smiled to show she was fine, and sipped again.

The older man frowned. 'You shouldn't be alone now – is there someone you could call? Or shall I get you a taxi?'

Sharon thought. In spite of her automatically humorous reply she still felt weak. Suppose something like this had happened when she was crossing the road, or walking beside the river? There was nothing funny about that.

She glanced at her watch. Good, it was almost lunchtime. 'I'll call my husband – he's an optician; he owns the shop at the top of the High Street.'

Craig was concerned and promised to collect her straightaway. Sharon ended the call and nodded at her rescuers.

'Sorted. I'm Sharon Morrison, by the way.'

The older man perched on a chair beside her. 'I'm Jeff Horne and this is Phil Waterson, who is supposed to be with his Over-60's Course right now.'

He jerked his head and Phil gave a mock salute before jogging back to a group of older people at the rear of the shop.

Jeff Horne was staring at her bump. 'When's the baby due, then?'

Sharon pulled a face. 'End of June. I'm beginning to wonder if I'll last the pace.'

He nodded. 'It'll be worth it, though, when the baby's here.'

Sharon pulled out a tissue and dabbed her face. What a mess she must look – that face pack was going to have its work cut out. Hopefully the rest of her pregnancy wasn't going to be like this, or she wouldn't be able to put a foot over the door. That would be the last straw.

'I suppose so,' she said. 'Look, there's Craig now. Thanks a million, Jeff. If I ever need an internet café, I'll come straight to you.'

He helped her up from the chair and picked up her bag. 'I hope you will. We do courses too – you could come and learn something. Or we could start a mother and baby group, now there's a thought.'

Sharon took her bag and did her best to smile. Mother and baby group – what a nerd. But he was only trying to be funny, and he'd saved her from passing out on the street, which would definitely have involved an ambulance and a trip to hospital. She should be grateful.

Craig ran up from the car. 'For God's sake, Sharon, are you okay? Let's get you home and phone the midwife. Someone should check you over. And the baby, of course.'

Sharon settled into the car, closing her eyes as Craig pulled away from the kerb. She would be fine, she knew. And the baby was fine too, if the kicks were anything to go by. No need for the midwife, but they could argue about that at home.

Jeff

Jeff stood in the doorway, watching as Craig's car accelerated down the High Street and turned right at the traffic lights. It had been a shock coming across a hugely pregnant woman like that; his failure to give Caro a baby was mocking him at every turn. It was a failure that wouldn't go away and it left him with a heavy, sick feeling in his gut. It was grim – all Caro wanted was to be pregnant, and Sharon had been so blasé about it. Not exactly brimming over with the joys of prospective motherhood, was she? Talk about ungrateful. Of course, it must be difficult, being enormous like that and passing out all over the place – was she really all right? It would be good to know for sure and he'd let her go without getting her number. Still – he knew Craig worked in the swish little optician's that had been a dairy when Jeff was a child. He'd gone there most days after school and spent a couple of pence on sweeties.

The Over-60's group were getting ready to leave and exchanging banter with Phil. Jeff escaped into the staffroom and flopped into a chair. He still had to come to a decision about his own baby problem. Meeting Sharon had made him realise anew how bad things were. He tried to imagine Caro with a bump like Sharon's, but it wasn't easy; Caro was as thin as a rake. He would lose her if he wasn't careful and he couldn't, couldn't lose Caro. But she wanted a baby and he wasn't able to give her one... the usual way.

So. Maybe he should start considering unusual ways. Something he'd thought yesterday shimmered back into Jeff's head and his breath caught. Maybe he could – buy a baby. Maybe that wasn't such a way-out idea. Babies weren't all lovingly expected and wanted, were they? Somewhere, some woman or girl must be having a baby she didn't want to raise. All he had to do was find her. He could put a couple of feelers out on the World Wide Web right now; Twitter might be a good place to start. He could try different hash tags. He typed swiftly – good God, find a baby, get a baby, even buy a baby. They all existed. Jeff leaned back in his chair, mentally composing his tweet. With a bit of luck, they'd soon be a family of three after all. And Caro wouldn't be as blasé about it as Sharon was.

In fact, now he came to think about it, Sharon hadn't as much been blasé as unwilling. And although there was nothing to say that Craig and Sharon would want to pass their baby on to someone else, they had shown him clearly that not everyone was overjoyed at the prospect of becoming a parent. Sharon certainly wasn't, and Craig had rushed in swearing and only mentioned the baby as an afterthought. If these two were run-of-the-mill parents-in-waiting, it should be fairly easy to find someone even less keen who would provide him with an unwanted child. A baby for Caro to love.

Sharon had given him faith in unwilling mothers.

Jeff sat straight again and began to type. Operation Baby was about to begin.

Caro

Caro grabbed her handbag and almost ran towards the door of Rawlington Car Salesroom. Hallelujah, she had two whole hours away from Louise and the incessant baby talk. But that was unfair.

Poor Louise had been up most of the night with Anja, who was teething more violently than every other baby in Bridgehead and Caro knew that if things were normal – i.e. if she had any prospect of having a baby of her own – she'd have been both interested and sympathetic. As it was, she was glad to get away.

'See you at two!' she called, not waiting to hear Louise's reply.

It was pleasant outside, warm for the time of year. A lovely day to go shopping. Caro put on her sunglasses and turned towards the town centre. She and Louise often doubled up like this, one of them looking after the phones right through the lunch period, allowing the other a full two hours to do some shopping. At least, she was the one who did the shopping nowadays. Louise went back to her mother's for lunch and a visit with baby Anja. Lucky, lucky Louise.

Caro walked briskly through the park and emerged by the traffic lights at the bottom of the High Street. Where should she go first? There were summer sales all over the place now. She stopped for the red man, feeling herself slump inside. Shopping was just a pathetic attempt to distract herself from the disastrous turn her life had taken. She'd used up a lifetime of emotion in four short days, but now she needed to focus, decide what to do. Stay in childless comfort with Jeff, or...

Caro welled up again. The one, the only important thing in her life was – the no-baby. What was she going to do?

The lights changed and she started up the High Street, glancing at Cybersonics on the other side of the road to see if Jeff was anywhere near the front window. He wasn't, and she walked on quickly, feeling guilty. Only last week she'd have gone in, asked if he wanted a lunchtime sandwich too, suggested they go to the park together. It wasn't that she didn't like him. Caro swallowed hard.

Wanting – needing – to be a mother was an absolute gut feeling, as much a part of her as her need for oxygen, food and water. A baby was utterly and completely necessary for her future happiness. But so was being able to give her child – children – everything she'd never had herself and that simply wasn't possible as a single mother on the salary she was on. So Jeff was a necessary part of the family planning, whether he was fertile or not. And the chance that he'd agree to donor artificial insemination was zero. Maybe she should try IVF.

On the other hand, Jeff was showing her clearly that while he wanted them to recover from this near-fatal blow, all that was really important to him was that she shouldn't leave him. He wasn't taking her wish for a baby seriously. She'd lost the husband she'd thought she had and her comfortable marriage was beginning to feel like a prison sentence.

Jealousy and despair fighting for top place in her head, Caro pretended to stare into the sandwich shop window while she blinked the tears away. Jeff had everything. His own business, great prospects, and the home they shared now was his dream-come-true. Yet like hers, his start in life hadn't been the best. His mum had run off when he was ten and his dad started out on a series of live-in girlfriends, which only ended when he was killed in an industrial accident. Jeff went off the rails a bit then, and spent his teens living with his gran and his younger brother whilst having some pretty intensive counselling. In an odd way, Caro found this reassuring. He wasn't perfect and he hadn't always been rich. He'd had a dream too, and he'd achieved it – but now his dream was turning into Caro's worst nightmare.

Pushing the dark thoughts away, Caro went into the Puff Pastry and bought her lunch, then walked around the corner to the little square at the back of the High Street, where some jaded-looking benches were grouped round a patch of grubby gravel, flowers in tubs cheering the place up in all four corners. It was a popular spot to have lunch. The houses round about it were uniform grey stone tenements with door less, tunnel-like entrances opening onto the square, but it was amazing what a difference a few flowers and some sunshine could make. Caro had grown up here, her old home was right up there in the corner of the east side of the square. It hadn't been the happiest time of her life. She sat down on an empty bench and tried to pretend she was in Paris, lunching on the Champs Élysées without a care in the world. If only.

Egg and cress eaten, Caro dusted the crumbs from her front and dropped the sandwich packet into the bin by the bench. Now to spend some of Jeff's hard earned cash. She was walking back across the square when a glint of glass in the sunlight caught her eye – no, it wasn't glass; it was shiny plastic, one of those tiny bags that sealed themselves across the top when you pressed the sides together. It was lying on the ground beside a tub of petunias. Caro poked it with her foot, then picked it up.

There were five orange pills in the bag and Caro stared. They looked like – her throat went dry – they looked very like the pills she'd seen on a television documentary last week and those had been ecstasy. Was that even possible – a bag of drugs lying in the sunshine in Mortimer Square?

She looked round nervously. A couple of teenagers were sitting on the backrest of a bench on the other side of the square and two middle-aged women on the next bench were busy comparing what they'd just bought at Mirabelle's, but none of them were paying any attention to her and no-one looked as if they'd lost five ecstasy tablets. Caro closed her fist around the bag and turned towards the High Street, her heart thumping.

What on earth should she do now? Take the pills to the police? That was the logical thing, but for a moment Caro stood still, frustration welling inside her. Bloody hell, could nothing go right in her life? By the time she handed over the pills and made a statement or whatever, it would be time to go back to work. Her shopping trip had ended before it began.

'They're mine. Give them back. Right now.'

The voice came from behind, and Caro swung round to see a youth of about eighteen, a boy, almost, with short bleached hair and a poor complexion. Hands thrust deep into the pockets of his shapeless hoody, he moved round her when she stopped, blocking the way to the High Street.

Caro's mouth went dry. He was bigger than she was, and there was an aggressive, aggrieved look on his face.

'What – what do you mean?' Her voice had gone hoarse. Surely he wasn't going to mug her? This was the middle of town, practically on the High Street and there were people nearby. But would anyone come to help her if she screamed? Her legs started to shake.

The boy smiled nastily. 'Them pills. They're mine and you took them. That's stealing, Missus. That's wrong.'

Caro was too afraid to feel relief, but a tiny ray of hope allowed her to speak more steadily. He only wanted the pills. 'It's not, you know. I was going to hand them in at the police station. How was I to know they were yours?'

'Stealing,' said the boy firmly. He gripped her arm with shocking suddenness.

Anger chased the last of the fear from Caro's mind. The little wretch could go to hell and back as far as she was concerned. He was making a big mistake trying to accost her, because nothing could possibly hurt her more than the news about the no-baby – she didn't give a toss what this little thug did with his pitiful haul of E. Trembling with anger, she wrenched her arm from his grasp and flung the bag of pills to the ground at his feet, noticing with grim satisfaction the sudden shock on his face. She pressed her advantage home.

'Take your precious pills, then. I hope they choke you. But just you remember what's right and what's wrong, and remember too that not everyone's afraid of pathetic little yobs like you.'

His face livid, the boy swiped up the pills and raced back to the High Street.

Caro stood taking deep breaths. Now that the encounter was over, she felt almost as shaky as she had at the clinic on Friday.

'Are you all right, love? We saw what happened.'

It was the women who'd been on the square.

Caro swallowed. 'I'm fine, thanks. He was just being obnoxious.'

The woman patted her shoulder. 'You did the right thing. No use risking getting mugged. Will you be okay on your own?'

Caro managed a smile and a few more reassuring words and they went on their respective ways. They boy was nowhere to be seen on the High Street, and Caro heaved an enormous sigh of relief. What a horrible thing to happen. She would go back to the Puff Pastry and get herself a cup of something hot. Chocolate with cream on top. Comfort food.

Determinedly, she went on with her shopping expedition, even buying the trousers in Mirabelle's. So it wasn't quite a ruined lunch hour, though she still felt jittery. But what she'd said to that little tyke was true. She wasn't afraid of him, because the worst had already happened in her life. The shattered dream. No baby.

It wasn't until she was nearly back at the salesroom that another train of thought started in Caro's mind. That boy. He was just a kid, really. A kid on E? Was he a dealer or a user? Whichever it was, he needed help and all she'd done was fling five pills back at him, enough to end his life if he took them all at once. But then, he wouldn't. He would sell them and get enough money to buy more pills to sell on again to some other stupid kids. How would she feel if they were her kids? Maybe she should still report the incident. But it was ten to two; she didn't have time before work now.

Her feet carried on past the police station, not stopping until she was back at her desk in the salesroom reception.

'Good shop?' said Louise. 'It was mobbed here, four blokes all wanting test drives. I've only just sat down. What did you buy?'

Caro took a deep breath and produced the trousers, saying nothing about the incident with the boy. She would go to the police on the way home.

Work kept her occupied until six, when she and Louise left the salesroom together. Caro hesitated. Left to the police station, or right to the bus stop and home and Jeff and the no-baby?

'Forgotten the way?' said Louise, laughing, and Caro made herself laugh too.

'Silly. Well – see you tomorrow. Love to Anja.'

She turned right and walked towards the bus stop. This was the best way. Least said, soonest mended. Just forget the whole nasty business.

Sharon

'Are you feeling better now? Shall I get you something to eat?'

Craig was hovering in the doorway. Sharon sat up slowly, glancing at the alarm clock on the bedside table. She had slept for a good two hours after her dizzy turn in the High Street.

'Maybe just a cup of tea and some toast. I'm not hungry,' she said. 'I'll come through and blob on the sofa for a bit. You should have gone back to work, Craig. I'm fine.'

'Oh, for pity's sake – first you wouldn't phone the midwife, now I've done the wrong thing again.'

The exasperation in his voice was undisguised and Sharon blinked at him miserably. He wasn't enjoying this any more than she was, and who could blame him?

The peeved tone was still there when he spoke again. 'You should go back to bed after your tea. You're pregnant, you're allowed to have proper naps.'

'I've just had a nap,' she snapped. Hell. She was back to sounding like a hormonal teenie, moaning because a parent wanted her to go to bed early. Except Craig wasn't her parent, and having her husband suggest bed for a 'proper nap' was doing exactly nothing for her self-esteem. She must look really knackered.

They would have to talk about the whole having-a-baby situation. It was pitiful, the way they were behaving; it had been non-communication from the day and hour she'd told him she was pregnant. Craig hated confrontation, and she'd been trying to get her head round the fact that in eight months' time she was going weigh at least ten kilos more and would need a babysitter when she wanted to go anywhere. It had been downhill all the way from there.

Sharon pushed her feet into the pink flip-flops she wore about the flat, noticing with resignation that her ankles were swollen. Brilliant, her feet looked like they belonged to a hippopotamus now. She shuffled through to the kitchen and sat at the breakfast bar while Craig stuffed two slices of bread into the toaster.

She didn't know how to start talking to him anymore. Before she stopped work she would have started with the funny and exasperating things her students had said that day. But now the highlight of her week was tidying the bathroom cabinet, and who wanted to laugh about that? And the only 'date' on their horizon was the last antenatal class tomorrow evening, when they were going to have a labour and birth rehearsal. Not exactly sexy, was it?

Sharon watched glumly as Craig spread her toast with cottage cheese, put it on a tray with a cup of tea and a glass of juice, then carried it through to the living area for her. He wouldn't have done that before her pregnancy, what did it mean that he was doing it now? She eased herself into the blue squidginess of the sofa and lifted a piece of toast. Yet another meal for one.

'I'll go back to the shop for a bit now,' said Craig, pulling his jacket on. 'Hey, I thought we could go for dinner tomorrow after the antenatal class?'

Sharon stared. It seemed an odd thing to suggest after she'd practically conked out on the High Street – he was back to ignoring the whole nasty business now she was better. But on the other hand, a meal out sounded like a win-win situation. Best case, they could talk, and worst, she wouldn't have to play the dutiful housewife and produce dinner.

She smiled at Craig. 'Good idea. Let's go to Oscar's and have fish dips.'

The flat door banged shut behind him, and Sharon lifted her second slice of toast. Did all expectant parents go through the same kind of ups and downs? Or only expectant parents who hadn't wanted a baby yet? And here she was, home alone again.

At least tomorrow she'd have plenty to do. She hadn't told Craig about her planned lunch with the woman from the library. Maybe talking to Julie would give her some ideas about how to cope with a baby. Sharon pulled a sudden face. Julie appeared to be a single parent existing on what must be a lowish income, and coping brilliantly. They couldn't have much in common – she hadn't missed the shocked expression on the Julie's face when the other woman realised that Sharon would prefer not to be having a baby... Maybe it wouldn't be much of a fun lunch after all.

Jeff

The house was silent. Jeff dropped his car key on the hall table and went through to the kitchen. He was home first when he had a normal day shift, so dinner preparations were usually down to him. Actually, at the moment it felt like everything else around here was down to him, finding a baby to adopt being top of the list. He banged two pans on the stove and grabbed a packet of spaghetti and a jar of sauce from the cupboard. It wasn't exactly gourmet grub, but after the previous night's fiasco he didn't feel like cooking. Saving his marriage was more important.

Caro arrived home and one look at her face was enough to freeze Jeff. Her lips were that thin way, like she was trying not to rant about something, and she barely met his eyes when she came into the kitchen.

'Spag bol okay?' he managed, emptying the sauce into a pan.

'Fine.' She went upstairs, but when she came down again she hadn't changed into something comfy or glamorous for the evening, like she used to – before Black Friday.

Jeff drained the spaghetti. 'Let's watch the news. Big day in parliament, apparently.'

He tried to sound casual, but Caro only lifted the glasses and cutlery and went to put the TV on.

Jeff went to the fridge for the parmesan. At least with the news on he wouldn't have to make an effort to chat. And Caro certainly wasn't conversing, or even having a moan like she often did after a strenuous day. That bloody doctor – he should have told them more gently. Caro was still in a blue funk, Jeff could tell. At least he had started the baby-finding process, and the amount of information you could find on Twitter was mind-boggling. Jeff had gone into several serious – he hoped – forums about adoption and surrogacy, and posted a tentative query on each. Maybe he should tell Caro about it? But no – not until he found the baby, then she'd be all the more delighted. He couldn't wait to see her face.

Jeff dished up and took the plates through, but something stopped him joining her on the sofa tonight. He watched glumly from the armchair as the newsreader started an item about two teenagers who'd been caught in Indonesia with several condoms of heroin inside them, and how they could end up with long prison, or even death, sentences. Some pretty disgusting footage of drug addicts in a far-off city was shown, and Caro made a shaky, throaty sound. Jeff turned to stare, but she was on her feet, running from the room.

He slid his half-full plate onto the coffee table. They couldn't go on like this. He had to fix things, or he would lose Caro and that Could. Not. Happen. Heart in his mouth, he followed her upstairs.

Caro was standing at the bedroom window, staring out at a couple of teenagers lounging around smoking at the end of the street.

Jeff joined her. 'Okay, love? Look at those two. It's yobs like them that give the place a bad name. This used to be a…'

Caro turned on him, a vicious expression on her face. 'You don't know a thing about them! That's Tom and Jay and they're just kids. They have decent homes and with a bit of luck they'll be fine. Not like those kids on the news – they'll have been surrounded all their lives by people who don't give a shit about them. And you don't give a shit either, do you Jeff? About kids. Well, I do. And I just wish I'd never…'

She stopped there and glared at him with an expression that was somehow both furious and heartbroken, and then she marched downstairs. He heard her scraping the abandoned spaghetti into the bin.

Jeff leaned his head on the window. He had to find a baby very quickly. This urge for a child of her own was making Caro positively irrational.

Chapter Four

Wednesday, 25th May

Julie

Julie jogged down the High Street, Amy's buggy rattling in front of her. It was fortunate she was one of those people who could get by on five hours' sleep, because nowadays she didn't often get more. Last night had been a real bummer, with Sam up for hours after a nightmare, and Amy fussy with a tooth. None of them had slept much before three in the morning. Then this morning the child minder had phoned to say she couldn't have Amy because her own kids had some tummy bug. It was shaping up to be one of those days.

The green man beeped and Julie hurried across the road, catching sight of the town hall clock as she reached the opposite pavement. Oh no, it was five to nine already. Dee would be at the library by now. She always arrived early in case people were queueing up at the front door. As if.

Julie sighed. She knew how insecure her job was. Not many people used the library for study or research now, and you didn't have to look further than the World Wide Web to know why. The team had discussed a few plans to drum up custom after the summer holidays. The best way forward seemed to be to offer not only internet access for those few households who weren't online, but also services that weren't available online. Not an easy task. But if they didn't, someone on the staff might have to go, and Julie had been the last in. No way did she want to make herself conspicuous in a bad way, so hopefully Amy would be cooperative about spending a day in the library.

The main door was open as Julie rushed up the path, and she could see Dee standing motionless just inside.

'Dee, sorry I'm – oh no!'

Dismayed, Julie stood in the narrow hallway and stared through the glass doors into the library. Books lay everywhere, pulled from shelves and scattered across the floor, pages torn out and discarded, papers and pamphlets from the stand near the desk adding to the chaos. Paper and books were covering the entire floor – the place was an absolute wreck.

For a brief moment neither woman spoke, then Dee came to life, ushering Julie back outside and pulling out her phone.

'Vandals,' she said grimly. 'What an absolute bugger. I'll phone the police.'

Julie stared back into the building, glad it was Amy looking around with big eyes, and not Sam. 'Oh, no, Dee – who would do such a senseless thing?'

Dee was punching out nine-nine-nine. Julie peered through to the reception desk. The computer screen was shattered and lying on its side, which didn't bode well for the PC corner at the back of the main room. Thank goodness two of the machines were away being repaired at the moment.

Her legs shaking, Julie sat down on the edge of a stone tub of begonias. It was a wonder it had survived the attack, but the little pink and red flowers were bobbing in the breeze as they always did.

Dee finished her call and sat down beside her. 'Are you okay, Julie? You look a bit pale. And what's with Amy?'

'Rona's kids are all sick,' said Julie. 'And Sam wasn't great this morning either. He had a bad nightmare, poor thing – he was up half the night.'

'And poor you were up with him,' said Dee, patting Julie's clasped hands. 'We'll see what the police say when they come. The library won't be open today, that's for sure, so you can probably go home and rest.'

A police car swung into the parking bay at the side of the building. Two uniformed officers emerged and strode towards them. Julie and Eve stood up.

The taller man spoke. 'Morning. I'm PC David Spiers, and this is PC Steven Banks.' He listened as Dee told them about discovering the break-in. 'Okay. If you'll just wait here.' Both men vanished into the library.

A couple of minutes later a yell came from within, and Julie seized the buggy and ran inside after Dee. The two officers were bent over something on the upstairs gallery where the study section was.

'It's a kid, he's unconscious,' shouted PC Spiers, dropping to his knees.

The other officer was on his radio, calling for an ambulance and back-up. A chill of horror swept through Julie. Someone was up there, hurt, and she and Dee hadn't noticed.

'Can we do anything? What's wrong with him?' Dee started to pick her way over books to the gallery stairs.

'It could be a drugs overdose – he's vomited. I'm not sure he's breathing.'

PC Spiers started chest compressions, his face pale. Dee stood at the bottom of the stairs, and Julie parked Amy by the desk and went to join her.

The other officer stared down through the wooden bannisters. 'Can you open the doors to let the ambulance crew in, please? Then wait outside.' His colleague was still thudding up and down on the boy's chest, grunting as he did so, and Julie felt sick. She and Dee did as he asked, then went back outside with Amy. It was good to be away from those dreadful noises up in the gallery.

The next half hour passed like some kind of bad dream. The ambulance arrived and two green-clad paramedics dashed in, followed by a couple of more senior policemen. Julie and Dee sat on the flower tub, turning away the handful of people who arrived to use the library and wondering what was going on upstairs. Who was it, fighting for his life on the gallery floor? Had he vandalised the library, or had that been his friends – or his enemies, maybe? How had he got in? Was he going to live?

It seemed to take forever before they heard the sound of feet clattering down the wooden gallery staircase. The paramedics

manoeuvred their trolley out while a new, older officer was rep[
developments into the radio attached to his uniform jacket.

Fighting back tears, Julie looked at the face on the trolley. It was just a boy; he couldn't have been more than seventeen or eighteen. He was a terrible colour under the oxygen mask, but he was breathing. Thank goodness, she couldn't have borne it if someone – a kid – had died like that in the library.

The paramedics loaded the trolley into the ambulance and drove off, sirens howling and blue lights flashing.

The older officer turned to Julie and Dee. 'He's alive, but they said he's not very stable. We'll need to go over the whole place now and see if we can find out exactly what happened. We've had some trouble with local gangs recently and this might be part of it. I take it you didn't recognise that kid, or know anything that might help us? Anything out of the ordinary happen in the last few days?'

Dee shook her head. 'It's all been perfectly normal.'

The officer looked inquiringly at Julie.

She shook her head. 'Nothing. It seems so – so pointless.' Oh, help, she was crying now, her tiredness and the shock were catching up with her.

'We'll find out what happened, don't worry.' He took their details quickly, writing in a small black notebook. 'Okay, we'll need one of you to stay here.'

'I'll do that,' said Dee, turning to Julie. 'You can go home, Julie. Could you let Head Office know we're closed today? An email would be best, then they've got it in black and white. I'll start phoning round the rest of the staff.'

'Sure,' said Julie. 'I'll do it on the laptop at home. Let me know what happens.'

Dee gave her a rueful grin and nodded. Julie turned the buggy and trailed back down the path, her cheeks tight where the tears had dried. It was definitely one of those days.

The High Street was quiet as Julie strode along, barely noticing the warm May sunshine on her shoulders. What a ghastly thing to happen. A break-in was bad enough, but to have someone hurt, maybe even dying, then just lying there on the gallery floor where she worked every day – it left a sour taste in her mouth. They could only hope the doctors would be able to do something for that poor boy. What had happened in his short life to make him end up like this – and how could she be sure that something similar wouldn't happen to her own children one day? Julie shivered at the thought.

Sam's school was down the next street, and Julie's steps slowed. He must be almost as shattered as she was, even if he had youth on his side. Four-year-olds often had more energy than their mums, she'd noticed that before. But she would pop in and see how he was.

Sam's classroom was on the ground floor, a big, sunny room with windows down one side. Julie stood in the corridor, peering through the narrow glass strip in the door. The children were milling around, it seemed to be one of the free-play sessions Sam was so enthusiastic about. But today he was sitting on a floor-cushion by the bookshelf, leafing through a picture book, his face pale.

Miss Cairns, who was younger than Julie and always seemed terribly efficient, spotted her and came to the door. 'Hello, Mrs Mayhew, I was wondering if I should call you. Sam's not his usual bouncy self this morning.' She gestured towards the little boy.

A lump came into Julie's throat. 'He didn't sleep well. I'll take him home for a nap now, if that's all right.'

'That's exactly what he needs. Sam! Look who's come to collect you!'

'Mummy!' Sam dropped his book and scrambled to his feet. 'Are we going home? Why aren't you at the library?'

Julie knew she would never get him to sleep if she started talking about break-ins and policemen. 'Change of shift,' she said briskly. 'Get your things and let's go.'

They left the building, Sam trotting beside the buggy, relief making Julie feel almost light-headed. She should never have sent him to school this morning, but oh, thank goodness he hadn't come to the library with her. And at least Miss Cairns had been tactful enough not to make her feel like the world's worst mother.

Approaching the traffic lights, Julie spotted the internet café on the other side of the road. Maybe she should just scoot in there to send her email. The Wi-Fi at her flat had been unreliable lately, and it would be awful if it was uncooperative today, when she had an important email to send. Julie sighed. One of these days she'd be able to afford a mobile phone package that included internet.

Gripping Sam's hand on the buggy handle, she crossed the road and went into the internet café. It was a pleasant, spacious room, computers set out at regular intervals on long tables along cream painted walls. A small group of women at the back of the room were listening to a young man explaining something.

Another man was at the desk, clicking around on the keyboard there. 'Hi, can I help you?'

'I need to send an email,' said Julie, looking in her bag for the card with the important work email addresses.

He indicated a computer at the end of the table. 'Sure. You pay per fifteen minutes – give me a shout when you've finished. I'm Davie.'

'Oh, um, hi. I'm Julie. Come on, Sam.'

She left a drowsy Amy by the desk and sat Sam on a stool beside her computer before giving him an envelope and a pencil from her bag to draw something. Sam could read a few words; she didn't want him peering over her shoulder and noticing things like 'police' and 'ambulance'. It only took a few minutes to write her email, and she clicked 'send' with a sigh of relief. Time to go home and sleep.

Replacing the address card in her bag, she looked round for Davie. He was crouched on the floor in a corner doing something with a cable, and Julie had taken two steps towards him before her stomach cramped in fear as she realised what was wrong. No – no! She stared wildly round the room, then ran outside, where High Street shoppers were meandering around as usual. Nothing. No, no no no no. Julie stood in the shop doorway and screamed, her voice ringing across the street, making Sam scream in terror too.

Amy and the buggy were gone.

Sharon

Sharon unplugged the iron and sank down on the sofa. The silence was deafening. Quite possibly she was the only person in the entire block right now – it was a place where young professionals lived, ambitious people on their way up the corporate ladder. Like she'd been.

Sharon clasped her hands over her bump. She'd done some thinking while the baby was turning somersaults in the night. Here she was, the world's most reluctant mother-to-be, married to a guy who'd once been the perfect partner but had now turned into the prospective father from hell. Living in a great place was no compensation for that. A wave of homesickness for her old life washed through Sharon and she reached for a tissue.

They couldn't go on like this. She and Craig were about to become parents, mainly because termination had been a non-issue from the start. And she wasn't about to leave the baby in a box on the church doorstep either, so this child was going to be a big part of her life for the next eighteen years, or however long it took kids to grow up. So she could either make herself miserable for a couple of decades – or find the good parts to being a mother.

Imagining her child living with them for the foreseeable future was something she hadn't done before, and Sharon blinked. There would be nursery school, and birthday parties, and Brownies – and then later, arguments about going out, and make up, and boyfriends... with her in the middle of it all, a mum. And it would start the minute the baby was born.

And – happy thought for the day – when the baby wasn't inside her any more, she'd be able to get a babysitter. She could go back to work after her maternity leave, too. The thought was the one bright spot on Sharon's career horizon. She'd been so busy trying to come to terms with what was happening to her, she'd almost forgotten the most important part – she could have a life as well as a baby. So right now she was going to cheer up if it killed her, and today it should be easy. She was having lunch with

Julie, then tonight she and Craig had the last antenatal class and a table booked at Oscar's.

They could plan the next few months, make a shopping list of baby equipment and most importantly, start communicating again. As intelligent people, they would manage that, wouldn't they? If Craig wanted to communicate again. But he would. He must.

Determinedly happier, she took the newly-ironed maternity top through to the bedroom. Twenty-six days to go.

Jeff

It wasn't something he'd planned in any way.

He arrived at Cybersonics for the late-morning shift, thinking about the queries he'd put out on those forums yesterday and wondering if he'd find something useful in today's responses. There must be women expecting babies they didn't want, but there was nothing to say that any of them had seen his posts. Homeless, desperate girls were unlikely to have an internet connection, so he may have to extend his campaign beyond the net. But how on earth would he go about that? He could hardly put a card up in the newsagent's, or place a 'wanted' notice in the small ads section of the local paper.

With this running through his head, Jeff stepped into Cybersonics and saw the baby in the buggy, just sitting there at the front desk with nobody paying any attention to it – and something short-circuited inside his brain. In less than ten seconds he had both buggy and baby outside, and was striding round the corner towards his car. Now if this was his baby he could take it home to Caro and they could live happily ever after, just the three of them. Judging by the outfit it was a girl, too – Caro would love a little girl.

A woman's scream came before he'd gone twenty metres, and Jeff darted into the entrance of a nearby close, hauling the buggy up the two worn steps and into a warm, smelly dimness. The baby was silent, her eyes staring up at him.

'Good girl,' he said, taking the buggy right up to the back of the close. No one would see them now unless they came right inside. He was safe and he had a baby. Not so difficult after all, was it? What a great life they could have, him, Caro and the baby. Amazing how he'd been able to grab the opportunity the moment it presented itself. A baby for Caro.

More screams came from the High Street and Jeff's brain jerked back to reality.

What the shit was he doing? This was no way to deal with things; he would need a careful plan before the baby – any baby – came home. He thundered down the close, shoving the buggy in front of him, and ran back up the High Street. A young woman was rushing up and down outside Cybersonics, shrieking hysterically and dragging a little boy behind her, and Davie was diving about the middle of the road.

Jeff yelled at the woman as he approached. 'Is this your baby? I found her round the corner.'

The woman plucked up the child and rocked it in her arms, her face blotchy red and her hands shaking visibly.

'Thank God,' said Davie. 'Come back inside, love. Did you see what happened, Jeff? It could only have been two or three minutes ago.'

Jeff shook his head. 'It was a bunch of hoodies. I saw them shove the buggy into a close and then run off. Probably took her for a sick joke.'

Anger was welling up in his head. It was disgraceful. This woman didn't deserve a baby any more than Sharon did. Imagine sitting in an internet café – she was probably faffing around on Facebook or something equally mindless, leaving her baby to be taken by anyone who happened to pass by. She was lucky it hadn't been hoodies. Caro would never do anything like that. And that poor little boy with tears running down his face – Jeff knew exactly what that felt like. It was heart-breaking; some people just weren't fit to be parents.

'Do you want me to phone the police, love?' said Davie, and the woman shook her head.

'The police'd never find them now,' she said, her voice trembling. 'I want to go home and get my children safely into bed for a nap.'

She turned to Jeff, wiping her eyes on a scrunched-up tissue. 'Thank you more than I can say for bringing her back.'

Jeff nodded, not trusting himself to speak. She stared at him, her eyes widening. Quick, he had to say something normal here or she might get suspicious. He cleared his throat. 'I'm Jeff Horne. Davie and I own this place. Don't worry, your baby was in her buggy all the time – I'm sure she's not hurt.'

That was true, at least. The baby was now back in her pram, lying there blowing bubbles, oblivious to what was going on. The woman nodded, and Jeff watched as she left the shop and turned towards the east side of town, pushing the buggy with one hand and hugging the little boy to her side with the other.

And now he would go and see what results his queries had brought.

Julie

Her heart was still pounding away as Julie strode towards the flat, Sam whimpering at her side. What a disgusting thing to happen – ghastly yobs, playing a vile trick like that with a defenceless baby. She would never forget the feeling of absolute terror when she'd realised the buggy really was gone. It had been all she could do to remain upright; the world had spun around her and her bowels felt loose. Her baby, her Amy… sickening visions of perverts and paedophiles had stabbed through her brain – and then Jeff Horne rushed up with her little girl. Such blessed relief.

Julie shivered, remembering Jeff's face as he stood there behind the buggy, watching her cuddling Amy. He'd seemed completely stressed out too. His smile was nowhere near his eyes, and there were lines around his mouth that would have looked more natural on an older man. And when his eyes had moved to Sam he looked suddenly devastated, as if something really tragic had happened to him and Sam was mixed up in it. It was a creepy, disquieting feeling, to see a stranger look at her son with such an intimate expression on his face.

Julie gripped Sam's hand more tightly. The guy had found her daughter; she should be more than grateful. And she was, of course, but she could still see that there was something a little – odd – about Jeff Horne. Did he have a child? Or – had he lost one? Or possibly he was divorced and didn't often see his children.

Sam sobbed aloud beside her, and Julie forced herself to speak brightly.

'Come on, lamb-chop, panic over. It was just big boys being silly, and we're nearly home now. We'll have a nice nap before lunch, won't we?'

It was after twelve when Julie awoke, Sam and Amy both still asleep on the bed beside her. She'd needed their closeness, and Sam at least had needed hers. His face was flushed in sleep now, one thumb just touching his lips.

Julie eased herself off the bed and boxed Amy in with pillows. She was looking out a clean top when she remembered – no! She was supposed to be meeting Sharon on the High Street in – oh heck, in fifteen minutes. She would have to cancel; no way was she going to wake Sam and Amy and drag them to the Puff Pastry for lunch. How awful, she should have thought to call Sharon before they'd all crashed out on her bed.

She lifted her phone. 'Sharon, I'm so sorry, but the kids are both asleep in bed. Can we shift lunch to another day?'

Sharon's voice was bleak. 'Oh – I'm just on the way to meet you. Well – poor things. I hope they're not ill?'

Guilt crept through Julie. This wasn't Sharon's fault, and she was having a tough time too. Maybe they could compromise.

'Just tired. Suggestion – why don't you get some stuff at the Puff Pastry and come here? It's second on the left after Mirabelle's. Number 22.'

Sharon agreed gushingly and Julie put the phone down, wondering if she'd done the right thing.

Sharon

Sharon watched as Julie wiped cream cheese from Sam's mouth and fingers before the little boy raced through to the living room and his cars. Being in Julie's home was like getting off the bus at the wrong stop – she knew which town she was in, but everything looked foreign and unfamiliar.

It was clear there was no money to spare here. The flat was on the fourth floor and the lift looked like the first lift ever. Sharon had hesitated, but she couldn't walk up four flights and fortunately the metal cage had clanked its way to the top without incident. Julie's tiny living room was crammed with toys, and the kitchen where they were now was long and narrow and could have done with a complete overhaul. The contrast to her own shiny units and tiled floor was almost embarrassing. Talk about different worlds.

At least she'd chosen the right kind of lunch. A selection of fillings on brown and white bread had gone down well with both Julie and Sam, and Sharon had bought some individual trifles too, for dessert. She and Julie chatted about babies and child minders and going back to work, and Sharon was beginning to realise how much she'd got things out of proportion. According to Julie, a baby needn't mean the end of the old life. There was no reason she and Craig couldn't go right on enjoying the things they'd always enjoyed. Except maybe long holidays in exotic places, but they could do that again when the baby was older.

Over the course of lunch Sharon cheered up about three hundred per cent, and it was only when Sam left the table that she realised Julie wasn't sharing the joy.

'Are you okay?' she asked tentatively. Maybe it was an imposition, her coming here, even if she had supplied lunch. Julie was pale and her mouth looked tight.

'I've had the morning from hell,' she said in a low voice, pushing the kitchen door half shut.

Sharon listened, feeling her eyes widen when Julie talked about the library break-in and Amy disappearing. 'Julie, you should have called the police. If those yobs think they got away with it, they might try the same thing again.'

Julie pushed thin fingers through already tousled hair, and Sharon's hand strayed up to check her own head. Would she be like this in four years' time? Stressed-out and not caring what she looked like? Her euphoria nose-dived.

Julie slid her plate to the side and leaned her elbows on the table. 'I know. But I didn't want Sam to be even more scared than he already was. I'll talk to the police at the library about it later. That kid on the gallery floor, Sharon – he really got to me. Not very long ago he'd have been four years old and cute, like Sam. Life's just the pits some days, and today was one of them.'

Sharon nodded. 'You're giving Sam the best possible start in life. You can't do more.'

The doorbell rang while she was speaking and Julie stood up. 'That's probably Dee, my boss. Let's go through.'

She led the way to the living room, pressed the button to admit the caller four floors below and went out to the landing.

Sharon lowered herself onto the sofa and was immediately roped into Sam's game. She sat with a car in each hand, listening as footsteps coming up the stairs came closer. It soon became clear they didn't belong to a woman, and Julie made an apprehensive 'who on earth is this?' face through the door. Sharon joined her on the landing as a suited young man with blond hair appeared, panting slightly as he strode up the last flight.

'DS Max Sanders. Wish I'd known you were right at the top,' he said to Julie, waving his identification.

Sharon relaxed. This must be to do with the break-in at the library.

Julie grinned. 'I make a point of walking up once a day at least. Saves me the bother of going to the gym. This is my friend Sharon Morrison. Is there any news about the boy?'

The officer nodded to Sharon, then turned back to Julie. 'Can I come in for a moment?'

He followed Sharon and Julie into the living room, and Sam leapt to his feet.

'Mummy?' He reached for Julie's hand and she ruffled his hair.

'This is, um, Detective Sergeant Sanders from the police, Sam. There was a break-in at the library last night and a young man was hurt. The police are trying to find out what happened.'

Sam stared, his eyes as round as saucers. 'Was he shot?'

Sharon winced in sympathy. This was just what Julie hadn't wanted.

'For heaven's sake, no, of course not. He was just – ill. Sam, can you be very good and play in your room while we talk?'

Sam kicked the sofa, not letting go of Julie's hand. 'I want to stay with you.'

Sharon could see that Julie was almost at the end of her patience, and was about to suggest she could go with Sam, when Julie pointed to the door. 'Five minutes, if you want to watch telly tonight. You can set the timer. Scoot.'

Sam scooted and Julie joined Sharon on the sofa. Sharon could see she was upset and thought she knew why, too. What kind of a world was it when a four-year-old saw a policeman and heard about someone being injured in a break-in – and immediately thought about guns?

Julie's voice was shaking when she spoke again. 'Is that boy okay?'

DS Sanders leaned forwards in his armchair and spoke in a low voice. 'I'm afraid not. He's still unconscious, and they're concerned about brain damage. He'd taken ecstasy. We reckon a whole gang of kids broke into the library, trashed it for a laugh, then settled down for a nice trip that went wrong for our lad. And the others left him there. This may be connected to a drugs death in Glasgow last week, so CID has taken over the investigation. We need to talk to all the library staff, but your phone seems to be switched off. Could you come back to the library this afternoon?'

Julie nodded. 'Of course.'

Amy cried out from the bedroom, and Julie went to lift her. Cradling the baby in both arms, she sat down again on the sofa.

A lump came into Sharon's throat – how natural Julie looked, her baby in her arms. She glanced across at DS Sanders, who was staring at Amy with a little smile on his attractive face. Good grief, here was another baby fan – was she the only person on the planet not completely convinced that having kids was a good idea?

Sam sidled back in and looked shyly at DS Sanders. 'Is the young man who wasn't shot in prison?'

To Sharon's amusement, the detective blinked twice and swallowed before replying. Julie caught her eye, and Sharon realised that for all their differences, they had the same sense of humour.

DS Sanders gave Julie a hunted look. 'Um, no, he isn't. He's in hospital and the doctors are looking after him. His mum and dad are there too.'

Sam considered this for a moment. 'My dad went away and he never came back,' he said, and Julie hugged him.

Tears burned behind Sharon's eyes. Please God her baby would never have to say that.

'I'm sorry to hear that. Well, Sam, I'd better go and see how things are at the library.' DS Sanders looked at Julie. 'Um – would you like a lift there?'

'Thanks, but we'll walk. It's just five minutes away and I'll need to change Amy first. But later, I need to tell you about something else that happened this morning.' She gestured significantly towards Sam as she spoke.

The little boy's expression was anguished. 'A lift in a police car? Mummy!'

Max Sander's lips twitched. 'Maybe we can show you one later on, Sam.'

Sharon watched as Julie showed him out, then laughed aloud as the other woman came back and looked at her sheepishly. 'He fancies you, Julie.'

Julie wrinkled her nose. 'You may be right. But my priorities have to be Sam and Amy.'

It was all baby talk after that. Sharon walked back towards the library with Julie and the children, then waved as they went their separate ways. Well. That had been a good two hours —she felt much better now.

Home came into sight round the corner and Sharon set her shoulders. She had to hold on to this positive mood, which might not be easy once she was echoing around in the flat all by herself. Then there was the small matter of persuading Craig that all he wanted in life was a baby daughter and several years-worth of holidays in a non-exotic, child-friendly resort.

Hm. That part sounded like the impossible dream right now.

Jeff

Jeff craned his neck to check that Davie was coping in the front shop, then settled down in the staffroom and opened his laptop. He would have another quick look to see if any more responses to the Operation Baby queries he'd posted yesterday had come in. He'd had six replies already, but none were actually offering babies.

It was maddening, because a baby was no longer an optional extra. Probably that was why he'd had a brainstorm and grabbed that buggy this morning. No, a baby was an absolute must if he wanted to keep Caro. She'd been pretty silent since the weekend and then last night... She had really scared him, saying he didn't give a shit. They'd never had such a freeze-out before. It was crazy, because he wanted them to be a proper family too, with a baby. If only Caro would agree to adoption – surely they would grow to love a two-year-old just as much as a baby? But Caro had made it very clear she wanted her own biological baby. Jeff's stomach churned. He mustn't lose her.

Forcing his mind back to the present, Jeff opened the first forum he'd placed his query on. He could hear his heartbeat in his ears; all this stress wasn't good for him.

Right, here was his baby-post and – another eleven replies! Maybe this time...

Jeff started to scroll through the list, his excitement fading rapidly. Same old, same old. Five were from American agencies wanting to put him in touch with a surrogate mother. No use at all; he wasn't even sure if it was legal in this country – and you heard all the time about people doing that, and then the surrogate mother kept the baby in the end. Caro would never agree to that. Jeff pressed a hand against his mouth. How he wished Caro would be content with just being loved. But no, she wanted a baby too, and he'd never felt so helpless, or so scared. He checked another forum, finding a few more replies from cranks and weirdos, or well-meaning idiots suggesting fostering or adoption. Two were from women purporting to be pregnant, exactly what he was looking for – but the price! One wanted $75,000, the other $80,000! Not including medical expenses. And both were in America, too.

Disappointment and frustration mingling inside him, Jeff thumped the table then blew on his hand. This was only the first day, and if he got seventeen answers every day surely a useful one would appear eventually. Maybe even tomorrow.

Sharon

Sharon glanced at the clock on the microwave. Craig was late; it was after six. The antenatal class didn't start till seven, so there was still plenty of time… but still. Here she was, full of joie de vivre and good intentions, determined to make the evening a success, but now the old feelings of frustration were rising again. It was all very well for Craig, he hadn't had to leave his business and he hadn't got fat and hormonal – she was doing all the hard stuff for this baby they hadn't planned. The least Craig could do was show up when he was supposed to.

It was nearly twenty past before he arrived home, dumping his briefcase in the corner and diving into the bedroom to change. 'Sorry, sorry. It was the under-sixteen five-a-side football championship in the sports centre last night, and they all came in with broken specs after school this afternoon. Times like this I wish I wasn't a one-man business. Be right with you.'

Sharon sniffed, then pulled herself together. What she needed for the next couple of weeks was a mantra, something to repeat when things got tough. *You can do this, you're strong, you're in charge.* Something like that. Although – right now she wasn't sure she could do anything much, she definitely didn't feel strong and as for in charge... It was the baby who was calling the shots these days.

She made herself speak brightly. 'Loads of time – and I'm looking forward to our meal out.' He looked surprised; he must have been expecting to have his head bitten off. Sharon smiled to herself. Maybe she did feel a tiny bit strong...

The antenatal classes were held at the Health Centre, and were a joint effort between a midwife and a physiotherapist. Sitting cross-legged on her mat, Craig beside her but not touching, Sharon was very aware of the other eight couples. They all looked calm and happy; damn it, they all looked like they were having the best time of their lives. Like she and Craig had, once upon a time.

The first part of the class was a birth rehearsal. Sharon lay on her side with Craig kneeling behind her, massaging her back in slow, regular circles.

'That looks fine,' said the physio, doing the rounds. 'Feels good, huh, Sharon?'

Sharon smiled and nodded, and the physio went on to the next couple. Sharon closed her eyes, trying to imagine what a contraction would be like. There was a lot of giggling going on in the room; no-one else seemed to be taking the practice very seriously – but then, none of the others were as far on in their pregnancies. She and Craig had started classes late, because Sharon hadn't wanted to go at first, and Craig hadn't cared.

After the rehearsal they had the opportunity to ask questions, and Sharon nodded at Craig when someone asked about dizzy turns. Again, he looked surprised. Had she been so horrible to live with recently that her being halfway nice was unexpected? Something to add to the list of things to talk about.

When the class was finished they drove back across town to Oscar's, a fish restaurant overlooking the river. It was famous for miles around, and the summer months saw it full of tourists and locals alike. There were a couple of tables outside on a tiny terrace just above the water, but Craig had booked a window table inside. Sharon was glad – the evenings were still pretty chilly. They ordered a selection of fried fish to dip into various sauces, a speciality of the house which Sharon loved. This was exactly what they needed, a nice meal and quality time together.

They sat opposite each other and dipped and ate and talked about favourite restaurants and holiday food, and for a while Sharon almost forgot about the baby. This was fun. How long was it since they'd had proper fun?

But people with children had fun too, didn't they?

'Oh Craig,' she said suddenly, grabbing his hand. 'We'll be okay, you know. I was talking to a woman I met this week, she's got two kids, and I'm sure we'll manage a lot better than we've been thinking.'

It had burst out of her. He stared across the table, a frozen expression on his face, and Sharon felt fear twist inside her gut.

'I don't know, Sharon,' he said heavily. 'I've been thinking too, but I can't imagine what it's going to be like, stuck at home for years on end with a baby. And the flat isn't exactly child-friendly, is it? If I thought I would end up living in a three-up two-down semi with toys all over the place and a garden with a swing set, and holidays in wherever-on-sea – I'd shoot myself.'

Sharon took a deep breath, feeling the baby kick. What a cruel thing to say. She glared at Craig. Was this the beginning of the end of their marriage? Maybe she'd end up a whole lot more like Julie than she'd been anticipating. A single mother struggling to make ends meet in a pokey little flat and no husband.

It was hard to keep the anger from her voice. 'No, Craig, it's not what we planned. But it's happened, and I'm the one doing the hard bit. I thought today I'd got things in hand. I was feeling more positive. This baby's going to be born soon no matter how we feel about it, and you need to start feeling positive too. We have to start communicating again or we aren't going to make it as a couple. I don't want that to happen.'

For a moment he stared, a muscle working at the corner of one eye, and then to Sharon's dismay he slammed his glass down on the table then strode towards the gents. Sharon gaped after him, shock making her heart race uncomfortably. Just what the hell did he think he was doing? Was she supposed to run after him? Anger surged through her and she signalled for the bill, aware that several people were staring. Poor pregnant woman whose husband had thrown a tantrum and left her… holding the baby. How bloody dare he.

You can do this, you're strong, you're in charge.

If she thought it often enough she might start to believe it.

Chapter Five

Caro

Caro reached out and switched her alarm off. It was only twenty past six, but she wasn't likely to doze off again. Jeff was snoring beside her so she eased out of bed, grabbed her clothes and tip-toed through to the bathroom.

Thank goodness Jeff was on late this morning – with any luck he wouldn't get up before she left the house. She wouldn't even risk waking him by having a shower; last night's prolonged soak in the tub would have to do for today too. The bath had turned into her refuge and comfort, which was pretty sad. Jeff had been at Cybersonics until late yesterday evening; she'd been in bed when he came home and she'd pretended to be asleep, so they hadn't spoken all day. What was happening to her marriage? Okay, Jeff had always been the one more in love, but she'd been as keen as he was to settle down. He was a lovely, good-looking guy who would give her and her children all the advantages neither of them had enjoyed as youngsters. Except now all they had was the no-baby…

Caro buried her face in the towel. The prospect of childlessness wasn't the only thing upsetting her now. Those poor kids who'd been arrested in Indonesia on Tuesday – what must their families be going through? And the boy on Montgomery Square; he was just a kid too. She shouldn't have chucked those pills back at him.

Downstairs, she made coffee and switched on the radio to catch the weather forecast. The news was still on and she was about to turn the sound down when the word 'Bridgehead' made her listen more carefully.

'…unemployed eighteen-year-old man appears to have taken an undisclosed amount of ecstasy and is still in a coma. The library will remain closed until further notice. The sewage works at…'

Caro frowned. Teenagers and ecstasy again. What was all that about? She reached for her iPad, and horror crept down her back as she read about the break-in at the library. Dear God in heaven – that boy – he could easily be the one who'd threatened her on Tuesday. The age was right, and the ecstasy –that *couldn't* be coincidence, could it? She'd flung those pills to the ground at his feet, and now look what had happened. Caro raised cold hands to her face, her breath coming fast. If this was the same boy, she could have prevented it. Why hadn't she gone to the police? She'd been too, too – what was the word? Bored? Lazy? Uncaring? That was it, she simply hadn't cared enough to report the incident. She was no better than all the other sickos in this sick world.

Choking back sobs, she clutched her coffee mug to her chest, searching for comfort in the decreasing warmth. Was this boy's overdose *her fault*?

But even if she had reported the incident in Mortimer Square, the police might not have been able to stop what had happened. And it could be a completely different boy. Bridgehead was more than large enough to have several youths like him running the streets.

But if it was the same boy… She had given him the pills back and those two women had seen her. She hadn't reported it – supposing they did?

Caro dumped her mug in the sink and grabbed her bag. It was time to go to work – but how was she to find out if it was the same boy? If he was going to be all right? It was suddenly very important that he was, because maybe even now the police were looking for a youngish woman with curly brown hair who'd given a – oh God, supposing he was still legally a *child* – a packet of ecstasy.

Chapter Six

Saturday, 28th May

Caro

Caro searched through the last of the newspapers she'd bought that morning in the newsagent's at the bottom of the road, then pushed it away impatiently. Nothing again. And nothing online, either. This was the third day in a row she'd leafed or clicked through every newspaper available to see if there was anything about the boy who'd been found in the library, but apart from yesterday's brief item that the library was re-opening on Monday and the police were still investigating, there hadn't been anything. Apparently, a kid overdosing in a public building wasn't big news. What lousy reporting – was this really such a run-of-the-mill news story that no-one was interested after the second day?

But she was interested. Caro gathered the newspapers and stuffed them into a plastic bag. She would dump them somewhere later. If Jeff found them here he'd think she'd gone completely bonkers, buying all those papers, but she didn't trust the online versions to include every last piece of local news. It had been easier during the week; she'd read them in her lunch break at work then left them in the recycling there.

She glanced at the kitchen clock. Just on two. In a couple of hours Jeff would be home. Business varied at Cybersonics on Saturdays; sometimes the place was packed and sometimes there was hardly anyone in at all. Today was chilly and dull, so it was probably one of the busier days. Caro flopped down on the sofa and picked up the TV magazine.

What would they do tonight, her and Jeff? Usually, when he'd worked all day on Saturday they just crashed in front of the box in the evening. A bottle of wine, a nice dinner, and a comfy evening at home. Now she dreaded being alone with him because the no-baby was always there too, huge and important and smothering all conversation. She hadn't even told Jeff about the ecstasy pills and the boy.

Her comfortable, well-off marriage was disintegrating, she realised dully, and there didn't seem to be anything she could do about it. The no-baby had marked the beginning of the end for her and Jeff, and the end of her dreams; it had changed how she felt about their relationship, about – everything. It had become one of those events you measure your life by – before the no-baby and after. Jeff was different too. Of course, it must have been a cruel blow to his pride; imagine how it must feel for a man to be told he was firing blanks. He'd definitely been a bit off ever since. More than a bit, in fact.

The real question was – where would they go from here? Would she be able to persuade him that a sperm donor was the only way forwards? That didn't seem likely. And if she couldn't, she'd have to decide which was more important to her – the money and her marriage, or the no-baby.

But she knew already, didn't she? Caro grabbed a tissue to wipe away the tears spilling down both cheeks. The no-baby. The baby she would never have with her husband was more important than he was.

Sharon

Sharon stood at the living room window, half-watching one of Bridgehead's few sightseeing boots chugging up the river with a group of cold-looking tourists on board. The summer season was starting, and several coach tours found their way to Bridgehead every week. As a destination for an afternoon's outing it had quite a lot to offer. There was the river, with boat trips to the weir, and on the other side of town was the Museum of Childhood, which was staging a dinosaur exhibition this summer. Sharon heaved a sigh. In spite of her resolution to be more positive, she was finding it hard to drum up enthusiasm for anything right now.

Craig had apologised for his behaviour as soon as he returned to the table at Oscar's on Wednesday, but that was all he'd done – apologise. Back home, Sharon tried to talk about the future while Craig sat staring at his hands, obviously wishing he was anywhere else but here, and in the end she'd given up. Now she was beginning to wonder if her new-found optimism about the baby was real, or if she was deluding herself because it was just too painful, living a life you were hating.

Sharon massaged her bump and the baby moved beneath her hands. The movements were more gentle nowadays; there wouldn't be room for big stretches in there any longer. She had grown a baby girl, and if she was born right now she'd be fine, apart from the fact that her father didn't want a child and her mother was putting on the biggest brave face ever. Was that living a lie? Oh, good grief, all this introspection was giving her a headache. Maybe she should go out after all.

Sharon turned back to the room. She'd planned a nice healthy walk in the park this afternoon, but the weather today was more like April than almost June. The sky matched her mood – grey. But she would go anyway. Being stuck in the flat all by herself was doing her head in and although Craig usually shut the shop at lunchtime on Saturdays, this afternoon he was staying to organise the new frames that had arrived yesterday. At least that was what he'd told her, but it wasn't something he'd ever done before and it seemed a bit of a lame excuse for not spending Saturday afternoon with his pregnant wife.

Tears came into Sharon's eyes and she blinked them away impatiently. You're not supposed to get depressed until after the birth, she told herself fiercely. At this stage, you're supposed to be happy and eager and bubbling over with excitement. But today she was barely managing to be cynical.

In spite of her black mood she changed her shoes and set out, pulling her jacket round the bump, then fastening it all the way up when the wind hit her at the front door. Now she felt like a hippopotamus again. Look on the bright side, Sharon, in a few weeks you'll be able to get into normal clothes again.

Emma from the first floor flat, out watering plants on her balcony, waved enthusiastically as Sharon walked down the communal pathway. 'Not long now! Bet you can't wait!'

Sharon smiled and nodded, and rushed on before Emma took it into her head to ask her in for coffee. She couldn't be doing with baby small-talk, or people who still had marvellous jobs to go to asking condescending questions about how she was getting on without one. To the park, to the park. She turned right and walked as briskly as possible towards the end of the road. Her bump made anything quicker than a sedate stroll feel as if she was climbing Everest, and even walking along the flat was hard work today. Sharon clasped her hands under the baby. And they *still* hadn't chosen a name.

She reached the park and walked down the hill towards the seats by the duck pond. She would sit there for a bit and then she'd go home via the High Street, and buy salmon steaks for dinner. She would try again. Maybe she and Craig would manage to talk if she made a lovely dinner at home. She could even get a bottle of Prosecco to toast their new lives with the baby. Surely one tiny glass wouldn't hurt now.

Feeling a bit more positive, Sharon sat down and watched the ducks and swans swimming their aimless circuits. A family with three little girls arrived and Sharon looked on as the children scattered breadcrumbs in the water. It only took a moment before every creature on the pond had gathered round them.

'Careful, you three!' the father called. 'You're too near the edge – that water's pretty disgusting, you don't want to fall in.'

Giggling, the children moved back two steps, and Sharon smiled as the birds moved with them. Would she bring her daughter here too, in a year or so, and feed the ducks?

After a few minutes the bread was inside the ducks and the family went on their way. Loneliness crept through Sharon. Okay. That was enough fresh air. Time to go and buy those salmon steaks.

She hoisted herself to her feet and took a deep breath before starting back towards the gate. The hill seemed much steeper now she was going uphill, and she stopped for a breather halfway to the top, wishing there was a bench here too. Her legs had gone all wobbly on her. But short of sitting on the ground she couldn't have a proper rest until she got to the swing park by the gates.

On she went uphill, vowing not to return here until the baby was well and truly in its push chair and she was much fitter. This was almost as bad as the day she'd gone all shaky outside the internet café.

Come on, woman. *You can do this, you're strong, you're in charge.* And you're nearly at the top now. Five more steps should do it…

The pain came from nowhere, gripping her womb, squeezing relentlessly and viciously. Sharon dropped to her knees, panting, huddled over her enormous belly, palms supporting her weight on the damp gravel pathway. No, no, what was happening? Was this a contraction? The start of labour? But it wasn't supposed to start like this; it was supposed to start gently and gradually to let her get used to the contractions. And it was three weeks too early; it couldn't be the baby.

The pain eased off almost as suddenly as it had started, and Sharon breathed more freely. Thank goodness. She sat back on her heels and brushed the gravel from her hands, looking round to see if anyone was within shouting distance. There was no-one in sight, and she swallowed painfully. Home. She had to get home as quickly as possible and phone the midwife. And Craig. Oh, please don't let it be the baby. She forced herself to her feet, reaching for the mobile in her pocket, and everything went black.

Julie

'Well done, folks. Great team effort and we're done now, so it'll be business as usual on Monday.'

Julie joined in the brief round of applause when Dee finished speaking, then pushed the books trolley into its place beside the desk and grinned at her boss. 'I can't believe the time it's taken to get the place fixed up again.'

'I know,' said Dee. 'But you've all been brilliant.'

'I helped sort the picture books, didn't I, Mummy?' said Sam, sliding one hand into Julie's. 'Can we go for a picnic now?'

Julie glanced outside. She'd used the bribe of a picnic in the park to keep Sam motivated, but the weather had turned out distinctly non-summery.

'Tell you what. We'll go to the swings for a bit before we go home, and keep the picnic for a nicer day. Okay?'

'I'll join you,' said Dee. 'I could do with some fresh air, even if it is sub-Arctic.'

The park was deserted. Sam ran to the climbing frame while Julie joined Dee on a flaky green bench, jiggling the buggy in an attempt to keep Amy asleep a little longer. Dee shivered and Julie laughed.

'You're living in the wrong country. A nice sunny balcony in Italy would suit you better than a freezing cold swing park in Scotland.'

'Mm. If we were in Italy we could be sitting on a piazza, drinking chilled white wine and complaining about the heat. Let's emigrate.'

'Chance would be a fine thing,' said Julie. 'Can you speak Italian? And what would we live on?'

Dee gave her a little push. 'For pity's sake, woman, where's your spirit of adventure? Look, was that a raindrop? I think we should buy some nice gooey cakes and head back to my flat for coffee before we freeze to death. How about it?'

'I'm in,' said Julie. 'Sam! Time for cream cakes!'

The little boy was on his scooter now, flying round the border of the playground. 'Can we go down to the pond first?'

A spatter of fat raindrops had Julie pulling the rain hood over Amy. She called to Sam. 'Come on, Sammy-boy! We'll do the pond tomorrow too. You can bring a bag of crumbs for the ducks.'

Sam scooted towards the park gates and Julie turned the buggy while Dee held an umbrella over them both. It was time to get out of the rain.

Jeff

Jeff strolled round Cybersonics. The place was well filled, as usual on chilly Saturday afternoons. He could go home any time. Davie and Phil were on late today, and there was nothing happening that needed his personal attention. Jeff chewed on a thumb nail. He didn't want to leave his safe little cyber-cocoon. Home seemed to mock him now, continually pointing out his failure to provide Caro with a family; home was a nice little yuppie house on a nice little street where all the neighbours were nice little families with masses of nice little kids. And on Saturday afternoon all these kids would be biking up and down their cul-de-sac and playing skipping ropes or football, and if they weren't doing that they'd be yelling at their parents to let them play on the computer or watch telly. Oh, it was a great place for families, and if he didn't do something about getting a baby, he would lose both his ideal life and his wife.

Jeff stopped at the door and looked out. Families galore on the High Street, too. He drummed his fingers on the wooden doorway.

His queries about finding a baby had been out for nearly a week and he'd had no useful replies whatsoever. Oh, it *would* be possible to buy a baby, but comfortably off as he was, he couldn't spare the kind of money that babies seemed to cost. Was it really so difficult to get hold of a reluctant pregnant girl who only wanted a good home for her child, and not tens of thousands of pounds as well? He could afford a couple of K, but the mortgage on the house was pretty steep and a lot of his money was tied up in the shop, too. He couldn't even withdraw a few thousand without Caro finding out, as a trained accountant, she did most of their bookkeeping. The whole situation was making him ill, and Caro wasn't looking so hot these days either.

He found himself thinking again about the pregnant woman who'd had the dizzy spell last week. Sharon. She hadn't been over the moon about being pregnant, had she? But then there was probably a long way between not being over the moon and wanting to sell on your baby. What a failure he was.

He trailed through to the back of the shop and packed his briefcase. Maybe he could just walk by the optician's and ask Sharon's husband how she was after Tuesday's upset. No harm in that. He would take those glasses someone had forgotten last week as an excuse to go in, yes. He pulled them from the drawer, a blue case containing a pair of steel-rimmed specs. And look, there was even a sticker inside with the optician's name on it. Craig Morrison. Perfect. This was meant to be. Cheered, Jeff called goodbye to Davie and Phil and left the café.

In spite of the weather – it was raining now – the High Street was thronged with Saturday afternoon shoppers, but the optician's was empty when he arrived. Jeff pushed the door open, a bell clinging as he did so. He looked around appreciatively. Nice little place. Shiny wooden floor, black granite counter and tables, and rows of frames along the walls, mirrors behind them. There was serious money here. How unfair was that? This Craig had a flourishing business *and* a pregnant wife.

Sharon's husband came through from the back. 'We're not actually open this – oh – you're the bloke from the internet café, aren't you? I never did thank you properly for being so kind to Sharon last week.'

Jeff couldn't have wished for a better opening. 'No problem. I just happened to be in the right place at the right time. How is she now?'

Craig Morrison smiled, then shrugged, his eyes sliding towards his mobile on the counter. 'Fine, fine. Tired, of course.'

Jeff stiffened. The other man was uncomfortable with the question, so much was clear. He should do a little prodding here. How right he'd been to come. He nodded sympathetically. 'I thought she looked a bit drawn on Tuesday. But she'll be excited too, I expect. Is it your first baby?'

'Yes, it is. I'm sorry, I've forgotten your name.'

Jeff re-introduced himself, and pulled out the pair of forgotten reading glasses.

Craig examined the glasses. 'I can't tell off-hand, but I should be able to find the owner in our system and give them a call. Thanks for bringing them in.'

'No problem. Well, I hope everything goes well for Sharon. That's a lucky baby, you know. So many babies aren't welcome. I saw a news report the other day that would turn your hair grey. You'd think people would want to give their own kids the best possible start in life, wouldn't you? But I won't keep you – you'll be wanting to get home to your wife. Tell her good luck from me.'

He left the shop, hearing a ringtone as he closed the door behind him. A quick look back showed that Craig was staring after him with a strained expression on his face, completely ignoring the insistent ringing of the mobile phone on the counter.

The High Street seemed a much brighter place as Jeff hurried back to the car, dodging shoppers with enormous umbrellas. Maybe there was something to be done with Craig and Sharon after all. He would keep an eye on the pair of them, yes, and on their baby too.

Sharon

There was water running down her face. Sharon forced her eyes open, but closed them again when all she saw was a green and grey swirl. Nausea flooded through her as realisation dawned. Lord no, she had passed out in the park, that contraction, oh help, no – was the baby coming? She had to get home. But her arms and legs didn't belong to her and her head was spinning. No way could she stand up yet.

She took a deep breath and shouted. 'Help! Can somebody…' Her voice came out a thready caricature of its usual self, and Sharon's throat closed in despair. No one would hear that.

For a moment she lay still, listening to the raindrops pattering on the path, feeling them run down her neck and soak into her trousers. She could smell the mustiness of wet undergrowth around the group of trees and bushes to her left. No one would come to the park now, and this path wasn't even a short cut that people might use to get home quicker. Hell, what was she going to do? Her phone. She had to call an ambulance.

Sharon rolled onto her back and thrust her right hand into her pocket. Thank God, here was her phone. But as soon as she opened her eyes, dizziness overcame her and she closed them again. She began to sob, her teeth chattering with cold and shock. Deep breath, Sharon. Relax for a moment and try again. She counted breaths up to ten, then opened her eyes very slowly, holding her phone in front of her face. At first everything was swimming in front of her, then the world swung into focus, and God, no – she must have fallen on her phone. Dozens of thick and thin cracks were criss-crossing the screen and it wouldn't switch on. Sharon sobbed aloud.

Maybe she would manage to crawl along the path. If she got to the top of the hill, there was a chance that someone would see her from the pavement outside the park. It was only fifty metres away, surely she'd manage that?

Taking a deep breath, she heaved herself onto all fours. The sick, dizzy feeling lurched back, but it wasn't as bad as before. Right. All she had to do now was move one limb after another, uphill.

As soon as she pushed herself forwards she fell again, hitting her cheek hard on the gravel pathway and crying out with the sudden pain.

'Help! Can somebody help, please?'

Nothing. The rain was heavy now; her trousers were soaked and she could feel dampness spreading inside her jacket. Oh God, no. There was nothing more she could do. Still sobbing, Sharon lay cradling her bump.

The baby wasn't moving. Heavy fear crashed into her gut and Sharon moaned again. 'Come on, baby, please be okay. Are you okay?'

This was the baby she hadn't wanted, except that wasn't true anymore because the thought that her baby might not be okay was the worst thought in the world. Oh yes, she wanted this baby, but she was helpless to do anything to get them out of this God-awful situation.

Just when she was thinking that things couldn't possibly get any worse, another contraction hit and Sharon writhed in pain. No way could she do her breathing in these circumstances. Choking, she moaned through the pain and lay exhausted when it was over. Was she going to die right here in the park? Would the baby die? But maybe it was dead already. Her daughter. Blackness swirled into Sharon's head and she fought to remain conscious.

Voices. She could hear voices.

'…must have fallen out of my bag when we were down at the pond…'

Swift footsteps were approaching and Sharon moaned again.

A child screamed. 'There's a lady down here and she's dead!'

'Hello? Can you hear me?' It was a man's voice now.

Several young voices were crying in distress as strong hands pulled Sharon over on her side. The relief was incredible. Help had arrived. She could hear a woman now, calling for an ambulance while the man spoke again.

'She's not dead, girls. She's breathing nicely. Go to the top of the hill with Mummy and wave to the ambulance when it comes.'

It was the family she'd watched at the duck pond. Sharon felt fingers on her wrist, and forced her eyes open again. A dark head was above her, but his features were blurred.

'Hello, love, just lie still. An ambulance is on its way. Can I phone someone for you?'

Shivering, Sharon whispered Craig's number and he repeated it back to her as he keyed it in.

After a moment he patted her shoulder. 'No answer, I'm afraid. But here's the ambulance.'

Sirens were shrieking down the High Street and through the park gates. Sharon lay panting, cradling the baby, but it still wasn't moving. The fear was numbing – *was her baby alive?* Different hands were touching her now as she listened to the man explaining that she'd been conscious enough to give a phone number.

'Right, my love. Can you open your eyes? No? Move your arms and legs for me? Good. We'll just pop a collar on your neck and get you into the ambulance. We'll be at the hospital in ten, don't you worry.'

Sharon lay passively as an uncomfortable hard collar was put around her neck. She felt herself being lifted, then another man's voice was speaking, reassuring her as the ambulance rolled off, siren wailing again.

Julie

'Can I have the last éclair?' Sam was gazing up at her, leaning against her chair as he wheedled.

Julie tapped his nose. 'You may not. You'll be sick if you have any more and we don't want that, do we?'

'I won't be sick,' said Sam, pouting.

Dee winked at Julie. 'Tell you what, Sam. We'll put it in a freezer bag and you can take it home for tomorrow.'

Julie watched as Sam considered, head to one side, then nodded and trotted off to help bag up the éclair. She relaxed back in her chair, cuddling Amy. Dee was brilliant with kids, despite not having any of her own.

'Want a job as surrogate grandma?' she said, when Sam and Dee returned.

'You bet. Julie, I know you lost your parents, but – aren't Matt's folks around either?'

Julie shook her head. 'His dad died of pancreatic cancer when he was only fifty-two, and his mum lives with her sister in Cornwall.'

'Well, consider it a done deal. Just don't call me Granny, okay?'

Julie blinked as unexpected tears welled up, but a muffled ringtone in her bag interrupted them and she pulled out her mobile. It wasn't a number she recognised.

'Hello, I'm Angela Baird, one of the midwives at Bridgehead Infirmary. We've got Sharon Morrison here. She's in labour but we can't get hold of her husband, and she'd like you to be with her.'

Julie gripped the phone, shocked. 'In labour! But I've got my kids here, I can't just leave–'

Dee was leaning forwards, looking at her significantly. 'Grandma, remember?'

Twenty minutes later Julie was running into the maternity unit at the hospital. Dee had insisted on treating her to a taxi, which seemed a bit OTT even for an ersatz-Grandma, but they could fight about that another day. She wasn't sure what she was doing here, either. She and Sharon had barely known each other two minutes – wasn't there a closer friend to accompany Sharon through labour? And what on earth was the poor woman's husband doing that he couldn't be contacted when his wife could give birth any time?

Her new friend's opening words explained the first point, anyway. 'Oh, thank you, Julie. I wanted someone who knows what it's like, and none of my friends have had babies.'

Julie sat down and gripped a cold hand. Sharon looked terrible, her pallor emphasising the redness of her swollen nose and the long, vivid graze on one cheek. Her voice was half-hysterical as she told Julie what had happened.

Julie winced. 'You poor thing. But don't worry, I'm sure they'll get hold of Craig in time. First babies always take ages.'

The midwife was adjusting the heart-rate monitor belt around Sharon's middle. 'I've a feeling this one might be in a hurry. But don't worry, Sharon. We've left a message on his phone, and everything is under control now.'

Sharon nodded briefly. Julie sat holding her hand, remembering her own experiences when Sam was on the way. Matt had brought her here; it had been well past midnight and the streets were deserted. Julie took a deep breath. She'd had an intact family then.

The next hour passed slowly. Sharon didn't want to talk, but was obviously grateful for the stream of comforting remarks Julie and the midwife kept making. The pains were about six minutes apart now and Julie breathed through them with Sharon. She was relaxing back in her chair after a particularly hefty contraction when the door jerked open and a dark-haired man strode in. Ah. The absent husband.

'Christ, Sharon, are you all right?'

Sharon's face had gone red and her voice was shaking. 'Where the hell have you been? This is your baby too, you know.'

'I went home to get your case with all your stuff for hospital as soon as I knew, didn't I?'

Julie stood up to give him her chair, and he flopped down and glared at Sharon, who was glaring right back.

Julie felt like shaking them both. 'Hi, Craig, I'm Julie. Sharon, honey, the important thing is that Craig's here now, and you two are going to have to start helping each other. Having this baby's all you need to think about for the moment.'

'Right on,' said the midwife. 'Labour doesn't have a pause button. You've done the classes, Craig, you know what to do.'

His shoulders slumped. 'I'll do my best, if you think I can help.'

Sharon nodded, reaching for his hand as another contraction started.

Julie pressed her lips together, watching as they breathed together, loneliness creeping through her. How good it would be to be one of a pair again.

Jeff

The High Street was busy as Jeff walked briskly back towards the narrow lane beyond Cybersonics. He always parked there; it was a handy little place, especially when he was working the late shift.

In the car he sat for a moment, turning the key in his hand, aware of heavy reluctance in his gut. Caro wouldn't be expecting him home yet. He'd bunked off early today, not like him, but these were difficult times. This baby business was stress pure. On the other hand, he could be proud of himself and Caro damn well should be too. He had made something of his life. He had a business, a nice home, he had married the girl of his dreams, and if he could only produce a baby everything in his bloody garden would be completely and utterly lovely.

He started the car and pulled out into the High Street. What was he going to do? He would lose Caro if they didn't have this baby – any baby, really – and he couldn't bear that. He couldn't.

So a baby was a must. He would have to plan it logically, and fortunately he was good at that – computer specialists were logical people.

Start at the beginning, with the baby. The baby had to be. Fact. But they couldn't have one the usual way, and Caro wasn't up for IVF, which probably wouldn't succeed anyway. More facts. And because these were facts they were unalterable, and had to be accepted. Meaning that the baby would have to come from somewhere else. Jeff sighed. It always boiled down to the same thing. Somehow, he was going to have to beg, borrow or steal a baby. Or buy it.

He knew now that babies cost more than he could afford. He'd been naïve about that. Buying was out, then. Begging? Please, *please* give us a tiny baby to adopt? Unlikely to succeed, and definitely not in a useful time-frame. Borrow? A foster child could potentially be a permanent fixture in the family. But it would never be truly theirs, and the uncertainty would always be there, so that was out too. Which left stealing, and how did you go about stealing a baby? His one experience of that had been a complete fiasco.

This was where the logic and planning came in, he thought, turning into the road that led to the riverbank walkway. He couldn't go home yet; home only emphasised his failure. He parked in an empty space near the cruise boat kiosk and cracked the window open. A damp, slightly musty river smell floated into the car, and Jeff closed his eyes.

Maybe he should go down to London. With all those kids living rough, surely there would be a girl there, pregnant, not knowing what to do about a baby she hadn't planned. He could befriend her, and then when the baby was born he could take it home to Caro. Everyone would be happy, and how much better it would be for the baby. It wouldn't even be stealing.

Jeff rummaged in his pockets for the packet of mints he'd bought that morning. He could go any time; he was due some holidays. It shouldn't be difficult to find a girl like that – even normal couples didn't always want their babies. Look at Sharon – it was blatantly obvious she would have preferred *not* to be pregnant. It was infuriating; it simply wasn't right that people like that should be having unwanted babies at the drop of a hat, while he and Caro, who would be devoted parents, had to go through all this bother to achieve something that other people managed with no effort at all.

The more he thought about Sharon, the angrier he became. Surely she and Craig couldn't seriously intend to keep the baby? Maybe he should go by soon – with a little present for the coming baby – and have a friendly chat.

Sharon

She had never imagined it would be this hard. Lying on a high hospital bed, crying out louder with every contraction because she couldn't get her breathing under control, resenting Craig more and more with every word he uttered. Not that he was uttering many now. After the first hour he'd retreated into himself, going through the motions of helping her but offering no real support. Sharon had seen the midwife cast her eyes heavenwards several times. Her handsome husband had turned into a petulant teenager who went into a fit of the sulks when he didn't get his own way. The only good thing was she could hear the baby's heart beeping away on the monitor. In spite of their sojourn on the park path, the baby was okay.

Another contraction started and Craig stood up to massage her back. Sharon managed to breathe through this one without losing the pattern, and the midwife grinned at them both.

'You're getting the hang of it, team,' she said. 'Sharon, let's try a little walk before the next one. Labour generally goes quicker if you're active. Craig, take her arm and walk with her.'

Sharon nodded and the midwife helped her up. The labour room was small, with blue painted walls and the bed in the middle. It wasn't one of those super-modern places with birthing chairs and ropes from the ceiling, but there was room to walk up and down.

The next contraction started and Sharon leaned across the bed.

Five contractions later, she looked mutely at the midwife. Lying down had never sounded so appealing.

'You're doing so well,' said the midwife. 'Hop back on the bed and we'll check how far on you are.'

Sharon held her breath while the midwife examined her.

'Super,' she said warmly. 'Almost fully dilated. This baby'll be here before you know it.'

'Pain,' said Sharon, struggling to sit more upright. Craig supported her as the contraction intensified, and suddenly she was glad he was here. Okay, he wasn't saying much, but he was doing his bit like they'd learned at the classes. Maybe they'd get through this after all.

The next contraction was like none of the others, and Sharon yelled in agony, aware that Craig was cringing beside her.

The midwife gave her shoulder a shake. 'Sharon, when the next contraction comes – close your mouth, chin on chest, and push as hard as you can. Okay?'

Sharon nodded, feeling her heart start to beat wildly. The baby, she would soon see her baby.

'Here we go, *big* push, Sharon, that's it, a real big push now, push push push. Yes – wow, here she comes already! Stop pushing, *stop*, Sharon, pant for the head. Craig, you pant with her.'

'Panting,' said Craig, his voice shaking, and they panted together until Sharon gave a loud scream. She couldn't help it. Surely giving birth shouldn't feel like this?

'Brilliant, that's great, the head's here, one more push and we'll be done.'

Sharon collapsed back. One more pain like that would kill her.

'Okay, just a little push, Sharon – look, look, here's your baby!'

A thin baby wail filled the room, and tears rushed down Sharon's face as the midwife deposited a slippery, wet creature on her front and started to wipe it down.

'Here we are, a lovely little girl. You hold her, Sharon.'

Sharon peered at the baby. She had a mass of black hair, and her face was pink and squashed-looking. She was flexing tiny fingers, gripping Sharon's thumb already. The midwife tucked a fresh towel over the baby, and Sharon clutched her daughter, gazing into the hazy blue eyes looking straight into her own.

'Oh my *God*,' she whispered, blessed relief filling her heart. Her baby was here. Her girl. 'Craig? Look…'

But Craig had run from the room.

Chapter Seven

Julie

Sunlight was streaming into Julie's bedroom when she awoke on Sunday morning, and she rubbed her eyes. It wasn't like her to sleep this late, more especially, it wasn't like her daughter, but there was Amy still slumbering peacefully in her cot beside Julie's bed. A lump came into Julie's throat as she looked at the baby's pink cheeks and sleep-damp hair. Thank goodness Amy hadn't realised what happened to her the other day. The anguish had all been Julie's.

Stretching, she remembered the previous day's events. Should she phone Sharon? The baby must have arrived by now. Or – not necessarily, she realised, counting back. Sharon's labour had started around three o'clock yesterday afternoon, and first babies could easily take longer than seventeen hours to appear. Julie swung her feet over the edge of the bed. She would phone the hospital around nine.

'Mummy? Can we have breakfast now?' Sam's voice from the living room sent Julie swiftly towards the shower.

'Give me five minutes,' she called. 'You could lay the table, huh?'

Sunday breakfast was always special. It was a family tradition, dating back to their first days in this flat. Croissants, warmed in the oven, with butter and raspberry jam. Sam loved it.

After breakfast, Julie sat down with her phone. Hopefully they would tell her something at the hospital – she couldn't exactly say she was a relative.

She called the labour ward, and fortunately the midwife who answered remembered her from the previous day, and told her that Sharon had been moved upstairs. 'Mother and daughter are doing well,' she said cheerfully.

Julie thanked her and ended the call, grinning. A little girlfriend for Amy, how lovely. She would visit this afternoon; Dee had already offered to take Sam and Amy for an hour or two. Surrogate grandmas rocked. She stood up to fetch more coffee, and her phone rang in her hand.

'Hi!' said a deep male voice, sounding pleased. 'I'm glad I caught you – I tried a couple of times yesterday but you were switched off.'

It was DS Max Sanders. Why was he phoning on a Sunday? Surely not about the break-in at the library. Julie's palms were suddenly moist.

'I was – busy,' she said at last. 'How's the boy they found in the library? There's hardly been anything about him in the paper. Is he okay?'

'Not really,' said Max Sanders. 'His parents don't want any media attention, and fortunately for them the father is something quite high up in newspapers, so he's had more success blocking the story than you or I would. I'm afraid the boy's still critical.'

'Oh no.' The day turned shadowy.

'Um, Julie, I was wondering if you and the kids would like to do something this afternoon? The park, maybe? I promised I would show Sam a police car, and we didn't have time last week.'

Julie gripped the receiver more tightly. She hadn't dated since before her marriage, and the thought of getting to know a man again – but that was thinking way too far ahead. He'd asked her out to the park. With her kids.

'Sounds fun,' she said cautiously. 'It would have to be earlyish. I'm visiting a friend – remember Sharon? – in hospital later this afternoon.'

'Okay. How about a hamburger lunch and a walk in the park?'

Julie agreed, wondering if she was doing the right thing. On an impulse, she called Dee.

'Of course you are!' said her friend. 'You're going for a burger with a nice guy; it's not a marriage proposal. Someday you'll find someone who's right for you, Julie. It might not be Max the policeman, but maybe he's a good place to start.'

Julie rang off and rushed to her bedroom to rummage through her clothes. However long ago was it since she'd worried about what to wear on a date? Years and years.

Caro

As usual on sunny Sunday mornings, the kids playing in the garden next door woke Caro. It was Red Indians today, by the sound of it. She rolled on her side and pulled the pillow over her head to block out the sound of happy children. How inconsiderate – her own parents had never let them out to play this early on a Sunday, in case they disturbed the neighbours. But grousing about it wasn't fair; Caro knew if she and Jeff had kids she wouldn't be giving the shouts from next door a second thought. Grimly, she threw back the duvet and reached for her bathrobe.

At least she had the place to herself; Jeff was on the early shift today. He'd come home late yesterday afternoon, but they barely exchanged a word during yet another meal eaten in front of the television. Afterwards, he vanished upstairs into the spare room, where he kept his computer stuff. The room where the no-baby would never sleep. When Caro went up after watching the late-night film, he was already asleep in bed, and in spite of the mild night she lay shivering, huddled on the edge of the mattress with the shared duvet barely covering her back. She was married to a man who was rapidly becoming repulsive to her. Was this her punishment for entering into what was more a marriage of convenience than a love match? Sleep, when it came, was dogged by uncomfortable dreams she no longer remembered.

A cappuccino calmed her nerves, and Caro sat at the kitchen table listening as two cowboys and one poor Indian ran around the garden next door. The day stretched empty in front of her. When Jeff was working on Sundays she usually either blobbed here at home, or visited Jeff's grandmother, whose sheltered housing flat was a short bus ride away. Iris was a lovely lady, and she'd done all she could to welcome Caro to the family, but a visit today would be impossible. Caro knew she'd never be able to act the part of cheery granddaughter-in-law today, with Iris so happy and excited, planning her eightieth next Sunday. She had invited all the family – Jeff's brother and his family were going, and Iris's sister and some cousins. Caro pressed her fist to her mouth. She couldn't spoil it for Iris.

As usual when she was perturbed, she turned to cleaning to vent some energy, and banged around the ground floor before hoovering her way up the stairs. Landing, bedroom, bathroom… now there was only the room that belonged to Jeff and the no-baby, and Caro hesitated. If she went in there she'd end up howling, and it was really up to Jeff to keep this room in order. But she'd done every other room in the house and it seemed silly to stop here.

Determinedly closing her mind to the mental picture of how the room would look if their family planning had been successful, Caro vacuumed the beige carpet and reorganised the cuddly tiger on the sofa bed. Now to empty the bin – what a load of paper Jeff had stuffed in here. This should be in the recycling.

She pulled a wad of thick, white paper from Jeff's waste bin, then sat down suddenly, her mouth dry. This was one of these expensive paper carriers, almost an *exclusive* carrier bag, and it had come from The Rocking Horse. The biggest, poshest baby shop in Edinburgh. Had Jeff gone all the way to Edinburgh to buy something in a baby shop? If he had, then *why?* And when? Or had he found the bag somewhere and used it? But it looked new, apart from the folds from being in the bin. Caro smoothed it out and looked inside, but no receipt was lurking.

She dropped the bag and searched around the desk top, but there was nothing there connected to The Rocking Horse. Caro shrugged. The most likely thing was that Jeff had used the bag to transport something from Cybersonics. Maybe this carrier had belonged to Davie and his wife.

Yes, that would be it.

Sharon

'He just upped and left! I don't even know if he saw her – I was kind of distracted by what was going on between my legs. And now he's not answering his phone. What a jerk. But I guess you've got that T-shirt too.' Sharon tried to smile, but she could see Julie wasn't fooled.

'Maybe he panicked. He's obviously scared of the responsibility.'

'Him and me both. The difference is I'm here with the baby, and he's not.' Sharon sniffed dismally. She hadn't believed it yesterday when the midwife went to get Craig back in but returned to say he seemed to have left the building. Okay, he wasn't over the moon about being a daddy, but to leave her literally in the middle of giving birth was something Sharon couldn't get her head round. Her first thought was he'd felt dizzy and hadn't wanted to faint – he'd never been good with blood. But as time passed it became increasingly evident that Craig hadn't simply gone out for some fresh air, and Sharon's rage grew. How dare he leave her like this?

The midwives tried to be reassuring, but Sharon could see the shock in their eyes. What kind of man would rush off like that – and stay away? She lay clutching the baby, who gave a couple of squawks then settled down, apparently quite happy to lie listening to Sharon's heart pounding as her anger grew.

'Give him till tomorrow,' the nurse said when they took her up to the ward and settled her into a single room. This was probably where they put the women whose babies were sick or deformed or dead… and now she had it. The woman whose husband ran off as the baby emerged.

The ward sister brought her a cup of tea, and fussed around unpacking Sharon's case for her while she drank it. 'He's had a shock, Sharon – typical bloke, eh? If childbirth was up to them the human race would die out.'

It didn't sound very convincing, and Sharon was glad when the woman eventually left her – and the baby – to their own devices. Which meant the baby slept on and Sharon lay staring at the wall. What was she supposed to do now? Wait until tomorrow was the only answer. No way could she leave her bed, discharge herself, find Craig and kill him that night.

Now tomorrow was here and Craig wasn't. Sharon spent the day learning how to care for her daughter, and trying Craig's mobile every ten minutes.

She had never been so glad to see a friendly face when Julie arrived at four o'clock, clutching a box of chocolates. Julie kissed her and oohed over the baby and it was all very comforting, though the other woman's sympathetic expression was hard to bear.

'Oh no, Sharon. Do you want me to go and see if Craig's at home?'

'No. Thanks. I need him to come back because he wants to. But that doesn't seem very likely, does it? It's almost a whole day now.'

'He might need more time to recover. Just wait up, Sharon. And try not to chuck something at him if – when – he does come back. The baby needs you both.'

Sharon stared at her daughter, asleep in the plastic crib by the bed. All those months she'd spent wishing there was no baby. She didn't feel like that anymore, but Craig obviously did. He was probably wondering how best to get rid of them both.

Chapter Eight

Jeff

The DJ was gabbling away about traffic congestion on the Bridgehead Ring Road, and Jeff turned the radio off. Caro always put it on in the mornings, but she'd gone for her shower, and his head was splitting. He pushed a cup under the machine for a double espresso; that would help. It wasn't often he had a bad head, and just as well, considering the time he spent in front of computer screens. He'd have needed a different job if he'd been prone to headaches.

Caro came down while he was still sipping the strong, sweet coffee. 'What happened to the radio? I wanted to hear the local news.'

'I've got a terrible head,' said Jeff, leaning his forehead in his left hand. Now if only she would put her arms round him and show him how much she loved him. But she didn't.

'Try a couple of those pills Louise told me about last week. They're specially for tension headaches – they really helped mine on Saturday.'

She produced a packet from her handbag. Jeff took it glumly, consoling himself with the thought that at least she was being caring, if not exactly loving. He pressed two tablets from the foil wrapping and swallowed them with the dregs of his coffee.

Caro disappeared, presumably to finish getting ready for work, and Jeff made himself another coffee and took it to the table. He didn't start until after lunch today and he had big plans for the morning. It was time to do something about Sharon and Craig before their baby arrived. He was going to find out where they lived, and call around with the christening robe he'd bought

74

for them. It had cost an arm and a leg, but that didn't matter. If Sharon and Craig agreed to give up the baby, the robe would come back here along with it, and who knows, he and Caro might have more than one child in the end. The robe could become a family heirloom.

Jeff sat with his head in his hands, waiting for the pills to take effect and picturing a succession of generations being christened.

'See you late tonight, then.' Caro was standing in the doorway with her jacket over one arm.

Jeff went to hug her, but she dodged away before he had touched her.

'Mind my war-paint,' she said in the over-bright voice she'd taken to using recently. 'Go and have a shower, that'll freshen you up and help your head too.'

The front door slammed behind her and Jeff watched from the living room window as she tapped smartly up the road in those new sandals she was so fond of. She was gone and he still hadn't said anything important. They wouldn't have time to talk at all today; he was in Cybersonics from two right through until ten. This was dire. He had to make things all right again with Caro, he just had to. A baby was the only thing that would help with that.

Caro disappeared around the corner, and Jeff turned into the room. The sofa looked soft and inviting, and he slumped down in one corner. Dear God, what was happening to his life? They hadn't mentioned the word 'baby' all weekend. It was as if Caro was deliberately avoiding the subject, and of course he could hardly tell her that he might have found the perfect baby right here in Bridgehead, but if that didn't work out he would go to London and find a girl who was expecting a child she didn't want. Everything would be okay when he could tell Caro there was a baby on the way, but whichever plan he ended up using would need to be a lot more definite before he presented it to his wife.

London sounded complicated. It might take him ages to find a girl, and it would be difficult to keep in touch with her when he did find her. It would be so much better if Sharon agreed to hand over that baby.

So he would pay her a visit. Today. He would go to Craig's shop first and have a chat with him too, because he should be friendly with them both, and in the course of the conversation he would find out where they lived. He could use the flyers about the new autumn courses as an excuse to go into the optician's.

Jeff jumped up, enthusiasm surging through him. This was going to work; he knew it was. The baby was due in – two weeks or so? That would give him plenty of time to befriend the couple and persuade them that life with no encumbrances was infinitely preferable to parenthood.

Half an hour later Jeff was striding along the High Street, headache gone and a box of flyers in his briefcase. There weren't many people around; at least half of the shops were closed on Monday mornings. Cybersonics was open, of course, but he didn't go in. And he knew the optician's would be open too, because he'd somehow made a mental note of the opening times when he was there last week. As if he'd known even then that he would be doing this today. Funny how things always turned out for the best.

His happy mood evaporated when he stepped into the optician's doorway and found the security blinds down and the door locked. What was going on? It was after nine; Craig should be here by now. Jeff looked for the opening times on the door and saw the card hanging at eye level – 'Closed until Monday 6th June'.

Dismayed, he turned and walked back along the High Street. Were Craig and Sharon away somewhere? Having a little holiday before the baby came, just the two of them? He and Caro should do that, actually. A week in Spain before the baby arrived sounded like a very good idea indeed. Mind you, he was surprised that Sharon had agreed to go away, so close to the birth.

A woman pushing an old-fashioned high pram passed by on the other side of the road, and Jeff watched her, nodding to himself. They had known a thing or two about prams in the sixties.

Babies weren't squashed into three-wheeled contraptions and taken jogging like they were nowadays. When the baby came home he would see that it had a real, proper pram and all the comforts it needed. But he was forgetting… Craig and Sharon – how could he make friends with them if they weren't here? Imagine if anything happened, and Sharon had the baby while they were away.

And Sharon had the baby…

He stopped short, kicking himself for being so stupid. They weren't on holiday, of course not – Sharon had had the baby and was in hospital with it. Craig must have taken time off to be with her. Oh no, no. The baby that could be his and Caro's was here, and he hadn't known. Panic filled his head and he started to run, tearing down the High Street towards the traffic lights, then stopping abruptly when he realised he had no idea where he was going.

He stood outside the Post Office struggling to get his breath back, aware that people were staring. Calm down, Jeff. The thing now was to find Sharon and get to be a trusted friend fast. It wasn't too late.

Right. He would phone the hospital first.

He waited until he was home again – it wasn't the kind of call he wanted to make in the middle of the High Street, and it was complicated. He had forgotten what Sharon's surname was, so he had to look up the optician's number first. There it was – Morrison, of course. He found and punched out the number of the Maternity Unit and was confronted by the second hurdle. They would give him no information whatsoever.

'I'm afraid that's our policy,' said the receptionist or whoever he was speaking to. 'We can't tell just anyone who's here and who's not. You'll understand that security has to be our first responsibility.'

Jeff did understand, but it was still annoying. He sat for a moment, clutching his head in both hands. His headache was gone, but there was a peculiar kind of tightness across his forehead.

Was he getting migraines now? All this stress, it wasn't fair – what had he ever done to deserve all this? He forced himself to think about the baby again.

So, what now? He still didn't know if Sharon was in hospital or on holiday. Or – could she be at home, with Craig looking after her there? Jeff turned back to the laptop. Thank goodness for online directories, and just please God they were in it. Yes, they were. Riverside Gardens, very nice.

He punched out the number and let the ringtone shrill through his head twenty-two times before breaking the connection. Nothing was going right this morning.

Sharon must be in the hospital. He would go there and search until he found her – there couldn't be that many women in the maternity ward. Surely Sharon would be pleased to know her – was it a son or a daughter? – had a new loving… friend. And Caro would leave him soon if he didn't get her a baby, he could sense it. She wasn't his Caro any longer, and he wasn't her Jeff; they had turned into different people. But having a baby would help them. People did change when they became parents, so it didn't matter that he and Caro had changed already. The baby would bring them back together. Their little boy or girl. Jeff smiled fondly. It was going to be such fun.

His and Caro's baby had been born. Sharon would be so glad to have her life back again. He knew she would.

Julie

Julie waved as the last of the 'Under-Three Story Club' kids left the library, all accompanied by smiling mums, who'd just had an hour and a half to themselves. The group had been her idea and it had been well-attended right from the start. Even if it was a glorified babysitting service, it got the kids and their families into the library and borrowing books. It was also the most intensive hour and a half of the week. Time to make coffee; she'd earned one.

Dee came in as the first cup was ready, and Julie pushed it over the table.

'Here,' she said, starting the machine again. 'Your reward for having Sam and Amy yesterday.'

Dee sat down and sipped. 'Wasn't a problem. Amy was a joy, and Sam chattered away the whole time about having actually sat in a police car.'

Julie grinned, then bit her lip.

Dee pounced. 'What's up? I got the impression you had a great time with Max?'

Julie giggled. 'We had a wonderful time. Except Sam monopolised the whole thing. We had lunch in McDonalds and Sam asked Max questions about the police, then we had a walk in the park and Sam asked Max more questions, and then we sat in the police car and talked about Max's arrests and his weapons training, and Sam couldn't get his questions out fast enough. He had a ball, but Max and I barely exchanged three words. Mind you – I really don't know if I'm ready to start anything new yet.'

'Better make sure you have Sam with you at all times, then,' said Dee, laughing.

'I guess. Oh, I'm going to see Sharon again this afternoon. I'll take her the baby massage book.'

'Well done, a new customer. And Julie – if you ever want to talk things through, just say the word.'

Julie sipped her coffee. Dee was a good friend. 'Thanks.'

The rest of the morning passed swiftly and Julie was surprised to see it was twelve when she finished unpacking the latest consignment of new books. Lunchtime already.

A glance in the staffroom mirror revealed that the sneezing fit and accompanying watery eyes when she was emptying the dusty box of books hadn't done her appearance any good at all. Julie grabbed her handbag and went into the loo to repair the damage.

'Hello? Anyone here?'

A deep voice came from the desk and Julie froze. It was Max. She couldn't go out there, not looking like this. She could sort her face, but her grubby clothes were a different story. She didn't want him to see her in this state. Hardly daring to breathe, she listened as Max spoke to Dee.

'I've got some photos here for you and your staff to look at. They're all more or less local kids with drug problems of different kinds. You might have seen some of them hanging around.'

A rustling noise told Julie that the photos were being removed from their envelope while Dee spoke. 'The others are all at lunch. I'll get back to you, shall I? Oh, and I'm told you made a small boy's day yesterday.'

Julie could hear the grin in Max's voice. 'Reminded me of when I was a small boy myself.'

Julie's heart melted. Oh, he was nice. Not to mention good-looking. And not a hint of a leading question about her and the kids, so he was discreet, too.

Dee was apparently still looking at the photos. 'They're all complete strangers to me, I'm afraid.'

'Okay. Let me know if anyone else recognises any of them, will you? I'll collect them later. And say hello to Julie from me. I'm sorry I missed her.'

Firm footsteps told Julie that Max was leaving the building, and she crept back out. Dee was taking a large brown envelope into the staffroom.

'Julie, my lamb, that is one very nice young man,' she said severely.

'You think I should grab him with both hands, don't you?'

A wry smile passed over Dee's face and Julie sighed.

'Maybe I will. Soon.'

Caro

It was lunchtime before Caro heard the news. She listened every day now; the local radio station had short bulletins every half hour and longer ones on the hour. She wanted to hear something – anything, about the boy who was presumably still in hospital after the break-in at the library. How was she to find out if he was the same boy who'd accosted her about the ecstasy tablets last week? Because if he was, did that make her a – what did they call it? – an 'accessory after the fact'? Her gut twisted every time she thought about how she'd thrown those pills at his feet. That one thoughtless, truculent action could have harmed another human being irreparably. It was a horrible feeling, and the only way to get rid of it was to find out if they were two different boys. The local radio seemed a likely place to have the info, so as soon as Louise left to buy them both a sandwich in the shop across the road, Caro turned the sound up. There wouldn't be anything, though. There never was.

But today was different. As usual, the newsreader gave out the traffic situation first and then continued. 'The eighteen-year-old man who was hospitalised after taking an overdose of ecstasy during a break-in at Bridgehead Public Library last week, died in Bridgehead General Hospital this morning. Police are still looking for those who vandalised the library late last Tuesday evening or early Wednesday morning. Members of the public who may have seen or heard anything, or who have any relevant information about the case, are asked to call Bridgehead Police at 0800 470586, or any other police station... Bridgehead Town Council has...'

Caro snapped the radio off, her hand shaking. He was dead, that boy. If it was that boy. While she'd been having breakfast this morning or worrying about Jeff or sitting on the bus, the boy had died. It wasn't just an overdose any more. She could be to blame for his death. Caro buried her face in her hands. What was she to do? She couldn't live with herself, not knowing if she had played any part in his death. Maybe his picture would be in the papers tomorrow. Or maybe not, there had been virtually nothing about him up until now; that was unlikely to change now he was dead.

She could still go to the police, of course. They'd know what he looked like. But would they tell her? She had no right to know. And suppose those women who'd seen her fling the pills back at the boy had already reported it? She might be arrested on the spot, if she turned up at the police station now. What happened to people who withheld information – was it really illegal?

Caro choked back a sob, wishing with all her heart that she was knowledgeable about the law and what happened in situations like this. She'd never had any dealings with the police – hell, she'd never even had a parking ticket. And there was no one she could ask to help her with this. How she missed the feeling of Jeff being there for her, looking after her.

He'd been so strange these past few days. Hyper one minute, and then totally down the next, or else away in a dream, ignoring the world around him. Maybe it was his way of coping with their bad news, or maybe he sensed too that their marriage was doomed.

Caro folded her arms across her middle and gripped her elbows, trying to hug herself back to normality. But normal would never happen again. What with the grief about the no-baby, the worry about the boy and Jeff's strangeness, there was so much bad stuff going on in her life right now she didn't at all know how she was coping. Actually, she wasn't coping. She had never felt so alone. What was she going to do?

'Here we are. Tuna mayo on wholemeal for you, prawn cocktail for me, and they had some mini Danish pastries so I got a couple of those, too.' Louise breezed back into the salesroom and dumped a brown bag on Caro's desk. 'I'll get the bottles from the fridge. We can take the phone with us and go around the back to eat – it's lovely out today.'

Slowly, Caro gathered up her lunch bag and followed Louise out to the patch of ground behind the salesroom. It was a real suntrap, protected by buildings on all four sides. No breath of wind ever ventured here, and in July and August it was frequently too hot for comfort.

Louise was chattering away about her trip round the Royal Yacht yesterday, and Caro sat down heavily on the wall across the back of the yard, lifting her face to the sun and letting the words wash over her head. Louise was right, it was a beautiful day. And an eighteen-year-old boy was lying naked and cold on a mortuary slab; never again would he feel the warmth of the summer sun on his face, never again would he laugh or cry or… And she might be partly to blame. The thought made Caro feel sick. Somehow, she would have to find out who he was.

Maybe he had friends she could ask. That was a good idea, yes… Caro took a deep breath, relief and hope lightening her day. She would go back to the place she had seen him and look around for other kids, and she would go today. The boss was away all afternoon, and Lou wouldn't mind if she left half an hour early. And if that didn't work, she could always go to the dead boy's funeral. It would be in the 'deaths' section of tomorrow's paper, wouldn't it? She might be able to talk to someone there, and people often had photos on the order of service at funerals, too. One way or the other, she was bound to find out something soon.

The High Street was at its busiest at half past five when Caro walked along in the direction of her meeting with the boy the previous week. She rushed past Cybersonics on the other side of the road, not daring to look across in case Jeff was there and saw her. She didn't have the strength to talk to him now, because if he was acting strangely again she would have to worry about that too.

'I don't know Jeff anymore and I don't know myself either. I just want out of this marriage.' The thought was as clear in Caro's mind as if she'd spoken aloud, and tears sprang into her eyes. She'd been so happy at the start of the relationship, full of plans for her new family life. But now they had the no-baby, an enormous hurdle bang in the middle of her world, and it had changed everything. So maybe the happiness had only been superficial – it was easy to smile when things were going well.

The weird thing was, if there *had* been a baby, then she and Jeff would still be happy together, revelling in their child and probably planning another. The child that didn't exist, that never would, had changed her whole life. Did that make her a completely shallow person? Some uncaring, scheming woman who abandoned her relationship because she wasn't getting her own way? But what was happening to her now was too much to bear.

Today there was no shout behind her from Cybersonics, and Caro breathed again. Okay. Here was the Puff Pastry where she'd bought her lunch on the day she met the boy, and round here was Mortimer Square with the flower tubs and benches.

She stood still, her eyes tracking round the square. There were no lunchers now, of course. Two elderly women were sitting comparing purchases nearby, and a group of teenage girls were sprawled over a couple of benches at the other side, talking and giggling and playing with their phones. Nostalgia rose in Caro's heart and she blinked. Teen culture. It didn't seem long since she'd done something very similar after school every day. She walked round the square as slowly as she could, but no boys or youths were lurking today. Maybe she could ask those girls if they knew anything about the boy who had died. Caro hesitated. No. They were younger, thirteen or fourteen by the look of them. She'd only be setting herself up for an earful of abuse if she asked them.

It was on her second round of the square that she noticed the boy, and her breath caught in her throat. That was – hell, yes, that was Liam. Her brother's boy. He was sitting on the steps of an entrance close further down the square from the old family home, hunched over what looked like an exercise book, two years older than he'd been when she last saw him, but definitely her nephew.

Caro's mouth went dry. Pete and his family must still be in the area, then. Liam hadn't seen her; maybe she should just go… Pete had been the brother from hell when they were growing up, always mocking her and her sister, and not above the odd nip or slap. Both Caro and Rosie had left home as soon as they could, and avoided Pete as much as possible afterwards. When she met Jeff, Caro had dropped her brother – and his family – altogether. Jeff had never even met him.

Liam looked up and their eyes met. He was small, with a shock of dark hair and a solemn, pale face. Reluctantly, Caro walked across. If he lived here, he might be able to help her.

'Hi, Liam. Remember me?' He would be about ten now, maybe nine…

The boy nodded. 'Auntie Caro.' He stared at her indifferently, not getting up from his stony seat on the step.

'That's right,' said Caro, awkwardly. 'Um, do you live here now?'

Liam shook his head. 'Dad's away on the lorry a lot so I stay here with Alfie and his mum and dad till he gets back.'

Caro frowned. Pete must have traded in his job as a bus driver, but why wasn't Liam's mother looking after him? 'Where's your mum, then?'

He sniffed. 'She left a long time ago.'

Resentment robbed Caro of speech for a moment. How could a woman leave her child like that? She pulled herself together and nodded at the book on Liam's thin knees.

'Doing your homework?'

He blinked up at her, his mouth turned down. 'It's maths. I'm rubbish at it and there's no-one to help when Dad's away.'

Caro crouched down. This might not be a good idea, but by the looks of things, she wasn't the only one in this conversation having a bad time. 'Maybe I can help – I'm good at maths.'

Liam sniffed. 'There's this test tomorrow and I've forgotten how to do these.' He handed over the book.

Caro peered at the page, which contained six problems involving boxes of different items, then perched beside him on the step. 'Look – you're going wrong in the last part here. You have to find the number of pencils in four boxes, so you multiply by four. Then you add the extra pencils to that number and that's your answer. See? Like here, one box has fifteen pencils, so four boxes have…?'

'Sixty,' said Liam, after a few seconds. 'Plus five is sixty-five!'

'Good! You try the others now.'

The young face had brightened by about five hundred percent, and Caro laughed, in spite of her gloomy mood. Liam changed his answers and handed the book back.

'Correct!'

'Can you look at these ones as well?' He turned to the previous page.

Caro checked and corrected there too and he beamed. His face looked different when he smiled, and she cursed both Pete and Laura for leaving their son to fend for himself like this. She stood up again, rubbing her numb backside.

Liam's entire posture was more relaxed now and warmth flooded through Caro. She had helped one child, no matter what had happened to the other boy. It was the best feeling she'd had for weeks.

'Liam, I'm looking for a boy I saw here last week. Older than you, and he's white with bleached hair. I need to find him.'

If only he was still alive to be found...

Liam shrugged.

Caro tried again. 'It's a bit complicated, but I really need to know he's okay.'

'Who's that, Liam?'

Another boy appeared out of the building; a child of five or six, his voice hoarse and his nose in need of a wipe.

'A lady. Get back in, Alfie. Your Mam'll be mad if you're out when she comes home.'

Caro dug in her pocket for a packet of tissues and held one out to Alfie. 'Have a nose-wipe,' she said, trying not to sound shocked. Was no one looking after this poor little soul? Not to mention looking after her nephew. It was difficult to know what she should do. If she should do anything...

Alfie took the tissue without a word and scrubbed his nose with it.

'Is your mam still at work, then?' said Caro, stepping closer and handing the whole packet of tissues to the younger child. His eyes were shiny and feverish.

'She always works till after tea,' he said, sniffing.

Caro nodded, pity piercing her heart. 'Well, Liam's right. You should be inside. And you should be drinking lots. It looks to me like you've got a temperature. You should have a big glass of water, or something.'

She stopped. She couldn't interfere with Alfie. Even to Liam, she was all but a stranger.

Liam stood up. 'Come on, then,' he said to Alfie. 'You heard what she said.'

Caro opened her handbag. She had a packet of Fruit Pastilles in here, maybe the boys would like them. 'You can have these. If Alfie has a sore throat they might help.'

Liam took the sweets without a word, and the younger child coughed, then beamed up at Caro.

'Good luck with the maths test.'

Caro watched as the boys disappeared into the entrance, then moved away, not sure how she felt about the encounter. Her brother's child... It wasn't much of a place to live, an old tenement block behind the noisiest street in Bridgehead. And left alone while Alfie's mother was at work, too.

Did being Liam's aunt make it any of her business? No, she decided. But it was difficult not to feel outraged that any mother could leave a sick child at home, in the charge of another child, and go out to work. But who was she to judge? She knew nothing about them. For all she knew, there could be an aunt or a grandfather tucked away inside the house. Yes, that would be it.

Caro moved back into the High Street and mingled with the shoppers again. Back to the real world, her world. And she was no nearer to finding out about the boy with the ecstasy. But she would keep checking – if she came back at different times she might see him someday.

And maybe she would see Liam and Alfie again too.

Sharon

Sharon lay back in her hospital bed and gazed across to the see-through plastic cot. The baby was asleep, tiny hands touching just under her face, long fingers flexing every now and again, as if she were dreaming. Did babies dream? Was it possible to dream, when you knew so little of the world you'd been born into? Sharon caught her breath. How incredible it was that she should even care.

She pressed her lips together to stop them trembling. This was the baby she hadn't wanted. The baby who'd made its mother fat and resentful, and whose birth had frightened its father away. Craig still wasn't answering his phone and Sharon had decided to stop trying. He knew where she was. Her blood pressure was very low and the doctors wanted to keep her in for a day or two, so she'd be well-looked-after in the meantime.

The baby stirred and yawned, and Sharon smiled. How could she have been so distant, so uncaring towards her child? Thinking about her behaviour made her squirm now.

Donna, the Irish nurse, came in. 'Want to try another feed? She didn't take much last time.' She scooped up the baby and handed her to Sharon.

'Not much of a mum, am I?' Sharon took her daughter and kissed her, a tear trickling down her right cheek.

'No reason to think that. Talk to me, Sharon. Tell me what's wrong.'

Sharon felt more tears gather. 'I hated being pregnant, having my life messed up like that, and Craig felt exactly the same. He said he didn't want kids for years, but now I think he doesn't want them at all, and was scared to tell me. I don't even know if our marriage will go on. But I feel different about the baby now, and I wish I could explain it to her.'

The nurse pushed the pillow more firmly under Sharon's elbow. 'She's a baby; you don't have to explain anything to her. If you'd hated her she wouldn't be here now.'

Sharon looked down at the suckling child. 'I couldn't have got rid of her.'

'Exactly,' said the nurse. She lifted the still-blank pink name tag from the cot. 'Has she got a name yet?'

Sharon took a deep breath. She'd spent a long time thinking about this, because obviously it was something she couldn't put off too much longer without looking even more of a turnip than she did already. And if Craig objected, well – tough.

'Jael. J–a–e–l. After my godmother.'

The nurse printed the name carefully and replaced the tag on the top end of the cot.

Sharon stared at the baby. *This is my daughter Jael.* She would say that many times over the years, but how unreal it sounded today. But her daughter Jael would be part of her life from now on in, and Sharon was going to do her best by her. She would go to baby clinics and do baby gymnastics and make baby friends. Her maternity leave would make that perfectly possible, no matter what happened with Craig.

Julie arrived at half past four, a large plastic bag in one hand.

Sharon sat up. 'What's that?'

Julie laughed. 'Hello to you too!'

Sharon smiled guiltily. 'Sorry. Hello, Julie.' It was amazing how comfortable she felt with Julie – thank goodness they'd met.

Julie handed her the bag. 'A couple of mags and the Baby Massage book I mentioned. Have a go when you get home – it's great for calming them down.' She pulled out the visitor's chair. 'Any sign of Craig yet?'

Sharon stuck her chin in the air. 'Nope. I'm leaving him to it. He's a grown man; he knows what he should be doing.'

She was grateful when Julie said nothing more, merely reaching out and squeezing her hand before going to look at the baby. 'You've chosen a name! How d'you pronounce it?'

'Yah-ale. It's my godmother's name – she's from Switzerland. We hardly ever see her but it's a nice name, and not one you'll get three of in her school class later on.' Sharon leafed through the massage book, looking at the pictures and imagining herself sitting on the sofa at home, massaging the baby by candlelight, soft music playing in the background.

'I wonder if there's a course anywhere I could go to,' she said, and Julie nodded.

'I'll find out. We–'

There was a knock at the door and Sharon looked at Julie. Could this be Craig? What on earth could she say to him if it was, with Julie standing there? She pulled her cardigan around her. 'Come in!'

'Hello there,' said a deep male voice, and Sharon recognised the man from the internet café. He had a large bunch of flowers clutched in one hand, and a helium balloon with 'Baby's Here!' in yellow lettering in the other.

He presented her with both. 'Congratulations, Sharon. I was so pleased when I heard everything had gone well, I just had to come by and see you for a minute or two.'

Sharon allowed the balloon to float to the ceiling and stared at the bouquet. Long-stemmed red roses. Twelve of them. It seemed an excessive gesture for such a fleeting acquaintance; she couldn't even remember his name. And what on earth did he mean, he'd heard everything had gone well? Nothing had gone well. And who told him, anyway? He was still standing there with a big bright smile stretching from ear to ear, and she blinked uncertainly.

'Thank you, that's very kind. They're beautiful. This is my friend Julie, erm...'

Fortunately, he introduced himself, leaning over the bed and shaking hands with Julie. 'Jeff Horne. We met once in Cybersonics, didn't we? I hope your little girl was none the worse for her adventure.'

He moved over to the cot where the baby was sleeping peacefully. 'Oh – what a little love. She's just perfect. I'm so pleased for you.'

Sharon cleared her throat. What was she supposed to say to that? No words were necessary, though, because he wheeled round abruptly and gazed at her, his face solemn now, and Sharon suddenly felt like giggling. He was definitely a bit of an oddball, this Jeff.

'How do you feel about being a mother now, Sharon? Any better?'

Sharon almost jumped. The question was so unexpected, coming from a virtual stranger. How did he know she'd had doubts about it? She must have said something, that day she'd been dizzy in his café. 'Oh – fine,' she said, trying to sound convincing and aware that Julie was biting her lip in an effort not to laugh.

Jeff nodded. 'Good, good. Well – I'll leave you to it. I expect I'll see you again soon. Take care of little Jael, won't you?'

Sharon nodded, lost for words. 'Um – yes. Of course.'

He put out a finger and touched the baby's head for a second before saying goodbye. As soon as his footsteps were gone from the corridor Sharon caught Julie's eye and they both laughed aloud.

'Well – he's a funny bunny and no mistake,' said Sharon. 'But what gorgeous roses – smell them.'

Julie sniffed. 'Mm. He was the one who found Amy when some yob shifted her buggy, the day we discovered the break-in at the library. But you know, when I was in his shop, I had the impression he was unhappy about something. I mean really gutted. He was looking at Sam with an incredibly sad expression. I felt sorry for him but it was creepy, too, seeing him look at my child like that.'

The desire to laugh ended abruptly and Sharon blinked back hot, painful tears. Jeff Horne wasn't the only one who was gutted. 'Oh, Julie, what am I going to do about Craig? I don't know if I even want him to come back.'

Julie hugged her and for a moment Sharon allowed herself to lean into her. Bloody hormones – she was all over the place. She'd always had a way with words, but now she was bawling like a baby herself. If Craig had walked out on her at any other time she'd have had his head on a plate for tea.

Julie patted her shoulder. 'Whatever happens, I'll help you. And plenty of other people will too. You'll get through this, Sharon.'

Sharon nodded, placing the baby massage book on the locker. She would, because she had to.

A nurse came into the room with a jug of fresh water. 'Here you go. Oh – Sharon, I'm so sorry, but flowers aren't allowed here. Infection control protocols and all that. Maybe someone can take them home for you?' She eyed Julie.

Sharon shrugged. Flowers from Jeff Horne, lovely as they were, didn't rate highly in her life right now. 'You have them, Julie. As a thank you for being such a good friend.'

Julie lifted the roses. 'Wow – are you sure? I'd love to give them a home. Talking of which, I should get my kids back to mine, and you need your rest. When will you be discharged?'

'Probably Wednesday,' said Sharon, shuddering at the thought. Home. Alone. With Jael.

'I'll be in touch, then. Fingers crossed you and Craig will sort something out.'

Sharon waved goodbye as Julie left with the roses, their heavy perfume wafting through the air as she went. Sharon didn't know if she was glad to see them go, or sorry. Red roses were definitely a bit OTT in the circumstances. She didn't know the man yet here he was, visiting her like an old friend. On the other hand, at least someone was behaving like the stereotypical new father and bringing her flowers. It could be he was just rich, of course. Internet cafés were probably great little money-spinners.

But red roses were for lovers. Sharon closed her eyes.

Jeff

Whistling, Jeff ran down the steps at the side of the maternity building and trotted along the path towards the car park. That had gone rather well. Sharon had obviously been overwhelmed by the flowers, and more importantly – he had seen the baby. A little girl. And she was beautiful. Dark hair and a cute little button nose. Caro would love her.

It had been a good idea to turn up at the maternity department, clutching presents and pretending he'd forgotten his sister Sharon's room number. Simple, but effective. The woman at the desk had told him the number without batting an eyelid. Jeff manoeuvred the car out of the car park and turned towards the bridge. He'd seen the baby and affirmed his friendship with Sharon. A good afternoon's work.

And the best thing of all was, she had shown him yet again how unenthusiastic she was about being a mother. 'Fine' was all she'd said. No happy smile or gooey eyes as she looked at the baby, just 'fine'. It was all he needed to know – she was as unhappy as ever about the baby. The tightness in his head relaxed completely. This was going to work. And how typical; Sharon was friends with that Julie woman, the other callous mother he'd come across recently. Like calls to like, indeed.

He would leave Sharon for a day or two now; she'd be going home soon, where things would be even more difficult for her, with no nurses to do all the work. By the time he visited her again she would be well and truly ready to hand over the baby. She would, she would, he knew she would. And Craig would too – he was even worse than Sharon. He should be in that room taking care of his wife and child, like any loving father would.

Jeff stopped for a red light by the library, nodding and smiling broadly at the people crossing the road in front of the car. He had seen his little girl. Jael. A beautiful name for a beautiful baby. Yes, he would visit them on Friday and put forward his proposal. He might even be able to take the baby home that very same day. They would soon be a wonderful little family, him and Caro and their darling baby girl.

Sharon

At the midwife's suggestion, Sharon pushed Jael in her cot into the four-bedded room next door to have dinner, ham salad with boiled potatoes. She enjoyed exchanging stories with the other women until they started to talk about their partners, then it was all she could do not to run from the table.

Of course, they were all happily married with husbands who cooked, cleaned, took the dog out and brought home chocolates and theatre tickets every Friday. Sharon pasted a smile on her face as they tried to outdo each other with tales of domestic bliss. How futile it seemed. When they began to compare notes on how often they had sex she left them to it and returned to her room.

Jael was asleep, and Sharon lay on her bed and stared into the Perspex crib. Funny how fascinating it was, watching your child breathe, in and out, with one hand curled under a tiny chin. Who'd have thought it; she was falling in love with her daughter, but what the hell were they supposed to do? She'd have to get a taxi back to the flat on Wednesday – she didn't even know if Craig was still there. Sharon's fury expanded every time she thought about him. She could have understood that he'd panicked at the birth, but that was two days ago now. Nobody panicked for two days. Craig had either vanished into the dim and distant yonder, or else he was cold-heartedly ignoring her. Whichever it was, no way was she going to forgive him. She would phone her parents to come as soon as they could. She hadn't even told them the baby was here, which was unfair, because they'd be over the moon.

Damn Craig. How dare he treat her like this?

Visiting hours were nearly over when he sidled in the door. Sharon was nodding over one of the magazines Julie had brought, and the jolt she felt when she saw him was like an electric shock – and not in a good way.

For a moment neither of them spoke, then Sharon swallowed. Whatever the outcome was, they were going to have to talk to each other. They had a child; going completely separate ways was no longer an option.

'Craig. I wasn't expecting you.'

She saw him flinch at the irony in her voice. So he knew he'd behaved like a full-time wanker. Good.

He stepped in and stood at the bottom of the bed. 'I'm sorry. I should have been there for you. I just – I couldn't face this place.'

'I noticed. I didn't have the luxury of choice, myself.'

He nodded, his eyes sliding towards the baby in the crib and then back to her.

Sharon took a deep breath. A civilised agreement, that was what she should aim for while she was still in here. They could throw pans at each other in the privacy of their own four walls on Wednesday.

'Your daughter's doing well. I've called her Jael. We're coming home on Wednesday morning – shall I get a taxi, or will you manage to be here?'

'I'll come. We can talk at home, can't we?'

His voice was pleading now, almost whining, and Sharon felt her patience snap. What was he expecting her to say – there, there, it's all right, don't you worry? What a jerk he was being. He hadn't even asked how she was.

'I wouldn't count on it. Ten o'clock. And now I need some sleep.'

'Okay. I'll see you on Wednesday.' He stood at the end of the bed, hands twisting together.

Sharon lay back against the pillows. Obviously, he wasn't planning to visit tomorrow. So much for the happy couple – what had happened to them? Remembering how things used to be brought tears, and she closed her eyes for a moment to hide them.

When she opened them again, he had gone.

Chapter Nine

Caro

Caro hurried along the High Street. She had dry cleaning to pick up and bread to buy, and if she was very quick she'd have time to stick her head into Mortimer Square and see if Liam was around. How had the maths test gone? Caro remembered the way the boy's face had brightened when he'd understood what to do with his sum – it had brightened her day, too. She had helped a little boy, and if his father hadn't been such a scumbag to her, she could have been helping him all this time, too. But why hadn't Liam's teacher seen that her pupil hadn't understood the exercise?

She ducked into the Puff Pastry and bought a farmhouse brown. A stand of sweets by the counter caught her eye, and she put two packets of lurid green frogs beside the loaf. Just in case the boys were there. Smiling at the thought of little Alfie's face when she produced the pastilles yesterday, Caro joined the queue to pay.

At first she thought she'd be taking the frogs home with her, for no children at all were on the square this afternoon. She was later today, of course, the boys were probably inside with Alfie's mother. Disappointment heavy in her gut, Caro was turning away when she saw Liam emerge from the same entrance as yesterday and plonk himself down on the doorstep. She hurried across, pleased when he looked up and smiled.

'Hello, you – how did the maths test go?'

'Okay, I think. We get the marks back tomorrow.'

Caro fished in her bag for the sweets. 'I thought you and your little friend might like these. What's the homework tonight, then?'

Liam accepted his treat without saying thank you and opened one of the packets. 'English, but I've done it. We had to read a book to talk about in class.'

'What did you read?' Caro leaned on the wall, enjoying the conversation. What a bright little thing he was. She'd barely known him when he was younger, but then she and Rosie hadn't exactly been invited over regularly. Christmas visits to her parents, while they were still alive, had been the sum total of Caro's contact with Pete's son.

'Elidor. I got it in the library. It was cool. A bit weird, though.'

'Goodness, that's an old one. I read it too when I was about your age. Have you read—'

'Liam? What are you doing? I thought—'

Liam rose as a small woman appeared behind him and Caro smiled nervously. This must be Alfie's mother, and it was maybe a touch awkward that she, a stranger, had helped Liam with his school work.

'I just stopped by to see how the maths test went,' she explained, then realised by the other woman's blank expression that Liam hadn't talked about meeting her yesterday. 'I, um, helped him with his maths.'

'Oh. Thank you. He should have told me.' Alfie's mother stared at the sweets Liam was holding, but made no comment, and neither did the boy.

'It was no trouble, I enjoyed it. In fact, if he ever needs a hand again—' Caro rummaged for her business cards from the showroom, but Alfie's mother interrupted.

'It's all right, he can get any help he needs from me or his dad. Liam, your dinner's waiting.' She gave Caro a thin smile, gripped Liam's shoulder and marched him inside.

Caro stared, feeling snubbed. But Liam would explain things to the woman; she would understand when she knew that Caro was Liam's aunt. Caro hesitated, then turned back towards the High Street. She didn't want to interrupt their dinner. Chilly loneliness settled over her as she walked to the dry cleaner's. Maybe she could pop back tomorrow and introduce herself properly, and check everything was okay.

She was almost at home when she remembered she'd forgotten to ask about the teenager with the pills. She should definitely go back tomorrow. She'd hear then if the maths test really had gone well, too.

Sharon

Sharon sat beside her bed, staring at her mobile. She couldn't put off calling her parents any longer, it was going to be hard enough as it was, explaining why she had waited three days to tell them they were grandparents. A white lie might actually be best there; she didn't want to spoil her mother's pleasure.

She made the connection and spoke as soon as her mother answered. 'Hello, Grandma!'

Her mother's shriek sounded as if she was in the same room, not thousands of miles away in Cape Town. 'You haven't had it!'

'I have – her name's Jael, and she's 3.1 kilos, 55 cm, darkish hair but not much of it, and I'll make you a video the moment we're off the phone.' It was easier than she'd thought, sounding upbeat. Sharon listened, smiling, as her mother relayed the information to her father and enthused about 'their' choice of name.

'And how are you, darling? Was it okay?'

Sharon took a deep breath. This was where she had to act. 'It's fine now, but I was a bit under the weather after she was born on Saturday, so I waited until I was quite well before calling. I didn't want you upset, not with Dad's heart and everything.' Now she had to feel guilty for turning her father's recent heart scare into an excuse for her own shortcomings.

Fortunately, her mother accepted this. 'That was naughty – I could have cheered you up. But in a way it's good you waited, because Dad had the all clear just this morning, so I'll get right onto booking flights. Two pieces of wonderful news in one day! How's Craig enjoying being a daddy?'

Sharon hesitated. Her parents hadn't visited them since last summer and had no idea about the state of their marriage. But they would soon see for themselves what was going on, so there was no point pretending. 'He's, um – finding it difficult to adjust, to tell you the truth. But it's early days.'

Her mother snorted. 'Men! Don't worry, darling, I'll see to him myself.'

They chatted for a few more minutes, then Sharon had a word with her father before ending the call and making her video of a sleeping Jael. She pressed 'send' and sat back, feeling better. Her mother was pretty overpowering, but at least she was firmly on Sharon's side. Which was exactly what was needed right now.

Chapter Ten

Wednesday, 1st June

Sharon

'Got everything? Are you taking your balloon?' Without waiting for an answer, Donna the Irish nurse tied the balloon to Sharon's case.

Sharon was sitting beside the bed with everything packed and Jael dressed in a pink and white baby suit with hearts on the front. Craig was late. She managed to smile at the nurse.

'Thanks, Donna. You've all been great, but I can't wait to be home again.'

It was only half true, but at least being at home meant she wouldn't have to put on a brave face for strangers, kind as they were.

'Hi, there. Are you okay? All set?' Craig was standing in the doorway clutching the car seat they'd ordered online. He eyed the balloon, but said nothing.

Sharon rose and lifted Jael. 'Yes, to both. Not that you provided any extras to make my hospital stay more pleasant.' She strapped the baby in, then treated him to a hard stare. 'Jeff Horne from the internet café brought roses as well as that balloon, you know.'

A guilty expression crossed Craig's face, swiftly followed by one of puzzlement. 'Jeff Horne? Thought they didn't allow flowers.' He lifted her case.

'They don't. I gave them to Julie. My husband wasn't here to take them home for me.'

The guilt was back and Sharon smiled coldly. He could squirm a lot longer, his behaviour was inexcusable and she was only going with him now because there was nobody else to help.

It was nice to be out in the sunshine after four days in hospital, and Sharon walked towards the car park taking deep breaths. What a change from dull, grey Saturday. And how her life had changed, too.

Craig secured the car seat into the back of their Nissan, and Sharon got in beside the baby, perversely enjoying Craig's discomfort, knowing he was hating the uncertainty about what she was going to do.

The drive through Bridgehead was slow.

'You're driving like a little old lady,' was Sharon's comment, as Craig eased the car into the correct lane at the traffic lights, and stopped.

He looked round. 'Wait till you're behind the wheel for the first time with her in the back.'

Well. Sharon stared out of the side window. What did you know, he was nervous about driving his daughter. It was the first shimmer of hope that he might, after all, want to save the relationship. Yet he had never touched his child, never called her by name. There wasn't much hope, really. On the other hand, who was she to feel superior about being a devoted parent?

Back at the flats, Sharon lifted the baby from the car seat and carried her inside. 'Welcome home, kiddo,' she whispered, going through to the nursery. Hell, grey walls, and not a toy in sight. How uncaring she'd been. But that was in the past.

Craig had obviously done some work here since Saturday. The cot was made up, and the piles of clothes previously on the changing table had been organised into the chest of drawers. The table itself had been given a mat, and a selection of wipes and nappies was waiting for use. So, Craig hadn't quite ignored the fact that he was a father. In spite of her negative feelings towards him, Sharon was touched.

Craig was standing in the doorway. 'I'm sorry,' he said dully. 'I know I've done everything wrong. I don't want to give up on us, Sharon.'

She stared at him. He had deserted her, he had made her look foolish, and he had spoiled the first days of her baby's life. But he was Jael's father.

'I can't decide anything now, Craig,' she said. 'I want you to take your stuff to the other room for now. I need to recover from the birth and then – I don't know.'

He nodded and turned away. Sharon laid the baby in the cot. Craig was probably glad she hadn't kicked him out entirely, but that would have been cutting off her nose to spite her face. She would need help for a few days and he was the only one around to provide it.

In spite of her ambivalence towards Craig, the whole day seemed special. Sharon fed the baby and executed the first home nappy change, Craig hovering speechlessly behind her. Jael was awake for part of the afternoon, looking about with a serious little expression. It would be a few weeks before they got the first smile, Sharon knew.

But what a difference such a small person made to the place. The sounds and smells of the flat were entirely different, with the matching perfume of wipes and baby lotion in the air, Sharon's footsteps walking up and down with the baby, her voice talking, and, incredibly, singing to her daughter.

Halfway through the afternoon the doorbell rang. Sharon pulled a face. She was knackered; she didn't want any visitors today. Craig went over to the intercom by the flat door and pressed the button.

'Special delivery for you,' said a distorted male voice.

'Post,' said Craig over his shoulder. 'I'll go down.'

Sharon relaxed. 'It'll be flowers from Mum; I called her yesterday.'

A few minutes later Craig was back with a brown paper parcel. 'It was sent express,' he said, giving it to Sharon. 'Something for the baby, probably.'

Sharon pulled the paper away and revealed a large box of expensive Swiss chocolates, and a pink tissue-wrapped gift that must be baby clothes.

'I guess Mum phoned Godma Jael,' she said, looking for a card. There was none visible, so she opened the tissue paper. An ivory christening robe appeared, and Sharon gasped.

'This is silk. Wow. She must have won the lottery,' she said, forgetting for a moment that she and Craig weren't on speaking terms.

Craig shook out the tissue paper and a small pink card fell into his hand. He read it aloud and in a second, the day was tarnished.

'Welcome home. With love and thanks, Jeff.'

Caro

The two boys were kicking a football around Mortimer Square when Caro arrived after work.

Alfie saw her first. 'The sweetie lady!' He ran up to her, beaming, and Caro noticed with pleasure how much more energy he had today. He was such a cute little kid. His voice sounded normal now, her sweets must have helped there.

'I brought you some orange juice today. It's better for you.' Caro handed over the bag with the two small cartons she'd bought at the newsagent's on the way past. She looked at Liam. 'Well?'

He kicked at the ball, not looking at her, a grin pulling at his mouth. 'Seventy-eight per cent. It's my best ever maths test.'

Caro clapped his shoulder. The nonchalance was an act; satisfaction was shining right out of him. 'Very well done. Your dad must be pleased.'

'He doesn't know yet. And Alfie's mum isn't home from work, so she doesn't know yet either.'

Caro was caught between relief that Alfie's mother wasn't around, and indignation that the woman had apparently left the children alone on the square. 'Who's looking after you and Alfie, then?'

Liam jerked his head towards the other end of the square. 'Mary next door. She always does between school and when Alfie's mum gets back. I thought you might come, so I brought my maths again.' He ran over to a bench where the maths book was lying.

Caro followed and sat down, accepting the book. 'What is it today, then? Ah, problems.' She checked down the list of answers. 'Good work, Liam, these are all correct.'

'I like geography better,' he said, reaching out for the book. 'When I grow up I want to travel to loads of places and make a lot of money so I don't have to work away from home like my dad does. He's in Aberdeen now, but he's driving home tomorrow.'

Caro nodded, noticing with a jolt the red and purple marks around his wrist. 'That's a nasty bruise – what happened?'

Liam shrugged, and opened his juice carton. 'Nothing. Some kids don't like it when I get good marks. But I don't care.'

Caro was horrified. 'You mean other children did that to you? That's bullying, Liam. Did you tell your teacher?'

'No!' His face was shocked. 'They'd do it worse, then. You get good marks, you get picked on. End of. I can deal with it.'

Speechless, Caro watched as he drained the carton with a loud suck, and ran to kick the ball away from Alfie. The smaller boy yelled and chased after Liam, who was laughing now. Caro blinked. Well. Kids had problems too, but it looked like Liam was on top of his. What a pathetic little story, though. The absent father and the ambitious son. Maybe she should have a word with Pete. Caro looked round, remembering why she'd come back to Mortimer Square in the first place. But there was no sign of the teenage boy, with or without drugs.

Determinedly pushing depression away, Caro went to join the game of football, hoping that the unknown teenager was doing something similar. But even if he was, another kid was lying in the mortuary. It was a lose-lose situation.

'I'll maybe see you tomorrow,' she said, when the game was over and she was settling her hair back into place. 'I'm going out on Friday, so I can't come then. But tell you what, Liam–' She fished an old envelope from her handbag and scribbled both her mobile and landline numbers on it. 'If you ever need help with your maths when no one's around, give me a call.'

Liam stuffed the envelope into his pocket, grinned at her, and ran off after Alfie.

Chapter Eleven

Thursday 2nd June

Julie

The sky was relentlessly and unseasonably grey. Raindrops were spattering on the pavement as Julie hurried away from Bridgehead Primary and on down the High Street, frustration at her lateness mingling with relief at escaping this morning's pre-school tantrum. Sam had wanted to play when he should have been having breakfast, and was crabby and uncooperative when she insisted he get a move on. That was the worst part of being head of a one-parent family – every time a bad guy was needed, it was you.

The rain came on in earnest as she reached the traffic lights, and Julie cursed – her brolly was at the bottom of her bag. She dodged into a doorway to scrabble around amongst the million and one things she transported about town every day.

The placard outside the newsagent's opposite seemed to jump out and hit her as she turned back into the High Street: *Drug Death Inquiry*. Julie jerked to a stop. Drug death. . . surely not the boy from the library? But he couldn't have died, or she'd have heard about it on the news or from the police or something – wouldn't she? But then they'd been busy at work, and Sharon and the baby had occupied a lot of her time and attention this week. Oh no. . .

Julie crossed the road to buy a paper, not caring that she was definitely going to be late now. She stood in the shop and read.

It *was* the boy from the library and he'd died on Monday morning. How awful – he'd been dead for three days and she hadn't known. She'd stood and watched as he was loaded into the ambulance last week, and somehow or other she'd missed hearing that he'd died. But so had Dee. Why hadn't they been told? Julie crammed the paper into her bag and hurried on to the library.

One look at her boss told her that Dee had seen the paper too.

'It's a real bugger, isn't it,' said Dee, glancing up to the gallery where the boy had lain.

Julie nodded. 'I can't believe we missed it. I don't watch the early news on TV because of Sam, but I do sometimes watch the late news, and – hell.' She pressed cold fingers to her cheeks.

Dee pulled her into the staffroom. 'Let's have a quick coffee. I don't think we need to feel guilty about it, Julie. It's just – he was here, a young boy, and now he's dead.'

Julie accepted a mug. 'I suppose we'll never know all the whys of it.'

'You sit for a minute and catch your breath. I'll go back on the desk.'

Julie spread the paper on the table and sat down to read. There was only a short paragraph about the boy's death, the rest of the page was taken up with re-hashing all the teenage drug deaths that had occurred in the area over the last five years. Several kids had lost their lives. Julie read the whole page, then the part about the boy again. Eventually she sat back, a sick, heavy feeling in her middle.

That boy – he'd lived with his mother and his younger brother since his parents' divorce ten years ago. A one-parent family. Like her, Sam and Amy. In fact, a lot of those kids were from broken homes. And probably most of these parents were decent people who'd simply had problems in their lives and had to work through them alone afterwards. What guarantee did she have that her beautiful, dark-haired Sam wouldn't end up on a mortuary slab one day, having been marred for life because of what had happened to Julie's marriage? Or Amy?

Julie folded the paper soberly. What more could she do to make sure her children had the best start she could give them? And how, just how could Matt simply abandon his kids? Children needed a father and hers didn't have one. That was plain fact and there was nothing she could do to change it.

The library was busy, and she didn't have time to speak more than a few words to Dee all day. After work Julie had to rush off to collect Sam and Amy, and she changed into her outdoor shoes with the boy's death still uppermost in her mind. Maybe she and Dee could hash through the whole thing over a glass of something soon.

'Let's go somewhere at the weekend,' she suggested, looking round for her umbrella.

Dee shook her head. 'No can do, I'm afraid. It's my class reunion in Bedford, remember?'

Julie did remember. 'Of course – have a lovely time. Keep in mind that your liver isn't eighteen any more, won't you?'

Dee laughed. 'If you think I'm going to waste good gossiping time worrying about my liver then you're wrong, Miss. I'll see you Monday lunchtime.'

Julie grinned and started up the High Street. Hopefully Sam had got over his fretfulness of that morning. His bad moods didn't usually last long. That was the great thing about four-year-olds, they had this in-built enthusiasm and 'isn't life just the most interesting thing' attitude.

Wait until he's a teenager, she thought. That was the time of the real tantrums and problems. The time when a boy really needed a dad.

She glanced across the road to the internet café. There was Jeff, bringer of roses, sticking a poster up in the window. He saw Julie and waved, and she waved back warily. He'd definitely been a bit strange with Sharon, but maybe it was because he loved children, she thought, remembering the broken-hearted way he'd stared at Sam the other day.

Sam was waiting when Julie arrived at the After School Club, rain jacket zipped up to his chin and school rucksack clutched in both arms.

'Goodness, am I late?' she asked, checking the clock.

'You're bang on time and so is Sam,' said Katy, Sam's group leader. She winked at Julie over Sam's head. 'Sam wanted to show you how nicely he can be on time.'

'Oh! That's brilliant, Sam,' said Julie, dropping on one knee to hug him. 'Let's treat ourselves to pizza for tea, shall we?'

Sam ran ahead of her towards the supermarket, and Julie followed on with resolve in her heart. Sam was such a love; she *must* keep him safe.

Caro

Caro hurried away from the salesroom. It was still early, but Mr Wilson, the boss, was away at a meeting. Louise was waiting for her mother to arrive with the baby, and didn't mind holding the fort alone for the last half hour. Caro grimaced. She'd left Louise holding the fort a couple of times recently. It might be an idea to show her appreciation with a box of Lou's favourite soft centres. People didn't like being taken for granted.

The rain had stopped, but it wasn't exactly warm June weather, and Caro was glad she'd put on her jacket. She crossed the road and started off along the High Street, careful to put other passers-by between herself and Cybersonics on the opposite pavement. She didn't want Jeff to spot her.

He'd been away in a dream most of the past week, though admittedly he hadn't spent much of his time with her. It was difficult to tell because his working hours were irregular, but she had the distinct impression something was going on and he didn't want her to know about it. That bag she'd found on Sunday... Then on Monday he'd stomped in late and shut himself into his computer room upstairs without even saying hello. And to think that four short weeks ago they'd been happy, a normal couple, confident that modern medicine would soon help them have a baby of their own. It seemed incredible now. The no-baby had changed everything, and very soon she was going to have to make a hard decision about her life.

The Puff Pastry was busy with people buying something on their way home, and Caro tapped her feet as the queue shuffled forwards. She would get chocolate croissants for the boys today – she wouldn't see them again until Monday, now. She bought a croissant and a tube of Smarties for each boy, as well as two small cartons of orange juice, and hurried towards the square. And there they were, Alfie running around after an unpumped football, and Liam sitting on the back of one of the benches, large muddy trainers right in the middle of the seat.

Caro smiled and held out the bag with the chocolate croissants, watching as Alfie seized the biggest one. The voice behind her made her jump.

'What the hell, just what the bloody *effing* hell do you think you're doing, giving stuff to these kids?'

It was Alfie's mother. Caro's mouth went dry. The other woman's face was red, and the sharp blue eyes boring into her own were cold as ice.

'I – I just...' It was as if Caro's inside-out world stopped for a moment, shook itself, and then continued the right way up. What *was* she doing, actually? She should have introduced herself to the woman days ago. She opened her mouth to explain, but Alfie's mother was speaking – no, ranting – again.

'I had to take time off work just to wait here and tell you to leave these kids alone. What are you – some nosy, do-gooding...' She glanced at the boys and fell silent.

Liam had grabbed the bag from Alfie and was biting into his croissant, his face pink. Caro could feel his embarrassment. Hadn't he told Alfie's mum who she was? Probably he hadn't wanted the woman to tell his father – Caro could only imagine how Pete had spoken of her, over the years. She sat down heavily on the end of the bench, taking care to avoid the mud from Liam's shoes. Her happy mood was gone, replaced by something that felt more like this chilly, damp June day, a day that should have been warm and golden but wasn't.

'I'm sorry,' she said, her voice trembling. 'I didn't mean any harm. I'm Liam's aunt, though I haven't been in contact with Pete for a while.'

Alfie's mother stared at her, then sniffed. 'Then get in touch and organise it with him. Until then – leave us alone, please. My boy doesn't know you from Adam.'

Caro nodded, her cheeks burning. Stranger Danger. 'Never take sweets from strangers.' How often had her own mother said those words to them, as children? Yet here she was, teaching the boys – especially Alfie, who wasn't old enough to know what was safe and what wasn't – that it was perfectly okay to take things from strangers. And if *she* had children, what would she think if someone came along and fed them like she was doing?

How blind she'd been. Liam wasn't neglected or hungry, and he had neighbours to look out for him. Probably dozens of kids in Bridgehead were in the same situation. Why had she kept coming back? Because Liam might help her find the pills boy – if he was still alive – and Alfie was cute? Or was it more to do with the no-baby and her wish to nurture a child? Caro stood up slowly, not wanting to leave but knowing she must. She was lucky Alfie's mother hadn't involved the police.

'I'm sorry. I'll do that.' Caro glanced at Liam, but he made no move to join the conversation. How vulnerable he was, and she had made him even more so. 'Goodbye, then.' Caro walked away quickly so they wouldn't see the tears in her eyes. Neither boy replied. She didn't look back.

A hot, painful lump in her throat, Caro walked back down the High Street and stood at the bus stop, waiting for the bus that would take her back to the estate and Jeff and the no-baby. It wasn't fair. Liam might be her nephew, but she knew she wouldn't be calling Pete to ask his permission to visit the boy. She had only seen Liam a handful of times, but being with him and Alfie for those few short minutes each day had become important, more important than her quest to find out about the ecstasy boy. For a day or two, she'd been able to pretend there were children in her life who needed her. And yet – these were older children. She would never have thought a child of that age could get under her skin so quickly; she'd rejected adoption out of hand because the children available usually *were* older. Maybe she'd been wrong about that, but oh, it was much too late now. All she wanted was to love a child – didn't she want to love Jeff, too? Caro didn't know any more. She'd gone into the relationship with the aim of having a fun time with a nice guy, and bringing her children up in much better circumstances than she'd been in as a child. Love for Jeff hadn't been important then and it wasn't important now either. There was no going back. She didn't even want to go home, to the house where the door on her marriage was closing so quickly. She would have to talk to Jeff about it. After Granny's birthday do on Sunday – she would do it then. Then she could start the monumental task of rebuilding her life – without Jeff.

Caro got on the bus and sat by a window, noticing glumly that the rain was starting again. At least Alfie's mother was there to make sure the boys went inside, but – that was none of her business. Her business was to go home and spend an evening non-communicating with her husband.

Caro closed her eyes, feeling a headache start at the back of her neck as the bus trundled away from the High Street. She hadn't wanted any of this.

She'd wanted a baby, but she wasn't going to get one anytime soon.

Chapter Twelve

Friday 3rd June

Sharon

The book hit the floor with a thud and Sharon jerked awake. Rats, she had nodded off on the sofa again. She seemed to fall asleep every time she sat down nowadays, but that was apparently what happened when you had a not-quite-week-old baby to take care of, and a husband who was doing the bare minimum to help. Babies didn't sleep all night, Sharon had known that, but she hadn't been prepared for how exhausted she would feel after just two nights away from the help of the nurses.

She sat massaging her forehead and listening for the baby's small but penetrating voice. Craig had gone to deal with something at the shop this afternoon, so she and Jael were alone. A walk by the river was the plan, if she could muster the strength to push the pram.

An indignant voice called from the nursery and Sharon slumped, then grinned. Okay, she was half-dead and her relationship was in tatters, but who'd have guessed it – she was beginning to love having a daughter.

'There, my sweet, up you come.'

Sharon sat by the window, feeding the baby and watching as a tourist boat chugged down the river, followed by a couple of kids in a rowing boat. Shouldn't they be at school? It was funny how much more sensitive she was to all the other children out there, now she had a child of her own. If she wasn't careful she'd turn into a caricature of her former self, all floppy pullovers and leggings, making jam and clunky jewellery at every opportunity.

The doorbell rang insistently as she was rummaging in her wardrobe, looking for a clean top that didn't make her look like the side of a house. The sooner her figure got back to normal the better, and who could that be? Not Julie, she wouldn't have finished work yet. Oh, it would be Mrs Hutchison from along the road – she'd told Craig yesterday she'd come by soon with a little something for the baby. Sharon went out to the hallway and pressed the button to open the front door of the building.

A few moments later the welcoming smile died on her lips as she opened the flat door to find Jeff Horne on the doorstep. He was clutching another bunch of roses, yellow ones this time, and beaming all over his face, but... there was something funny about his eyes.

Apprehension washed over Sharon. No way did she want to be alone in the flat with him, but he strode in confidently without an invitation. At least Jael was waiting in the pram; he would see they were on the way out.

'Ah, my little princess,' he said, handing the flowers to Sharon and bending over the baby. 'I had to come and see how she's getting on. She's so lovely.'

'Yes,' said Sharon. 'We're off for a little walk now, out in the fresh air.'

He straightened up and gazed into her eyes with a frown on his face. 'Is that good for her? I'm sure you're not supposed to take new babies out much, the first week or two.'

Sharon gaped at him. She hadn't asked, but wouldn't the nurses have said, if fresh air should be off the menu for a bit?

'It's fine,' she said firmly. 'What lovely roses. Thank you so much, but you really mustn't bring us any more flowers.'

'My pleasure,' he said, and to Sharon's dismay he marched on through to the living area and settled himself down on the sofa. She followed unwillingly and perched on the edge of an armchair. It seemed churlish to ask him to leave; he was a funny bunny to be sure, but he'd been kind to them – all those flowers – and she should thank him for the parcel, too – but why was he *doing* all this?

'Thank you for the lovely gift,' she said, forcing herself to sound warm. 'But it was too much. We can't possibly accept such an expensive robe.'

He was staring across at her, frowning, and Sharon began to feel even more nervous. Was he offended? She'd still been deciding how best to refuse the christening robe, so this visit was embarrassing, but it was better to tell him in person. She was gathering her courage to ask him to take his robe and leave when he spoke again, and his words threw her completely.

'You look tired, Sharon. In fact, you look terrible. How are you coping?'

'Oh – well – the baby's up at night – I don't sleep well...' Somehow, she couldn't get a whole sentence out. There was something scary about Jeff Horne today, something she couldn't put a name to.

'Poor Sharon. This isn't the kind of thing you're good at, is it?' he went on, still staring, his voice soft and caring.

The hairs on Sharon's arms rose and she closed her lips tight to keep the shiver in.

Jeff was speaking again, the sound of his voice positively hypnotic. 'You knew you weren't going to enjoy being tied down like this, with all the responsibility of being a mother. It's nothing to be ashamed of. Lots of people don't want children.'

'I do want her,' said Sharon, beginning to feel panicky. 'It was a bit of a shock at first maybe, but–' She stopped. There was no reason to justify herself to this man. 'I love my daughter,' she said, trying to sound firm.

He smiled, leaning forwards and rubbing his hands together. A sour whiff of stale sweat wafted over to her, and Sharon recoiled.

'I'm sure you do, Sharon. But there's no need for you to take care of her yourself. If baby Jael was well-looked after and loved by another couple, a couple who'd always wanted a child of their own – why, your life could get back to normal just as quickly as you liked.'

Sharon clutched at the collar of her blouse. What was he saying? What 'other' couple? Was he suggesting she give her baby away? She stood up, feeling her legs shake.

'I'd like you to leave now,' she said, trying to keep her voice steady.

To her horror he laughed, leaning back into the sofa and looking completely at home. 'Sharon, Sharon, think about it. You could go back to work. Out to dinner. Lovely holidays with Craig. There would be nothing to tie you down, and Jael will be with people who love her. I'll organise it all for you myself.'

'No – how dare you–' Sharon heard her voice rise in fear, but before she could say another word her phone rang, and she grabbed it from the coffee table and connected without looking to see who it was. A lifeline, she had a lifeline. Please let it be someone she knew and not an insurance-seller calling from India.

'Hi, Sharon!'

It was Julie. Relief flowed through Sharon. 'Julie – I need help. Can you come straightaway?'

She listened to her friend's voice saying she'd be there in five minutes. Thank God – Julie had realised something was wrong.

Sharon tried to glare at Jeff. 'I want you to leave now.' Her voice was shaking with fear. What if he didn't go? Could she and Julie *make* him?

He stood up and gripped her arm, staring straight into her eyes. 'I'll be back,' he said pleasantly. 'For the baby. You'll see I'm right, Sharon, when you've had time to think. Your lives would be much better without a baby and you know it.'

'No!' she cried, but he was gone, striding through the flat as if he owned the place. Sharon didn't move until she heard the door close behind him, then she ran and blocked the Yale lock, grabbed Jael from the pram and crouched in the hallway, holding her child as tightly as she dared.

Julie

Calling to the other librarian that she had an emergency on, Julie grabbed her bag from the staffroom and ran down the path towards the main road. Something was wrong; Sharon's voice had been brittle. It couldn't be the baby – if Jael had been ill Sharon would have said. Had she had a bust-up with Craig? Could he have threatened Sharon? Or worse? Julie's breath caught painfully in her chest.

'Slow down, idiot,' she muttered, aware that people were turning in the street to stare at her mad dash. 'Pace yourself.'

She jogged on steadily and turned into Sharon's street, with the expensive riverside flats on one side of the road and the older, detached houses opposite. Both pavements were tree-lined, and Julie couldn't help comparing the area to her own fourth-floor flat in a grey sandstone tenement. She and Sharon didn't have the same problems, that was sure.

A woman Julie recognised as Sharon and Craig's neighbour was going out, and held the front door open with a pleasant, 'Going to see Sharon and the baby again? She's gorgeous, isn't she?'

The lift was on the ground floor and Julie rushed in and up. Calling Sharon's name, she banged with her fist on the flat door. Sharon opened up, a howling baby in her arms and her face sheet white.

'Sharon, love, are you okay? What happened?'

Julie pulled Sharon through to the sitting area and sat her down on the sofa. Sharon began to cry with loud hiccoughing sobs, and Julie rocked her in her arms for a moment before giving her a little shake.

'Come on, honey. Tell me what's wrong.'

Sharon rubbed her nose and sniffed. Julie handed her a tissue and took the baby while Sharon blew her nose.

'Sorry,' said Sharon eventually. 'I was so scared, Julie – I didn't know what to do. Did you see him? He might still be hanging around outside somewhere.'

'Craig?' said Julie, staring. Had Sharon kicked him out?

'Jeff Horne. Remember, the creepy bloke with the red roses at the hospital? Then he sent us Swiss chocolates and a really expensive christening gown too, and this afternoon he appeared with yellow roses and said he would take Jael and give her to a couple who wanted a baby. He said he knew I didn't want her really. He was so sure of himself – he was so weird, Julie.'

Julie patted the baby's back, rocking back and forwards as the howls died away. 'What a jerk. Where on earth did he get the idea you don't want Jael? He doesn't know you. Where's Craig – have you called him?'

Sharon shook her head. 'Not yet. He's stocktaking this afternoon, and he's having enough problems being a parent. He wouldn't help. I'm okay now.'

Julie shook her head. 'You don't look okay. You look as if you've had the fright of your life. I'll make coffee.'

Sharon giggled nervously. 'He said something like that too. He said I looked terrible. Oh, Julie, what'll I do if he comes back?'

Julie put the baby into her pram and went to rummage in the kitchen cupboards. Sharon sounded almost hysterical; coffee might not be the best idea. 'On second thoughts, let's have a nice cup of peppermint tea. How did he get in, anyway?'

'That was my fault. I was expecting the woman along the road and I let him in without checking who it was. I won't do that again.'

Julie looked at her thoughtfully. Even if Sharon did check, it would still be possible to get into the flats – look how she'd got in a few minutes ago. 'Maybe you should phone the police. After all, Jeff threatened you, didn't he?'

Sharon leaned her elbows on the kitchen table and clutched her head.

'I can't remember his exact words. It was so scary, Julie. And I can't phone the police without telling Craig first, can I?'

'I suppose not.' Julie sipped her tea, thinking fast.

'Tell you what,' she said at last. 'Remember Max Sanders, the policeman who came to my flat? We could phone him and see what he thinks. That way we could find out the best thing to do without it being official.'

'Okay. That's a good idea.' Sharon reached for a biscuit, and Julie saw with relief that the colour had come back into the other woman's face.

Julie made the connection, hoping Max wasn't at work. To her relief, he picked up on the third ring.

'Julie! How're you doing?'

Her heart-rate went up a notch. 'Fine, thanks. I meant to call a couple of days ago, but you know… And now my friend Sharon has a bit of a situation on, and we don't know if it's a police matter or not. Could you help us with that?'

'I guess. Tell me what's wrong and I'll tell you if she should go to the police. Is that what you want?'

'Perfect.' Julie put the phone on 'speaker' so that Sharon could listen in too. Briefly, she told the story of Jeff Horne's visit.

Max didn't speak until she had finished. 'I see. I think she should report the incident, but to be honest, it's the kind of thing we often can't do much about. He could deny the threats and Sharon can't prove anything. But she should report it, then we'd go and see him, and hopefully that would be enough to frighten him off.'

Julie listened, dismayed. 'Right, thanks. Is it stalking, what he's doing?'

'It's heading in that direction, though saying Sharon should give the baby up is a bit unusual. Tell you what – I'm on duty at five. If she calls the station then and asks for me, I'll deal with it myself. Stay with her until we get there, huh?'

Julie ended the call, feeling warm all over. Seemed like he hadn't minded Sam monopolising their 'date'.

She hugged Sharon. 'Chin up. Now we know what to do, and surely a visit from the police will bring Jeff Horne to his senses. I do think you should phone Craig now, though.'

She went back to the living area while Sharon phoned Craig. Jael was asleep in the pram, arms stretched above her head. Julie reached out and touched the little cheek, marvelling at the long lashes and tiny nose. Imagine anyone thinking Sharon would give her child up. What a weird person Jeff Horne was. Could he have lost his own child, perhaps?

'Craig'll be here in ten minutes,' said Sharon, coming up behind her to lift the baby. She sank into the sofa.

'That's good,' said Julie. 'I'll get off to collect the kids when he arrives, then.'

Craig appeared shortly afterwards, and to Julie's relief he put both arms round Sharon and she let him, leaning on his shoulder for a moment before breaking loose and pulling a rueful face at him. This definitely wasn't the time for them to continue their being-a-parent war.

Loneliness crept through Julie as she texted Max that she was leaving Sharon with Craig. How good it would be to have someone to lean on, just sometimes. Well, she had Sam. Look how he'd been ready and waiting after school yesterday, after his grumpy morning. That was him taking care of her. And right now, she'd better go and collect him, or she'd be the late one. Silently, she patted Craig and Sharon's shoulders and left them to it.

Jeff

Jeff wandered along the river pathway, hands stuck deep in his trouser pockets. The tourist boats were out in full force today, one steaming up the river, the other chugging along in the opposite direction en route for the weir, where it would turn, giving the occupants a prime view of rocks and spray. The pathway was busy too. He didn't enjoy having to weave round pram-pushing mothers, dog-walkers and running children – what were these parents thinking? Didn't they know how easily a child could fall into the water and drown? It was crass; there was no peace and quiet anywhere nowadays. Annoyance scorching through him, he stood back to let three chattering young women with babies in buggies pass. Every one of them was far too young to be a proper mother to those children. Where was the fairness here? Yobs and slappers having babies all over the bloody place while he and Caro...

Jeff rubbed his eyes. Somehow, his interview with Sharon hadn't gone as well as he'd thought it would. He'd imagined relief on Sharon's part, dawning realisation that here was the answer to all her problems, happy smiles through tears of gratitude. But she'd been positively off-putting. Really quite rude, in fact; it had started his headache off again. Ingratitude always riled him. He extracted his sunspecs from his inside pocket and put them on. The world was too bright today.

He couldn't put a finger on it, but there was something odd about his life now. Something had changed; something was wrong – if anything more could be wrong. Caro wasn't herself either. Last week she'd avoided him, hardly said a word. She'd been chattier this week, but that was all it was – chat. Neither of them had mentioned babies or hospitals. They were like two strangers having artificial conversations in the lobby of some anonymous hotel.

Which was why it was terribly important to find a baby quickly, and Jael would be ideal. Right here in Bridgehead, even. It wasn't as if Sharon was brimming over with motherly love and enthusiasm. She should be grateful to him.

He massaged his head, kneading the tight muscles across his scalp. It was awful, this stiffness in his head, like a continual buzz in his ears except it wasn't in his ears, it was behind his eyes. Maybe he was just tired.

At least he'd be able to rest over the weekend. Now that he'd told Sharon what he was going to do, he could leave her to realise she wasn't going to get a better offer. Yes, he'd go back on Monday, and if Sharon wasn't agreeable, well – he would have to be more assertive.

Determinedly, Jeff increased his pace, swinging his arms, and heard something clink in his jacket pocket. He pulled out a red leather key ring with three keys attached, and stared at it blankly. These weren't his keys. But he had seen this ring quite recently...

Today, in fact, yes, it had been on the small table by Sharon's flat door. He must have lifted it on his way out. Had Sharon noticed? Probably not, or she'd have called after him. Oh well, he could give it back on Monday.

He walked on to the bridge where he had the choice of continuing along the pathway, or taking a steep flight of steps leading to the end of the High Street. Jeff hesitated, then started up the steps. The car was still parked at Cybersonics. He would drive past and collect Caro from the salesroom on his way home. It wasn't often he was able to spoil his wife like that, and maybe they could have a nice talk on the way home – a real talk. They would have to talk more when they had the baby home, and Caro would want to then, anyway. She would be a happy mother, like all the others on the estate. Jeff smiled, then stopped so suddenly a couple of lads behind him had to swerve past. He was forgetting – Caro was going out tonight, meeting a friend straight from work. Ah, well. At least he'd have peace and quiet at home.

If only his head would stop buzzing. But he would pop into the chemist's on his way. A packet of magic pills would soon put everything right.

By quarter to five Jeff was home again, a couple of paracetamol inside him dealing with the worst of the headache, and a large wedge of Quiche Lorraine from the Puff Pastry waiting to be heated for his evening meal. He opened the fridge and reached for a beer, then decided against it and popped open a can of coke instead. It wouldn't do to aggravate his head. He poured the coke into a glass and took it through to the living room.

They'd need to change a few things in here when the baby came home, he thought, wandering round the room. Those plants on the window ledge weren't exactly toddler-friendly, and neither were the ornaments scattered about the bookshelves. But time enough for that. They would go on a lovely shopping expedition too, and buy everything a child would need. Caro would love that; it would make her happy again and that was all he wanted. Jeff sank into the sofa and reached for the TV remote.

The doorbell rang while he was zapping through the channels, looking for something to distract him from the dreariness of Friday evening home alone with the remnants of a headache. Jeff lurched to his feet.

Two uniformed policemen were towering on the doorstep. 'Jeff Horne? We need to speak to you about a complaint that's been made. Can we come in?'

Frowning, Jeff held the door open, then led the way back to the living room. Had there been a problem at Cybersonics? He couldn't think of anything, and Davie would have mentioned it if something had happened on his shift.

The older policeman introduced himself and his colleague, and Jeff sat down in the armchair, waving the two men to the sofa.

'Mr Horne, we believe you visited Sharon Morrison at Riverside Gardens this afternoon?'

Jeff stared. Had Sharon reported her keys missing? 'Yes. I took some flowers to welcome her home.'

'That's not how she saw it, sir. Did you threaten to take her baby?'

Jeff pulled at his collar. 'No! I – I'm a family friend and I–'

'She doesn't see you as a friend, Mr Horne.'

'I am!' Jeff began to sweat. What were they implying? 'I only want what's best for her and the baby, and she's not–'

'What's best for Mrs Morrison and the baby is that you stay well away in future. You seem to have forced an acquaintanceship to be in contact with the baby. That's very suspicious behaviour, Mr Horne and we don't like it. Not one bit.'

'No – you've got it wrong! She can't–'

The older policeman stood up, followed by his colleague. 'A piece of friendly advice, sir. Stay well away from the Morrisons. And their baby. Is that clear?'

His voice was hard as nails now and both men were glowering at Jeff. Nodding, he shrank into the sofa, unable to think of anything to say to redeem himself, his headache returning with a vengeance.

'We'll see ourselves out.'

Jeff sat motionless as they left the house and drove away. As soon as the sound of the car had gone he leapt up, yanked the drinks cabinet door open and poured a large slosh of whisky into his coke. That stupid, stupid woman. How *dare* she... She had convinced the police she was in the right, and she wasn't, she wasn't.

Jeff paced up and down with his whisky, heat filling his head and anger coursing through him. But he would get the baby. You only had to look at their two families to see who would be the better parents, and which the better home for Jael.

He would win in the end.

Chapter Thirteen

Saturday, June 4th

Caro

'Jeff? Jeff!' No answer came and Caro stared at him, sprawled on the sofa, his eyes fixed on the TV where two sports commentators were discussing last week's football results. Was that really so fascinating, or was Jeff away in his own world again? He was so strange at the moment – one minute he'd be talking about something completely everyday like the gas bill, then the next he'd be lost in a daydream, oblivious to everything around him.

Caro tried again. 'Jeff!' She strode from the kitchen and stood in front of him.

He blinked, then glared at her. 'Huh?'

'You know it's Granny's lunch tomorrow? We're supposed to be there about half one.'

He stared straight through her for a moment, then turned back to the TV. 'Yes, yes…'

Caro went back to the kitchen and shoved a mug under the coffee machine. This was scary. Something very strange was happening to her life. Had anyone else noticed how oddly Jeff was behaving these days? No one had said anything, but then, maybe they wouldn't. Was he working as usual? A couple of times last week she had wondered if he'd actually been at work, but his hours were so irregular it was difficult to tell.

And then there was last night.

She'd gone for a pizza and then on to the cinema with Rachel, an old school friend she saw occasionally. When she arrived home again just after eleven, Jeff was sitting in the spare room, in the dark. Caro nearly died of fright; she'd sensed he was in the house but he hadn't answered when she called his name – she'd had to search for him. He was terribly upset about something; his eyes were positively wild, but he'd only mumbled something about a headache. She'd been afraid to ask much about it. A few months ago, she'd have taken him in her arms and cuddled it out of him. But Jeff's non-existent sperm had altered them both so much she didn't recognise him anymore, and you couldn't cuddle a stranger.

Tomorrow. She would bring her feelings into the open when they came home from the birthday lunch. No way could she go on like this. Her life was brimming over with negatives – no marriage, no-baby. No Liam and Alfie. She had so much love to give a child. You couldn't love a no-baby, but oh, she did, she did, and it was killing her.

Julie

Telephone in hand, Julie stood at her fourth-floor window and stared down to the street below. The Saturday morning rush was starting, with people tripping towards the High Street and the shops, or down to the river for a day's relaxation by the water. A mixed crowd was going both ways – parents with variously-sized kids in tow, couples of all ages, and a lot of folk just by themselves. It was a real summer parade, t-shirts and tops in rainbow colours and even the odd picnic basket. Happy people, most of them.

Julie sighed and hefted her phone. To phone Max or not to phone? The real question was – did she want Max in her life?

Yes, she realised. That little flicker of attraction, the nervous, excited feeling she had when he was near – it was a long time since she'd felt like that. It must be worth taking a risk. And she wanted to know what was happening about Jeff Horne, too. And the dead boy from the library, what was going on there? Julie gripped the phone with now moist fingers and punched out Max's number.

The phone was answered on the third ring. 'Julie! I was just wondering if it was too early to call you!'

Julie laughed. 'The same thought crossed my mind the second your phone started ringing,' she said. 'Um, I wanted to ask what's happening about Jeff Horne? Were you able to talk to him about what he said to Sharon?'

'The boss-man nailed me for something else, unfortunately, but two of the other guys went. Jeff said it was all a big misunderstanding, and of course Sharon can't prove anything. But they were pretty severe with him, so hopefully that'll be the end of it. Sharon's going to warn her neighbours about letting people in at the front door of the building, too.'

Julie nodded. 'Good. Surely that'll be the end of it.'

'Yeah. Listen, why don't we meet later for another walk in the park? I'm off all day and it's great weather.'

It didn't sound as if Sam's questions had put him off. Julie thought quickly.

'Good idea. If we make it after lunch, I can drop Sam at his friend's birthday party and then he won't interrogate you to half to death again. I felt a bit guilty last time.'

She could hear the smile in Max's voice. 'He's a great kid, and Amy's a treasure.'

Julie took a deep breath. The way to any mother's heart was through her children… She made the arrangements to meet Max and rang off. Wow, she was looking forward to her afternoon.

Max was waiting at the swing park when Julie and the children arrived, and bounded across to meet them, his face bright. Oh yes, thought Julie, as he bent over the pushchair and tipped Amy's nose. There *was* something between them, but… It was early days.

Sam had a few minutes on the slide before they crossed the park and left him at his friend's house. Julie saw the interest on Ben's mother's face when she opened the door. It would be all round school on Monday that Julie Mayhew had another man in her life.

'Rather her than me,' said Max, taking over the buggy as they walked back towards town. 'Hosting a kid's party must be absolutely exhausting.'

'It is,' said Julie. 'Second only to Christmas Eve and Christmas morning. If you're lucky you get to sleep for three hours in between.'

Max laughed, then went on more soberly. 'It must be difficult, on your own.'

Julie glanced up at him. 'Sometimes it is,' she said slowly. 'But they both give so much back, and you know – you just do what you have to. I have to put them first.'

Max squeezed her arm. 'Let's take things nice and slow, then.'

They strolled down the High Street towards the river, and Julie asked about the boy who had died.

Max shook his head. 'Nothing new. His mates have been questioned, but they're keeping shtum about who got the drugs from where. Oh, we know a couple of possible dealers, the kind that sell contaminated stuff to kids. But there's no proof, and maybe there never will be.'

Julie sighed. 'Life sucks sometimes.'

She looked across the road at Jeff Horne's business as they went past. A noisy crowd of teenagers emerged from Cybersonics and ran off in the other direction.

'You know, I think he really likes kids,' said Julie thoughtfully, remembering how Jeff had looked at Sam. 'Jeff Horne, I mean. Maybe something bad happened to him, something to do with a child, and he hasn't got over it yet.'

Max stopped walking. 'You may be right, but if I were you I wouldn't go anywhere near him, Julie. He's definitely a bit more than your average weirdo, no matter what's happened to him.'

A shiver ran down Julie's spine. But surely, now that he'd been officially warned, Jeff would leave Sharon – and the baby – well alone.

Chapter Fourteen

Sunday 5th June

Caro

'Time we were off, love!'

Jeff shouted from the front door, his voice more cheerful than she'd heard it for quite some time, and Caro cringed. How could he call her 'love' like that, as if they were Mr and Mrs Perfect? And how she was to get through this birthday lunch at Granny's, with Jeff's whole family, including the kids, milling around, she did not know. She'd very much have preferred to cry off, but non-attendance wasn't an option. So they would go, and play their parts – or at least she would. She would try to act normally today, for Granny's sake, but tonight she would start to organise the rest of her life. Without Jeff.

But splitting up would bring a whole load of complications with it. This was Jeff's house, bought well before their marriage, so she'd have to be the one who left. Caro sighed. She could go to her sister's. Rosie was on her side, even if she was jealous of Caro's life of relative luxury, but on the other hand, Caro was jealous of Rosie's kids. They'd probably be at each other's throats in five minutes. Caro's stomach dropped. The next few weeks would be tough. Imagine packing all her things, deciding who'd get the joint stuff – the telly, the mixer, the furniture…

'Don't forget the present!' Jeff stuck his head round the living room door.

Caro made herself answer pleasantly. There was no point upsetting him now; she wanted the lunch to go well. 'I'll just get it.'

Keep it friendly, keep it normal, she told herself as Jeff drove towards the other end of Bridgehead. For Granny. Eighty years on the planet was an achievement, even nowadays.

The gears crashed, and Caro glanced across at Jeff. He was wearing his good suit, and nothing about his appearance suggested he wasn't his usual self. Only the erratic driving and the set of his chin were giving away that this was no normal Sunday visit to his grandmother.

Lunch was the usual noisy family affair, and to Caro's relief Jeff's older nieces and nephews kept him busy on their iPads. His IT expertise was always much in demand, and as he sat there, helping Ali gather material for her latest school project, there didn't seem to be anything out of the ordinary about him. Caro tried to relax. Just a few hours more.

At six o'clock the party was showing no signs of breaking up, so Caro decided to make the first move to go home. Jeff agreed instantly, confirming to her how superficial his normality was. Usually he loved family parties, but now he knew he'd never have a family of his own. Poor Jeff. Caro took the wheel, her shoulders tense as she reversed out of the driveway. It was difficult to pin down just why the whole infertility thing meant the end of their marriage. Other people had IVF or adopted older children, and Caro knew now she could love an older child, too. Liam's face swam in front of her eyes, and a lump rose in her throat.

Jeff was silent for most of the drive, and the minute they arrived home he headed for the garden shed and the lawnmower. Did he sense what was coming?

Caro made herself speak pleasantly. 'Could you leave that for a moment? I'd like us to have a chat first.'

They sat down at the kitchen table, his eyes that somehow weren't his eyes anymore locked on hers. Sweat broke out on Caro's brow and her hands began to tremble. She thrust them between her knees and forced herself to ignore the churning sensation in her stomach.

'Jeff. Things have been all wrong between us lately. Something's different; we've both changed and I can't go on like this. I – I want us to – separate. I think we'd be better apart for now.'

There. She had said it, using 'I' sentences like they always said in the magazines. It was out in the open.

Jeff jerked his head back, his nostrils flaring and eyes wide. 'No. No, Caro. You don't mean that. We'll be fine, you'll see. I'm going to give you a baby, don't worry.'

Caro frowned. 'What do you mean? You know we can't have one. Anyway…'

He leapt to his feet, breathing loudly, his chair crashing to the floor behind him, and Caro shrank back. She'd expected tears, anger, self-pity, not this wildness. He stood there, swaying slightly, bending over her. She could feel his breath on her face, hot and garlicky from lunch.

'Caro, please – just give me a day or two. I'll make it all right, don't worry. A few more days, that's all I ask, and then we can be a proper family.'

He straightened up and almost ran from the room. The spare room door slammed shut. And then silence. Caro buried her face in her hands. Where did this leave her?

All at once she was angry. He hadn't given her a chance to explain more fully, he hadn't asked about anything or even argued with her. He'd ignored everything she'd said about their relationship, and then he'd walked out. Well, she wasn't going to put up with that. She would give him half an hour to calm down and then she would start again. She would make him listen.

Thirty minutes' inactivity did nothing for Caro's nerves, sitting in the tidy, childless kitchen, listening to the neighbours' kids playing football on the street outside. Jeff was probably listening to them too. He needed time to realise what she'd said, for it to sink in a bit.

When the half hour was up she made a pot of tea and poured two mugs, putting two sugars in his. Right. Off you go, Caro-girl. Don't let him stop you having your say.

He did stop her, though. The spare room door was well and truly locked, and Jeff wouldn't open it. He wouldn't speak to her, either, though Caro knocked and thumped, speaking first calmly and then shouting – but nothing worked. It was as if he was pretending she didn't exist.

Twenty minutes later Caro was in tears of frustration. 'Don't say I didn't give you the chance to talk.' She gave the door a final thump, then choked the tears back, allowing anger to take over. 'I'm out of this, Jeff. I only ever started it for a baby. There's nothing left here for me now.'

Stamping as hard as she could, Caro went downstairs, staring round with tired eyes. This house had been home for over two years – she'd loved having so many nice things, and not having to scrape the cash together when she wanted something new. Jeff had given her everything she wanted, except the most important thing. Caro flung herself into an armchair.

The room looked so normal, but nothing would never be normal here again. And the stupid thing was, a lot of it was her own fault. If she'd agreed to adoption right at the start, maybe none of this would have happened. But it was much, much too late now.

Goosebumps rose on Caro's arms as she thought of the enormity of what she was about to do – end the relationship that had given her the only security she'd had in her life. She would go to Rosie's after work tomorrow. Jeff was often home on Monday mornings, but he'd go in to Cybersonics in the afternoon. She would come back here at lunchtime and pack some things, and this time tomorrow, she wouldn't live here anymore.

Caro raised clasped hands to her mouth and sobbed. No home, no Jeff, no-baby. It felt like she was on a tightrope, walking over an ocean of uncertainty, knowing she could fall in and drown.

But she had made her decision and she would stick to it. For better or for worse.

Chapter Fifteen

Monday 6th June

Jeff

Curled in a sweaty, uncomfortable ball in the spare room bed, Jeff waited until the front door banged shut behind Caro on her way to work. Only then did he feel it was safe to sit up, stretch, make a noise. He looked down at himself in distaste. Sleeping in his clothes like that. It was all Caro's fault. If she hadn't been so unreasonable last night – telling him their marriage was over! It was only a sticky patch; everyone had those. And what had she meant – she'd only started it because she wanted a baby? That wasn't true. It wasn't. They loved each other – didn't they?

He stood under the shower until the hot water ran out, massaging his head and shoulders. This headache was the pits. Something was twisting and tightening in his head – cramped muscles on the inside, maybe? Or migraine? He should have told Caro yesterday that he'd found a baby that could almost certainly be theirs. But *almost certainly* wasn't good enough; it would have to be definite.

It was a pity, but now he wouldn't be able to spend time talking to Sharon first, helping her see that she didn't want to be a mother. He would have to be masterful about it, tell her straight. She deserved a good talking to, actually. Reporting him to the police – he was angry about that. He hadn't been threatening her, not one little bit. He only wanted what was best for them all – especially for Jael. Sharon should be very grateful that her baby was going to such a good home. He'd told those two policemen on Friday evening that Sharon had misinterpreted him, and it was true – she hadn't understood at all how much better off the baby would be with Caro. But when Jael was settled here at home, even Sharon would see this was how their lives were meant to be, and everything would be all right again.

Jeff rubbed his face with both hands. The problem was, sometimes he didn't know any more what 'all right' was. It was often hard to remember what he was doing and feeling. The stress of being forced to produce a baby out of nowhere had done that – but it was nearly over now. The baby was waiting and today was the day.

At least he had a genuine excuse to call in sick; he couldn't possibly sit in front of a screen with a head like this. He needed fresh air and quiet, and a couple of pills with his breakfast would help too.

The question was, would Sharon give him the baby without a silly fuss? He needed it urgently now. If he and Jael were waiting when Caro got home tonight, all cosy and happy together – why, there would be no need for talk about things going wrong. They would be a family. Caro was going to be so happy.

But he needed Sharon on side when he arrived to claim the baby. Some more roses might help, white ones this time. And he would be very gentle, but firm, too. He would simply tell her what was going to happen; show her who was in charge. Yes.

Quickly, he slid his plate and mug into the dishwasher. It was well after nine now; he would go to the flower shop first, and then on to Sharon's. Humming in an attempt to drown out the headache, he lifted his jacket from its peg in the hallway. Something jingled as he thrust his arm into the sleeve, and he put his hand into the pocket.

The keys on the red leather key ring.

It was as if the sun had come out. Jeff drove towards town and parked further up than usual, by a little square just behind the High Street; look, they had benches and tubs of flowers here, how lovely. A good omen if ever he'd seen one. He would buy the roses for Sharon, and he would get Jael, but maybe he wouldn't need the persuasion.

He had the keys.

If he was careful, he could just go in and take the baby.

The High Street wasn't busy; it never was on Monday mornings, and Jeff walked briskly towards the florist's. You got much nicer flowers here than in the supermarket. More expensive flowers too, of course, but then Sharon was giving him the most priceless gift of all. The least he could do was leave her a few flowers.

He was slowing down, already reaching for his wallet, when the window immediately before the florist's caught his eye. The baby shop. He stood for a moment, gaping at the display. What a lot of things you could buy for babies nowadays. Silly, really – they only needed love. Well, love and… nappies and bottles, yes, and food. Baby milk. Actually, there were quite a few things the baby would need, and it would be easier to buy them now, before he had her with him. What a good thing he'd seen this place.

Chuckling to himself, Jeff turned into the shop doorway and stopped dead. 'Closed all day Monday.'

Oh. But he could drive to the big shopping centre outside town. Yes, he'd do all the shopping first and have lunch there, and this afternoon he would visit Sharon and collect the baby. He started back towards the car, a new spring in his step. Shopping would be fun – he could buy some lovely little girly clothes. Pink ones. Caro would love that.

And tonight, the two of them would be snug at home, a devoted daddy and a lovely little baby daughter. Waiting for Mummy.

Sharon

'Will you be okay?' said Craig, shrugging into his jacket.

Sharon nodded. The police had assured her that Jeff Horne had been warned off, and the neighbours were aware of the situation so there was no way for Jeff to get into the building. 'I'll be fine. I've got the baby clinic this morning and after that we'll just chill at home. Catch up on some kip.'

An uneasy peace had developed between her and Craig. He'd spent the weekend shadowing her, watching as she dealt with the baby. He was still sleeping in the spare room; there was a lot of mending to be done in the relationship before she would allow him into her bed again. But with her body still battered by childbirth, sex was the last thing on her mind anyway. Some help would have been nice, but Craig barely touched his daughter. Sharon shivered, in spite of the warmth in the flat. Maybe they should go for counselling.

She closed the door after Craig, then blocked the lock and attached the chain they'd had fitted, aware that she wasn't as confident as she'd sounded. Her gut still churned every time she thought about Jeff Horne's visit on Friday. Now she and Jael were alone in the flat for the first time since then. What if he did come back?

He won't, she told herself firmly. *You can do this, you're strong, you're in charge.* And right now, she had a clinic to go to.

It took ages to get herself and the baby ready to go out; teaching had never needed this much organisation. At last they were ready. Sharon laid Jael in the pram and looked round for her handbag and keys. The bag was on the sofa, but where on earth had her keys got to? She searched around the flat for a few minutes, then gave up. Craig must have taken them. He had a habit of grabbing the first key he could lay his hands on, ending up with his own, hers, and the spare set all in his pocket. Today at least the spare set were in their proper place in the airing cupboard. Sharon closed the front door firmly behind her and positively ran from the building.

To her surprise, she enjoyed the clinic. She'd been apprehensive that her care of her daughter wouldn't meet the nurse's expectations, but Jael was apparently thriving, in spite of her parents. The relief was liberating, like getting drunk, and Sharon was aware of the grin on her face as she walked home again. Craig texted to say he'd bring some quiche home for lunch, and hope swelled anew in Sharon's heart. Maybe they would find a way out of the resentment.

They managed to talk – about the business – all the way through the meal, which was encouraging, but Craig's face closed as soon as Jael started to cry.

'Why don't you lift her this time?' suggested Sharon, trying in vain to catch his eye.

He was staring out of the window. 'You go, you know how.'

Sharon shoved her chair back and left the room. So much for the supposed improvement; he was behaving like a teenager again. She changed the baby, fed her, then laid her back in the cot. Jael looked up fuzzily and blew bubbles before falling asleep with her usual suddenness.

Sharon grinned wryly. 'Wish I had your knack, kiddo.' She looked into the kitchen, where Craig was loading the dishwasher. At least he could still do that. 'I'm going for a sleep while she's down. I'm knackered, I was up four times last night.'

Craig nodded, his face a mixture of guilt and regret. 'If you go to sleep now you won't be able to attach the chain when I leave.'

Sharon hesitated, but her need for sleep was greater than her need for the chain. 'Double lock the door. Don't worry, if the doorbell rings I'll make very sure I know who I'll be letting in.'

He nodded, then to her surprise he hugged her briefly on his way into the bathroom. Sharon left him to it. Tonight, she would insist he did some of the baby-care, because left to himself, he never would. And if he refused... well, she would cross that bridge if she came to it.

She pulled off her jeans and shirt and slid under the duvet, feeling her body relax. Oh, this was what she needed. It was such a horrible dragging feeling, being so tired; how on earth did Julie manage with two little ones? For a few moments, she listened to Craig moving around the flat. Heck, she had forgotten to ask him for her keys back. Sharon closed her eyes, and blessed sleep overcame her.

Jeff

Jeff hummed softly as he guided the car round the side of the library and on towards the lights at the bottom of the High Street. His shopping expedition had been both time-consuming and expensive – he couldn't believe the price of disposable nappies, and as for baby milk… but it had all been worthwhile. He had enough supplies in the boot to last for weeks, including the best kind of baby milk – the assistant in Boots had been very interested in his story about taking care of his sister and her baby while she was recovering from a difficult birth. He'd found a little bouncy seat for the baby to lie in, too, and a small selection of clothes, just enough to last until Caro could buy some more. He was all set. They'd need a car seat later, of course, but today that wouldn't be necessary.

Sharon and Craig's building was sun-washed in a deserted garden area, and Jeff snorted as he approached the front door, the sports bag he'd prepared gripped in one hand. Look at the place. There was nothing child-friendly about it; it was yuppie-land pure, but it wasn't making Sharon and Craig happy – money couldn't buy you the important things. He pulled out Sharon's key ring and was able to identify the correct key immediately, so there was no conspicuous fumbling with the lock. The lift was waiting, and Jeff emerged on the fourth floor without having seeing a soul. He glanced around. There were two flats here and silence reigned along the long landing. He'd chosen a good time.

Another key slid into the lock on Sharon's door, and Jeff eased it round, his heart beating in his throat. This was the part that mustn't go wrong. One turn had no effect and his heart rate increased. It would be so much easier if he could get in and out without speaking to Sharon. He was doing the right thing, for Sharon and Craig as well as for him and Caro and Jael, but a silly fuss at the start of their new family life was best avoided. Another turn of the key and – yes, that was it. Jeff cracked the door open and listened for a moment. Nothing. Was she even at home? The possibility of finding an empty flat hadn't occurred to him, and he hesitated for a moment, then crept inside. Still nothing. He was busy wondering what kind of wicked mother took a days-old baby out when it should be having a proper lunchtime nap, when a slight sound came from one of the rooms. Jeff tiptoed up the hallway and into a small bedroom – and there she was, his little angel, lying there blinking up at him and waggling those wonderful baby fingers. He lifted her, hardly daring to breathe in case she started crying, but she snuggled into his arms as if she knew she belonged there. Tears ran down his cheeks. His little girl. Everything would be all right now – he had a baby for Caro.

Taking care to be gentler than he'd ever been before, he placed the baby in the sports bag and zipped it right up. She wouldn't suffocate in two minutes, would she? He would undo it in the car.

Quick, quick, away from here. He fled the flat on silent feet, the handle of the bag sliding on damp fingers. This was the dangerous part, getting the baby back to the car. Down in the lift… good, no one was about. Outside, round to the car… Jeff opened the passenger seat door and placed the bag on the floor where it couldn't fall down. Now to get home, as quickly as they could. How surprised Caro was going to be.

Julie

'Home-time,' said Dee firmly. 'Leave that computer, Julie, you must have megabytes coming out your ears by now. Let's go and have coffee in the park. We've scarcely had a minute to talk all day.'

Julie stretched thankfully. It was always nice, stopping work in time to enjoy some of the afternoon. Mind you, she'd spent quite a lot of work-time today day-dreaming about Max. It would be good to get her friend's input on Saturday's date.

They strolled towards the pond, sipping lattes-to-go. When they reached the benches, Julie sat down and patted the seat beside her.

'Guess what. I was out with Max again on Saturday – just me and Amy this time.'

Dee sat down, her face alive with questions. 'Good! Or – not good?'

'Oh, good. I think. Sam was at a party, so Max and I could talk.' She sighed. 'It's so complicated when you've got kids, Dee.'

'I can imagine. Julie, I know Sam and Amy come first, but… don't forego the chance of happiness with Max. I'll babysit for you as much as I can.'

Julie dropped her coffee beaker in to the bin at her side. 'You think I should stop being a wimp and grab a great guy while I have the chance, don't you?'

'You said it,' said Dee.

Julie nodded slowly. 'I thought I'd ask him to mine for dinner one night.'

Dee gave her a little push. 'Get on your phone and arrange a date soon, then. I'll see you tomorrow at work.' She walked off towards the hill.

Julie watched her for a moment, then reached for her phone. 'Soon' sounded good to her.

Sharon

A bang from outside woke her, and Sharon blinked the sleep from her eyes. The familiar sound of the bin lorry emptying the rubbish containers came in through the open window, and she relaxed. Well, that had been a good nap; she felt much better. A cup of de-caff and a digestive sounded good now. What time was it, anyway? She glanced at the alarm clock by the bed and froze. Four o'clock. *Four o'clock.* Craig would be home again soon. She had slept for over three hours – no wonder she felt rested. And how amazing that Jael wasn't yelling for attention. Or – oh heck – had her baby been crying, and she'd been too dead to the world to hear her? How awful. Or – no, no…

The ugly spectre of cot death reared up in Sharon's head, and she flung the duvet aside and ran through silence in the flat. Jael – Jael, sweetie, you're all right, aren't you? The nursery door was open, and Sharon skidded in, clutching the door frame for support. A scream in a voice she didn't recognise rang in her ears when she saw the empty cot.

Jeff

Humming, he pulled up in the driveway. Ah, this was better. Home was going to be so much more homelike with the baby here too. Careful with the bag, now, slowly does it. Key in the front door... There. He had carried his daughter into her new home.

'Here we are, sweetheart,' he murmured, lifting the baby from the sports bag and laying her on the sofa while he went for the rest of his shopping. When he returned, she was crying, her legs stiff and her face screwed up. Jeff lifted her – how natural it felt. The little head tucked under his chin, the warm little body leaning on his chest – oh yes, she belonged here. Was she hungry? Well, he knew what to do about that, thanks to the friendly shop assistant.

He took the baby into the kitchen and put her in the bouncy seat. She seemed to like it, so he lifted it onto the table and she lay looking upwards and giving occasional little bleats. Jeff poured boiling water over one of the new bottles to sterilise it, then made up a feed. Now it had to cool down before she could drink it. He put ice cubes into a jug and swirled the bottle around until the temperature seemed right – this baby stuff was complicated, boiling water and ice and powdered milk – but the feed was ready now. He lifted the baby, scraping the seat rather hard on the table top in the process, and carried her into the living room.

He had never fed a baby before, but of course he'd seen it done many times. It hadn't looked difficult. Jeff settled himself into a corner of the sofa, and offered the bottle to the baby.

To his delight, she sucked immediately and hungrily. Obviously, this was better food than she'd been getting. Sharon's milk was probably half sour. You couldn't nourish a baby you didn't want.

'Not too fast now, not too fast,' he murmured when the bottle was half empty. Weren't babies supposed to burp now and again? He held her upright, clean tea towel at the ready in case of dribbles, and rubbed her back gently. It was so amazing, sitting here with her baby solidness on his lap –and the band of tension in his head had disappeared at last. Yes, he was doing extremely well. Caro would be proud of him.

Jeff glanced over to the television table, where the framed selfie of the two of them at Louise's wedding stood. Big smiles and Caro's enormous hat. A good photo. But – where was the smaller one of Caro and Rosie that usually stood beside it? He gazed round the room, unease growing.

Several things were missing. The tiny wooden elephant Caro'd brought home from Thailand a couple of years ago. The chunk of quartz she'd bought in Austria. Two little enamel pictures of Brighton, and – the silver box Caro's grandma had left her! It was gone from its place on the book shelf. What had happened? Had they been burgled? Oh no – his computer stuff…

He left the baby on the sofa and charged upstairs. The spare room was the same as always, but one look in the bedroom told Jeff what had happened. Caro had gone. She'd taken a whole load of her things – both cases were missing from under the bed – no, no, where was she? He had to find her and bring her back home. They had a baby to think of now.

Back downstairs, he grabbed his phone and tried Caro's mobile, but it was switched off. Shit. But she'd be at work… He connected to the car salesroom.

'Hi, Jeff. No, she's taken the afternoon off. No, I don't know where she is. Sorry.'

He rang off immediately. That stupid cow Louise. Who else could he ask? Think, Jeff.

He didn't have many of her friends' numbers in his mobile, but he called those he did have. The answer was always the same.

'Sorry, Jeff, can't help you.'

It was all he could do to end the conversations politely. No one must guess what had happened, and of course nothing *had* happened, really, because Caro wouldn't, couldn't have left him. A sob rose in Jeff's throat as he stared at the baby on the sofa. She had fallen asleep, one little arm stretched towards him. He sat down beside her to think.

Caro must have gone somewhere. Probably Rosie's; that was the most logical place. He sat staring at Rosie's number in his phone. Even if Caro was there, Rosie might tell him she wasn't. He would go there later and make Caro come home. He would *make* her.

Sharon

The empty cot… No, no, her baby, her baby… Had Craig come home early and taken her out? But he would never do that; he was afraid to do more than touch her with one finger… Sharon stumbled into the living area and leaned on the back of the sofa. Her head was spinning, and waves of sickness were washing through her gut. The flat was absolutely still. The only sound was her own ragged breathing, and her heartbeat thumping, thumping in her ears. Where was Jael?

Sharon forced herself upright and stared wildly around, stumbling through the flat. Everything seemed so normal. The buggy was there by the door where she'd left it that morning. There was no sign of Craig, and no briefcase in the hallway, nothing in the spare room. He must still be at the shop.

Sobbing now, she hurried out to the terrace. No Craig, no Jael. Back to the bedroom – her phone, where was her phone? Christ, where the – there it was, on the chest of drawers. She had switched it off before she went to sleep. Sharon sank down on the bed, her fingers shaking and sliding on the screen as she turned her phone back on. Come on, come *on* – stupid device, why was it taking so long to boot up?

'Have you got her?' she screamed, hearing Craig's voice change from dull because he didn't want to speak to her, to sheer panic that matched her own. He hadn't seen Jael since quarter past one when he'd left them both asleep in the flat.

'Call the police!' he shouted. 'I'm on my way!'

He broke the connection and Sharon fell to her knees on the hard, wooden floor, her fingers trembling so much she could hardly punch out nine-nine-nine.

Jeff

A movement on the garden path outside made Jeff look up. Caro? Hope changed to horror when he saw the police car, and his heart crashed into top gear. Were they looking for the baby already? But they mustn't find her until Sharon realised that here was the best place for Jael to be. Swiftly, he lifted both baby and bottle, disappearing into the kitchen as the doorbell rang.

The baby chair was on the table; they would see that if they came snooping round the back. He thrust it into a cupboard, pushed the milk powder and all the bottle stuff into the sports bag, then wedged himself and the baby into the cupboard under the stairs. The police wouldn't see them here even if they did walk round peering in all the windows. Now if only the baby stayed asleep.

Fortunately, she did, and after a few shouts of 'Police!' and a walk round the back of the house, the officers departed. Jeff listened as their car reversed away from the house and drove off. He relaxed against the cupboard wall, wiping his face with one hand. That had been way too close for comfort. He couldn't stay here now, that much was clear. He lurched to his feet and pushed the door open, colliding with the shelf beside him. Something fell to the floor – goodness, his old pellet gun. He chucked it back on the shelf and carried the baby back to the living room. Where could he go with a baby and no Caro yet to help him? A hotel? B&B?

Suddenly he remembered the little square off the High Street where he'd parked that morning. There was a sign in one of the windows there, 'Rooms to let'. That would do very nicely, a furnished room if possible, where he and the baby could hide until Sharon came to her senses. This was all more complicated and messier than he'd intended, but the important thing was to keep his daughter with him. Caro would come back as soon as she realised he had a baby for her.

'Come on, little one. Into your lovely bag, and we'll go find somewhere to stay,' he said, collecting the baby's bits and pieces. It was time for them both to disappear.

Chapter Sixteen

Caro

Caro awoke early on Tuesday morning and for a second she couldn't think where she was. Then the events of the previous day slid back into mind and she sat up, pulling a face at her reflection in the dressing table mirror. This was Rosie's home; she had started new life without Jeff. And talk about bittersweet – the feeling of relief was intense; she literally felt lighter, and yet… it was the end of a dream. For her and for Jeff.

Rosie had been marvellous. She'd hugged Caro tightly and told her there was a bed here for as long as she needed it. They had three bedrooms and the third wouldn't be needed until one of the kids was old enough to want a room of his own. Caro eyed her sister's swollen tummy enviously. Well, now she'd be able to have one too. She was still young; there was plenty of time for babies.

A bird started to sing outside and Caro scrambled to the bottom of the bed where her cases were. She should get up now and be in and out of the bathroom before the others were wanting in. It wouldn't do to make a nuisance of herself.

A quick shower was invigorating and she stood in her room drying her hair. It felt strange, her things arranged in Rosie's tiny spare room. She'd forgotten her mousse, but she could go back today and fetch more of her stuff, and who knows, maybe Jeff would be ready to listen now. They'd have to talk properly sometime.

Rosie was in her dressing gown making toast when Caro went down. 'Going in to work today, are you?' She poured tea into a mug and pushed it towards Caro.

Caro nodded. 'I can't stay off again. But I'll go back ho– back to the house at lunchtime, get some more things and talk to Jeff, if he's there. We have to organise money and stuff, and then I can see about finding a place of my own.'

Rosie passed her a piece of toast. 'Jeff's place'll be a hard act to follow.'

Caro blinked back tears. This was true, but what else could she do? It was Jeff – or a baby someday. It wasn't a choice.

The news started on the radio and Caro listened idly as she ate. The usual boring political stuff came first, an attack on a head of state in the east somewhere, but the second item made her sit up, an uneasy churning starting in her middle.

'There is still no sign of the nine-day-old baby girl taken from her home in Bridgehead yesterday afternoon. Police are looking for an approximately thirty-five-year-old man to help with their inquiries. Anyone with information about this abduction, or who saw anything suspicious in the region of Riverside Gardens between one-fifteen and four o'clock yesterday afternoon, is asked to contact the police…'

'Sickening, isn't it,' said Rosie, reaching for the milk. 'Who would do a thing like that?'

She was distracted by the sound of her two-year-old upstairs, and Caro was glad of the time to think. She sat still, cold dread clutching at her heart.

It couldn't be – surely Jeff wouldn't – but he'd been so strange recently, so unlike himself. He'd changed – or had he gone crazy? But he wouldn't have taken a baby… would he? Caro pressed cold fingers to her lips. Jeff had definitely been a bit – erratic. What was it he had said about babies the other day, exactly? Something odd, anyway, but she couldn't remember; she'd been thinking about the no-baby.

Then there was that carrier bag from the baby shop. But *surely…*

Caro stirred more sugar into her mug, thinking hard. She would phone Davie in Cybersonics. Theoretically, Jeff would have been there all yesterday afternoon. Oh, please let Jeff have been safely at work yesterday afternoon.

She tried her best to appear normal until she left the house, and Rosie didn't seem to notice anything wrong with her sister's behaviour. Of course, she had just left her husband, thought Caro dismally, people wouldn't expect her to behave normally. As soon as she was out the garden gate she called Davie, forcing herself to sound upbeat.

'Hi, Davie. Um, this might sound odd, but I need to know if Jeff was in yesterday afternoon?'

'No, he called in sick in the morning,' said Davie, and Caro could tell there was more to come. Davie had never sounded so strained. 'Actually, Caro, he's been away a lot recently, and he's been a bit off too, if you know what I mean. I'm struggling to keep things going here. Is there anything wrong?'

Misery welled up inside Caro. 'I'm not living at home now, I'm at my sister's. And you're right, Jeff's been – different, lately. I'm worried, Davie. Is he coming in today?'

'He should be here right now, but he isn't,' said Davie. 'Hey, I'm sorry you're having problems. I'll get him to call you if he turns up, shall I?'

Caro ended the call and trailed across the road to the bus stop. The bus arrived and she sat downstairs, gazing blindly out of the window. Should she go to the police and say she was worried her husband might have taken the baby? But what if he hadn't? That would be an awful thing to do to Jeff, and it was going to be difficult enough to get things organised between them. No, she had to find out for sure first. She pulled out her mobile again and tried his number, but he didn't pick up. Caro scowled at her phone. Thinking logically, if Jeff had taken a baby home she would notice, even if he was out when she got there. So, she would go home and look, and she would do it right now. The next stop was just around the corner from the house.

On the way along the cul-de-sac she phoned the salesroom. 'I'm sorry, Lou, I'll be about half an hour late. I've got a bit of a crisis on. I've left Jeff.'

She heard Louise's swift intake of breath, and listened to the excited reassurances that she would cover for Caro as long as necessary. Lou would expect all the gossip later. Oh well, what did it matter?

The house was silent when Caro opened the front door. The car wasn't in the driveway, so hopefully Jeff was on his way to work. She went in slowly, looking around.

Well, there was no baby here. Jeff had been back since she'd left yesterday, she could tell. He'd left the kettle in the sink and there was a new scrape on the kitchen table. But apart from that, and a tea towel in the living room, nothing seemed out of place, or unusual. Caro shrugged. At the moment, there was no reason to think that Jeff had taken the baby. She could go to work with a clear conscience and try his phone again later.

She opened the front door just as a police car was pulling into the driveway. Caro stared, apprehension twisting in her middle yet again.

'Mrs Horne? I'm DS Sanders.' The older officer introduced his colleague too, and suggested they went back inside. Dumbly, Caro led them into the living room and they all sat down. DS Sanders leaned forward and spoke seriously.

'We need to speak to your husband,' he said, gazing at her steadily. 'Can you tell us where he is?'

Caro shook her head, tears prickling in her eyes. 'I've no idea. He should be at work. I – I've left him. I haven't seen him since, oh, since Sunday evening. We had a quarrel and he slept in the spare room. Then I left yesterday while he was at, um, out. I'm only back to – to get some more things.'

She couldn't bring herself to tell them she'd come to see if a baby had been here.

'I see,' said the policeman, glancing at his colleague. 'Was there anything troubling your husband that you can think of? Any problems? I should tell you we've had complaints of some pretty odd behaviour.'

Caro began to weep. She couldn't help it, the tears trickled down her face and she couldn't stop them. There was no point in not telling them everything. Oh God, what had Jeff done?

'He's been terribly upset because he can't have children,' she said, pulling a packet of tissues from her handbag and dabbing her eyes. 'We found out a few weeks ago that he's – infertile. It's been an awful time for him. He's changed since we got the news.'

The police officer's face was kinder now. 'That's very helpful, Mrs Horne. Now, you can help us more with a recent photo of your husband, and details of where you're staying in the meantime. Is it all right if we have a quick look round here?'

Caro nodded, sniffing, and went to get the photo she had beside her bed. Jeff in denim shorts and a red t-shirt, grinning at her on a breezy Arran beach last summer. That was when she'd thought they had a future.

The two officers joined her downstairs, and the older one took the photo. 'Thanks. I don't need to say you must contact us straightaway if you hear anything from your husband. It's absolutely vital.'

Caro nodded miserably. 'Has he taken that baby?' she asked, knowing the answer already.

'It looks like it,' said DS Sanders. 'We're going to have to seal this place in the meantime, so if you want any clothes or anything, you should get them now.'

Caro ran upstairs again and filled a bag with clothes and cosmetics, flinging things on top of each other any old way, squeezing in as many of her possessions as she could. The two men were waiting in the front garden, and to her intense embarrassment they checked through her bag right there before letting her go. She could sense curtains twitching all the way along the road. Her cheeks flaming, Caro walked back to the bus stop. She didn't want anything more from that house; it would only remind her that her husband was a child abductor who had got her mixed up with the police.

But surely Jeff wouldn't *hurt* a baby?

All she needed now was to be alone, but she had nowhere to go except work. The kids at Rosie's would give her no peace if she went back there this morning.

She would never forgive Jeff for this, never.

Sharon

Sharon jerked awake and was immediately alert, her muscles tense because her whole body was insisting she should be active, up and running, searching for her daughter. She rolled into a ball on her side and clasped both hands under her chin. The foetal position, and Jael's favourite sleeping pose. Every time Sharon closed her eyes, the scene in the flat yesterday played through her head like a horror movie caught in a loop. It was as if a long, sharp knife was twisting continuously in her gut. Was Jael warm enough, was she fed, comfortable, *was she alive?*

Sharon pushed the duvet away and swung her feet to the floor. It was impossible to stay in bed with thoughts like these running through her brain, but as soon as she stood up she collapsed back on the bed, darkness swirling above her. That would be the sedative the doctor had given her yesterday; she mustn't take strong medication like that again. She had to be ready to react the moment there was any news.

She rose more slowly and pulled on her robe. Was Craig awake?

He was sitting at the kitchen table, a half-empty mug of something in front of him, and the haunted look he gave her told Sharon all she needed to know. He hadn't slept any more than she had and he was worried sick. And the guilt, the terrible guilt, how very much more of that must be torturing his soul than hers? She at least had loved her daughter for nine days. Craig had spent that time in an adolescent fit of the sulks because his life had changed.

Sharon slumped down opposite him and held her head with both hands, elbows on the table. He reached across the table and gripped her hands, and she held on tightly. There was nothing she could say to him, and nothing he could say, either.

Her breasts were aching with the need to feed her child; she would have to go and pump off milk, Jesus Christ – the doctor had said she should keep it. Freeze it. For a baby who might never come home to drink it – oh, God, how could she bear this? The police had assured them yesterday that infant abductions more often than not ended with the return of the baby, but there was no hundred percent about anything, was there? Her baby might be dead. So here she was, not knowing what had happened to her child, and there was no yukky nappy to change, no little face to wipe, just silence in an almost-empty flat.

Sharon choked back a sob. Her baby's absence left a hole so large she could fall into it and perish. And she had loved this baby for only nine days, after resenting it for nine months. What kind of a person did that make her?

The last thing she wanted was breakfast, but the doctor had warned her yesterday that she should eat. She had to think positive – the odds were the police would find Jael today and bring her home. If… but of course she was still alive; she had to be. Think *positive*. Sharon rose and poured muesli into a bowl, but at the first mouthful she pushed it away, gagging.

They'd phoned their families yesterday evening, Craig's mum in Ireland and Sharon's parents in South Africa, all much too far away to get here in five minutes and be supportive. Mum and Dad already had a flight booked for next week, but of course now they wanted to come straightaway. Sharon told them to wait and see what the next day or two brought. She couldn't face the thought of witnessing her mother's fear and grief. Shivering, she cradled a mug of tea against her chest. Please God the time wouldn't come when she'd be glad of family to support her through a funeral. Jael *must* be found soon – a baby couldn't be hidden away. Babies cried, they needed things like nappies that came in huge, obvious packets – someone would notice a baby had arrived in a place where there hadn't been a baby before.

But a dead baby made no sound and needed no nappies…

Her tea finished in painful swallows, Sharon sat limply at the table, her brow cradled in both hands again. Had Jeff Horne taken Jael? The police hadn't committed themselves one way or the other, but it did seem likely. And if it was Jeff, he wouldn't hurt her, surely? But even if Jeff – if he had Jael – didn't hurt her deliberately, he might not take care of her properly, and that could hurt her too. And what could she, the baby's mother, do to help her child? Nothing at all.

Sharon's phone rang in the bedroom, and Craig leapt up, almost upending the table in his hurry to get to it. Sharon followed him. Was it the police? Had they…?

But it was Julie, calling to ask if there was any news yet. Craig passed the phone to Sharon. Her voice wobbled as she spoke to Julie, who started to cry too.

'Oh Sharon, this isn't real. Shall I come round later? Or do you want to be alone?'

Sharon rubbed her face. 'I don't know. I can't do anything to help her, Julie. I can't stand this. But yes, please come.'

'Okay,' said Julie, sniffing down the phone. 'I'll bring you something for lunch, something that'll just slip down. About twelvish. See you later, honey.'

Sharon sat on the bed for a moment, then lurched back to the living room for the things the midwife had brought her yesterday. She would bloody well pump milk for her baby, because it was the only thing she could do. Another sob rose in her throat. For a moment she stood at the window looking out over the town. Bridgehead, waking up to a normal summer's day. The river, the library, the crowded High Street… Thirty thousand-odd inhabitants going about their business, and somewhere in amongst them was her daughter – if she hadn't been taken even further away by this time. And that wasn't impossible. Jael might have been sold and abused by now. The thought made Sharon retch. There was no guarantee that their baby had been taken by Jeff – or anyone who'd look after her.

Sharon sat in her room pumping lukewarm milk into a plastic bottle, fuzzy exhaustion giving way to agonising hope and apprehension when the doorbell shrilled into the flat.

Craig's footsteps ran to the intercom. 'Hello?'

'It's the police,' he shouted, and Sharon heard him press the buzzer to let them into the building.

She put the pump down. 'Oh God – have they…?'

He appeared in the bedroom doorway, his face sheet-white. 'I don't know.'

'Go and let them in, then.' Sharon reached for the clothes she'd been wearing yesterday, fumbling into her blouse and listening as Craig led the officers into the living area. Julie's friend Max was there and Anita Grant, their family liaison officer, who was to help them and keep them up-to-date with what was going on during the search for Jael.

'Is Mrs Morrison all right?'

'She's getting dressed. She'll be through in a moment.'

'Good. We've come to suggest that you – preferably both of you – do a TV appeal today, ask whoever has your daughter to give her back, and tell the viewer's exactly what has happened. In our experience that's a very good way of increasing public awareness and sympathy, and we often get useful information sent in afterwards. If you're agreeable we can do it at half past one at the police station, or here if you'd prefer. It would be aired as part of the national news bulletins.'

Craig mumbled something unintelligible as Sharon pulled on her trousers. He was obviously close to tears. Shivering, she went through to the living room, where Max and his colleague were sitting upright on the sofa and Craig was slumped in an armchair.

Sharon lowered herself into the other, her unpumped left breast heavy with milk, and aching. 'We'll do anything you think might help. Anything. Is there any new information at all?'

Anita leaned towards her. 'Mrs Morrison. Sharon. We have strong reason to believe that Jeff Horne has taken your daughter. If he has, he's taken her because he wanted a child of his own. It's more usual for a woman to abduct in those circumstances, but I want you to know that cases like this are more likely to end well than not. Horne doesn't want to hurt your daughter, he wants a child of his own, and sooner or later someone will become aware of her – that's where an appeal always helps – and report in to us.'

Sharon nodded. It was something to hang on to, at least. 'But you're not absolutely sure he's got her?'

Max spoke. 'There's no proof yet, but we're pretty sure. It all adds up. He had opportunity to take the keys. He wanted a baby and couldn't have one. He met you when you were pregnant and forced an acquaintanceship; he even suggested you give up the baby. His wife has left him because he's been 'strange' recently, but he isn't at home. I think we can be fairly sure he's got Jael.'

Sharon took a deep breath. 'I want to do the appeal here. I don't want to go out yet.'

'No problem,' said Max, getting up. 'We'll come over with a camera team just after one. We'll write the text with you, and don't worry, we'll film it again and again until it's right. You can sit here on the sofa, so don't wear anything blue or you won't come out right on film. And if there's anything else we can do…'

'Would you like me to stay here with you?' asked Anita.

Sharon shook her head. A stranger would only make the situation worse. 'Please go and join the search for Jael. The more people who're looking for her…'

She watched as Craig went to the door with the two officers. 'Find our baby. Please.'

He did care. Sharon rose, hands over her aching breast, and went back to the bedroom. She would finish pumping now. Julie was bringing something for lunch, and then they would do the appeal. Then…

A throaty, painful sob escaped her lips. After that, there would be nothing left to do but wait.

Jeff

Jeff paced up and down the narrow room, holding the baby against his shoulder. Five steps to the window, turn, five steps to the door, turn… It was all there was space for in here. But if he sat on the bed, or tried to lay the baby down, she started to cry. Again. It had gone on like this for most of the night, and he was more exhausted than he'd ever been in his life before. The only thing that was keeping him going was the wonderful, incredible fact that he had his baby girl here with him. The daughter he'd almost never had.

And what a blessing he had found this place. They would be safe here, he was sure of that. The landlord was an incredibly ancient Asian gentleman who spoke very broken English and had scarcely glanced at Jeff the day before when he'd inquired about a furnished room. He'd left the baby in the car while he was asking, so Mr Bhandari didn't even know Jael was living here too. Jeff had paid four weeks rent up front and signed a false name.

His room was on the first floor, on a dark and narrow corridor between a two-roomed flat that seemed to house at least ten people, judging by the noise, and another single room whose inhabitant he had neither seen nor heard. The room was tiny, with barely enough space for the narrow bed, one wooden chair, and a low cupboard near the door. There was a radio, an electric cooking ring, and a chipped mug holding a wooden spoon and a stained vegetable knife. But at least he had his own loo. He would manage. Except the baby wouldn't settle, and he had nothing at all to do except walk up and down with her, and wait.

Maybe another bottle would do the trick. He heated one in a pan of water and offered it to the baby. She sucked half-heartedly, but she was quieter now, her eyes half-shut. Jeff relaxed, and switched on the radio that looked as if it had been gathering dust on top of the cupboard for the past forty years at least. The local news would be on soon. He didn't know whether to hope there would be something about Sharon and Craig and the baby, or not. Surely they'd soon realise it was better like this. He had to know when it would be all right to go back home and show Caro their little girl, and the news online wasn't telling him much. Jeff rubbed his face with one hand. He missed his home, and Caro, and the feeling of being safe.

The second news item was about Jael, but they didn't name her. They just said that the police were looking for a man – was that him? A sick feeling rose in his middle. Sharon must still be deluding herself that she wanted to be a mother – what a fool the woman was. Oh, well. What did it matter if it took a few days longer? She would see sense in the end, and afterwards he and Caro would have a lifetime ahead of them with their daughter.

Jeff stared at the small bag of food supplies in the corner. If the police *were* looking for him, it wasn't even safe for him to leave this room. He was very near the High Street here, and a lot of people there knew Jeff Horne, co-owner of Cybersonics. And maybe the next news bulletin would name him. He'd better get some supplies in right away, enough to last a week at least. And the car – it was parked in a narrow little alleyway behind Mortimer Square. He should move it a lot further away.

Jael finished the bottle and he lifted her upright for a burp. Even a day's experience had taught him this was a necessary part of the routine. Miss it out and she'd be grizzling for hours. The burp came, loud and windy, with it a messy load of baby-sick that landed on the baby's cardigan and Jeff's trousers. Lord. How on earth was he going to get things washed here? He mopped them both as well as he could with toilet paper, and flushed it all down the loo.

Fortunately, the baby fell asleep then, and he laid her on the middle of the single bed and covered her with a pullover. Warm and snug. Right. Time to go shopping.

It was good to be outside, and alone, the sun hot on his back. A free man doing his own thing. He hadn't realised how tiring babies were, or how much they restricted you. Probably nobody did until they had one of their own to look after.

Jeff drove to the shopping centre just outside Bridgehead and filled a trolley with food, and more baby milk and wipes. That should last them quite a while. Now he would take the shopping back, unload, then park the car somewhere else for the duration.

The square was busier when he returned, and Jeff saw that a lot of people seemed to use it as a place to sit and chat and have lunch. He frowned. It wasn't so ideal here after all. But often it was easier to hide in a crowd than somewhere quiet and deserted. He parked on a double yellow line outside the front door of the flats, and unloaded his purchases on to the pavement. A dark-haired boy came over and looked at the car. Jeff grinned to himself. Probably he'd never seen a virtually new one this close.

'Bunking off?' he said briskly. 'Don't blame you. Want to earn a quid?'

'I came home for a book,' said the boy, then squinted up at Jeff. 'What for?'

'Watch my car while I take the shopping upstairs. And keep an eye open for traffic wardens.'

'Two quid,' said the boy, hands in his pockets.

Anger surged up in Jeff's head. Little bastard. But he had no choice now. He didn't want to come down and find his tyres slashed, or his paintwork scraped.

'Two quid it is,' he said, forcing himself to sound pleasant. 'In fact, here's a fiver. But you have to forget you ever saw me for that.'

'Done,' said the boy, pocketing the money and leaning on the building beside the car.

Somehow, Jeff managed to lift all his bags at once, and went up the dark flight of stairs two at a time. The baby was still asleep, thank goodness. He dumped the shopping and ran downstairs again. Now to shift the car.

'Just remember,' he said, tapping the boy on the shoulder. 'You didn't see me. Or else. What's your name, anyway?'

The boy scowled. 'Liam,' he snapped. 'I didn't see you, right?'

Jeff relaxed. That was how little criminals were made and developed. Fact of life.

He drove swiftly to the hospital and left the car in the Maternity car park. He'd noticed last week it never seemed to be empty, so maybe the police wouldn't find it there for a while. Now he had to get back before the baby woke up and started howling. A taxi from the hospital to the High Street wasn't too much of a risk, surely.

It was after one by the time he got back to the room. The baby was lying there with her eyes half-closed, and Jeff started to put his shopping away. There wasn't much space. He thrust the bread into the little cupboard under the cooking ring where a few more pieces of cutlery and a couple of grubby looking plates were stacked, then picked up the vegetable knife and laid it on the shelf beside the door, just in case. There. He was ready for a long siege.

And now he was back to having nothing to do except fiddle with his mobile, and he couldn't do much of that because he'd forgotten his charger. He should have bought one while he was out. He sat on the bed and looked at his phone. The police could trace calls made on mobiles, so it was actually better not to use it unless he had to. He would wait another day or two before calling Caro – and Sharon. Sighing, he went to the door to check it was locked, then lay down on the bed beside the baby. A nap would do him good.

Julie

Julie sat cuddling Amy as Sam dealt out seven dominoes each and then piled up the others at the side of the table. The little boy had made a set at school, and insisted on trying them out as soon as they arrived home.

'Miss Cairns said I did a very good job,' he said proudly, showing Julie the ragged cardboard dominoes with their crayoned dots.

'They're brilliant,' said Julie. Oh how bittersweet this was, cuddling her baby and playing dominoes, while across town Sharon and Craig were sitting in a silent flat.

Sam played his first domino and looked at her expectantly. Julie organised hers, fixing a happy expression on her face. Sam didn't know yet that Jael was missing, but she would have to tell him today. The kids at school might be talking about it by tomorrow, and she didn't want him to learn about it second hand. It was tough; there was no way to soften news like this. The bogey-man had struck. Still, they could have a game of dominoes first.

It was difficult to concentrate and Sam won the first game very quickly. He beamed at Julie and tears welled up in her eyes. Oh, if only Sharon was able to play dominoes with Jael in a few years. Please let there be a happy ending. Two strange police officers had come earlier that afternoon to ask her about the couple of times she'd seen Jeff Horne, and it had really brought home to Julie that Jael was gone. Abducted, and no-one – except Jeff Horne – knew where she was. Lost baby.

Sam groaned when Julie's phone started to beep, but Julie sighed in relief. Her heart wasn't in this game.

'Always happens, doesn't it?' she said to Sam. 'Tell you what, you go and find some chocolate in the kitchen cupboard while I answer this.'

It was Max, and Julie's heart started beating faster.

'No news yet,' he said at once. 'Listen, why don't we bring our dinner together forward to tonight and go to a restaurant, if you can find a sitter? I thought we could go at six and give Sharon and Craig some moral support while they watch their appeal being aired. Then afterwards the two of us could go for a pizza, and you can cook another time.'

Julie agreed straightaway. Sharon had eaten a few mouthfuls of the pasta dish Julie had taken them at lunchtime, but she was still pale as death. The appeal had been on Julie's mind all afternoon. Poor Sharon, having to lay her heart on the line, and have some stranger film her while she was begging for the return of her daughter. There was nothing anyone could say to help, either. It was the worst possible thing that could happen to new parents – barring the death of the baby, of course.

'Good idea,' she said to Max. 'Dee's not going out tonight – I'm sure she'd babysit.'

'I'll pick you up about half-five, then.'

Sam was still occupied in the kitchen, and Julie called Dee, who offered to come round right away.

'Be prepared to play umpteen games of dominoes,' said Julie, smiling drearily.

She called Sam back from the kitchen and finished the game quickly, allowing him to win again.

'Well done you,' she said. 'Listen, Sam, this is important. Dee's coming over to look after you and Amy for a while, because Max and I are going to help Sharon and Craig tonight. They're pretty upset, because someone they don't know very well has taken their baby away, and they don't know where she is.'

Sam stopped putting the dominoes back in their box. 'Why? Who took their baby? Where is she?' He stared at her, wide-eyed and incredulous.

Julie hugged him with the arm that wasn't holding Amy. At least he didn't seem afraid, though that might come later. What kid wouldn't dread being taken away from home?

'It's a man they know a bit. He likes babies a lot and he wanted one of his own, and he's sort of stolen Jael. I'm sure he won't hurt her, but of course Sharon and Craig want her back as soon as possible.'

'Is Max looking for her?' Sam pushed his hair out of his eyes, and Julie could see the worried little frown start on his forehead.

'All the police are out looking for her and I'm sure they'll find her soon,' said Julie, amazed she was able to keep her voice level. 'It's a case of hanging on in there. Now, are you going to be very good and let me help Sharon?'

Sam nodded, his face glum.

Julie hugged him. 'Thank you, sweetheart. And when Jael's home we'll all go for a big ice cream in the café on the High Street; you, me and Amy, and Sharon and Jael, okay?'

'Tomorrow?' said Sam, blinking up at her.

Julie sighed. 'Well, no, not tomorrow. The police have to find Jael first, and then I think Sharon'll need a day or two's peace and quiet before she wants to go for ice cream. But soon, I promise.'

Was it wrong to promise? She only wanted him to be quite sure that the anguish was temporary.

But supposing it wasn't?

159

Caro

Caro watched Bridgehead pass by as the bus meandered along on its way to Rosie's district. It was a longer journey from the salesroom, but it was restful, just sitting here with no one yakking in her ear. Louise had been one big question mark all day. Had Caro seen Jeff yesterday – what was she going to do now – was there any chance they'd get together again? And the killer remark, as far as Caro was concerned – maybe starting a family would help? Caro closed her eyes. Even for Lou, that was crass. A baby would definitely have helped, but that wasn't the point.

Her phone buzzed, and Caro opened her bag. Had the police–? It was a strange mobile number, and she made the connection, turning towards the window and speaking in a low voice. 'Hello?'

'It's me.' A young voice.

'Liam? You shouldn't–'

'I can't do my maths again.'

'Maybe your dad can help? Isn't he back now?'

'He's out and he won't be home till late. Please, Auntie Caro.'

Caro bit her lip. 'Okay. What's the problem?' She would be the one with a problem if he kept calling her for help. His father would know now that Caro had turned up at the square, because Alfie's mother would tell him, even if Liam hadn't. What had Pete thought?

It was money this time and Caro sighed with relief. At least it was an easy fix. 'Change the pounds into pence, Liam, then divide, and then change the answer back into pounds and pence. And if it doesn't work out, ask your teacher to help you. Okay?'

'Okay. I never thought of that. Thanks, Auntie Caro.' The connection broke.

Caro dropped her phone back into her bag, not knowing whether to laugh or feel frustrated. If only she could help herself as easily.

Julie

The look of admiration Max gave her made Julie forget for half a second that this wasn't an ordinary date. But then reality hit home. They were going to watch the appeal.

Max's car was parked on the other side of the road, and he took her arm as they crossed over. 'Have you told Sam?'

Julie nodded. 'It's awful, when you have to shatter your child's confidence that they live in a nice place and all grown-ups are good.'

'Kids have to learn how the world works,' he said, starting the engine. 'I'm sure Sam knows not to speak to strangers.'

'Oh yes,' said Julie miserably. 'But stranger danger's the theoretical part. What's happened to Jael is the whole horrible thing put into practice.'

They were silent for the rest of the short journey, sad thoughts about lost babies and grieving mothers floating through Julie's mind. It must be the worst, the most unbearable grief of all, for a child, a baby you'd carried inside you for nine months. Your own flesh and blood.

It was ten to six when they arrived at Sharon and Craig's flat.

Craig let them in, his face pale. 'I'm glad you've come,' he said to Julie in a low voice. 'This afternoon was horrific. I don't know how Sharon's going to react when she sees it all on TV.'

The appeal was aired as part of the national news. Julie and Craig flanked Sharon on the sofa, with Max on the arm beside Julie. Sharon was outwardly composed, but Julie could feel the shivers that shook the other woman's body. She gripped Sharon's hand hard.

The appeal started with Sharon holding a blown-up photo of Jael and Craig explaining what had happened. Afterwards they both begged the kidnapper to bring Jael back, or leave her somewhere safe.

'We've only had nine days with her, please, please give us our baby again,' said Sharon at the end of the film, her cheeks wet and her voice almost inaudible.

The camera zoomed in on the photo of Jael for a few seconds and the appeal was over. The newsreader started the next news item.

Julie couldn't hold back her tears. Sharon was sobbing too, her head on her knees.

Max got up and touched her shoulder. 'That'll help, you know. There are always masses of calls after an appeal about a child. Everyone wants to help – millions of people will be thinking about Jael now, and the calls will start coming in.'

Sharon nodded, but her eyes were bleak. 'Thanks. Everyone has been so kind.'

Julie squeezed her hand. 'You'll get her back. Just hold on to that. Jael's with someone who wants a baby. He's not going to hurt her, and the police will find her.'

She felt Max's hand grip her arm and stopped, glancing up at him. His face was quite neutral, though, and Julie fished in her bag for a tissue to wipe her eyes.

They left the flat twenty minutes later.

'Sharon did that well,' said Julie, as they walked down the corridor. 'I'm sure I couldn't have spoken as eloquently.'

Max took her elbow again as they entered the lift. 'If you had to, you would,' he said flatly. 'Everyone does. It took us a while to get the version you saw. And Brian – my boss – realised half way through that I was sort of privately involved too, through you. He thinks I should back off the case.'

'Sensible, I suppose.' It was difficult to know what else to say.

'But frustrating. I'm going to do my best to stay involved. Okay – is pizza all right, or would you prefer Indian?'

Misery closed Julie's throat. She wanted to go home; this didn't feel at all like an evening out with someone she was attracted to. To her dismay, Max took her hand and squeezed it as they walked from the lift to the front door.

'I wish we could have some normal time together. Without all this hanging over us, I mean.'

Julie nodded, hardly trusting herself to speak. 'I'm sorry. I want to go home now, Max. Maybe some other time, huh?'

His eyebrows rose. '*Maybe* some other time? What's wrong, Julie?'

Tears were imminent again and Julie blinked hard. She mustn't cry here, because if she started she might not be able to stop. Then disappointment and – yes, anger, took over. Why didn't he understand?

'What's *wrong*? The very thought of anything like this happening to Amy makes me feel sick. I need to protect her and Sam, and how can I be sure I'll be able to do that? You don't know what this feels like.'

He held the door open for her, and she walked out, startled to see a tear run down his cheek.

'Max?'

He didn't meet her eyes. 'I know better than you think.'

He rubbed his face, and Julie stood still just outside the building, waiting. What was coming now?

'I was nearly a dad, two years ago. Except my ex didn't want to be a mum, and she got rid of the baby without telling me. It was the worst day of my life.'

'I'm sorry.' Julie put a hand on his arm. It all made sense now. He hadn't come to terms with his loss, and helping Sharon and Craig, and even doing ordinary things like going to the park with Sam and Amy was giving him the feeling of having a child – a baby – in his life. Poor Max.

She searched for words to help him. 'Some people are just – like that. There's nothing you can do about it, Max.'

He looked at her, his face tragic. Jeff Horne's face looking down at Sam flashed into Julie's mind and she caught her breath. That day... Amy had disappeared from the Internet café – Jeff Horne's café. And he had brought her back... Had *Jeff* taken her, then realised he wouldn't get away with it? If that was true, it could have been her doing the TV appeal, sitting in her flat going mad with grief and fear, not knowing if her baby was still alive. Julie's stomach churned.

Max was still staring at her, but somehow it was all too complicated to even start talking about now. Julie turned her head away and pressed a fist to her mouth.

Max stuffed his hands into his pockets. 'Maybe we should just – mark time for a bit,' he said, and she nodded.

This time he didn't take her arm on the way back to the car.

Chapter Seventeen

Wednesday 8th June

Jeff

The bread was as hard as a brick already; it was the heat in this place. Jeff tossed the dried-up loaf into the bin and flopped down on the bed. The baby, shaken by the sudden movement, began to whimper. Jeff covered his ears. Please, baby, please be quiet and good again. He didn't have the energy for another crying fit right this minute – living here was so much more difficult than he'd thought it would be. The baby-care part wasn't too bad, he only had to keep her fed and clean and she was reasonably content, and God knows he didn't have anything else to do. It was looking after himself that was the awkward part. He thought he'd bought enough food to last forever, but he hadn't.

The latest radio news bulletin informed him that a number of calls had been made to the police after yesterday's TV appeal by Sharon and Craig, but he had no way to know if any of those calls had been about him. The police must suspect him. Jeff smiled grimly at the high, dusty ceiling. They wouldn't be looking for him around here, anyway. They'd think he'd go further afield, to Glasgow or London, where it would be easier to be anonymous. Or up north somewhere where no-one was around to notice a baby. Staying in Bridgehead was a smart thing to do, but against this was the fact that his was a well-known face on the High Street, and he would be forced to go out shopping again soon. Had his photo been on TV? If only the room had a TV as well as a radio, but it hadn't, and he was afraid to use his mobile to find out what the general public had been told about him. He should have brought a laptop; you'd think he of all people… He'd taken off without thinking about anything much, except the baby. And now shoppers in the High Street could already be keeping an eye open for him, whispering his name, looking over their shoulders to make sure Jeff Horne wasn't behind them. They would go and peer in the window of Cybersonics to see if he was there. And Caro – what was Caro doing? Did she realise he had the baby? If she did she'd be over the moon, dying to be a mum to her daughter. It was odd how she'd deserted him like this, when she was the reason he was here. He'd done what he had to, he'd got a baby, and it was Caro's baby now. Jeff rubbed his head. A thin little voice was whispering in there, insisting this *wasn't* Caro's baby. He lifted the grizzling infant and rocked her in his arms. That helped them both. Jael, little girl, Daddy's girl. It would all be worth it when he got her home. Don't forget, Sharon hadn't even *wanted* this baby. It *would* be all right in the end, it was just the lack of sleep making his brain so woolly. New babies did that to their parents, everyone knew that.

The baby fell asleep again and he laid her down at the top end of the bed. Maybe he could slip out to the supermarket while it was still early. Undecided, he stood at the window and looked down into the square. The boy Liam was there, a tattered-looking school rucksack in one hand. Jeff had a sudden brainwave. He opened the window and whistled, beckoning frantically when Liam looked up. The boy shrugged, then trotted across the square and disappeared inside Jeff's building.

Jeff grabbed his wallet and went out to the landing. He started to talk as soon as Liam appeared up the stairs. 'Could you do me favour? I'm not well and I need a couple of things from the shops. You get them and bring them back to me at lunchtime and I'll give you a tenner.' He made his voice as authoritative as he could while remaining pleasant.

The boy stared at the wallet. 'Okay. What d'you want?'

'Bread, cornflakes, a carton of milk, and some cold meat.' Jeff pulled out a ten-pound note, then changed his mind and scrabbled some coins together. Better not give this little tyke too much opportunity to steal from him. He forced himself to smile at Liam. 'You buy them and bring me the receipt, and I'll pay you then.'

The boy considered, obviously wondering if he could improve the deal.

'Bread, cornflakes, milk, cold meat,' said Jeff firmly. 'Half twelve or so.'

'Okay, okay,' said Liam, and vanished down the stairwell.

Jeff went back to his room. He should have added a newspaper to the list. But if he paid the kid for each errand there would be no limit to what he could demand. Would a boy like Liam be able to lend him a lap top or a phone? Probably not, but it might be worth asking.

He would have to heat some soup for breakfast. Strange days indeed. He stood stirring a battered pan on his one ring, his mouth watering at the smell. It seemed like ages since he'd last had a decent meal. That had been at his grandmother's party on Sunday. Half a lifetime away now.

The morning passed slowly. Jeff listened to the radio and played with the baby when she was awake. She was a pretty little thing, with black hair and dark, dark blue eyes that would maybe turn brown later. She wasn't much like Sharon, that was sure. But then, Caro was going to be her mother now, so that would be all right. Caro was dark-haired too. The baby looked at him seriously when he spoke to her, only sometimes appearing to focus on his face. What could she see? When did babies start to smile when you talked to them? This one wasn't smiling yet, or not at him, anyway. Jeff sighed.

He fed her just before twelve, reckoning she would fall asleep and give him time to deal with Liam again at half past. He was getting good at the feeding bit now. They had a little routine going, him and the baby. Clean nappy first, then half the bottle, up for a burp, then the other half and another burp to finish off with. That way, she fell asleep without any problems. Usually.

Now, however, she seemed to sense that he was nervous, and grizzled and cried and wouldn't lie down to sleep. Jeff rocked her in his arms for the fortieth time at least, it seemed, then laid her down on the bed – and off she howled again. Jeff looked at his watch, dismay and impatience making it impossible to stay calm. Liam should be here in five minutes and he wanted to be on the landing when the boy arrived. No way could he bring a visitor, even a child, in here. The baby had to stay a secret. Without a doubt.

He would have to leave her crying; it was the only thing to do and it wouldn't take more than a couple of minutes. His mind made up, Jeff put the baby in the middle of the bed and reached for his wallet, wondering if the howls could be heard from the square below. The lunchtime people were there now. Supposing someone heard her? But even if they did, well, babies cried. No one would think anything of it.

Briskly, he opened the door, then reeled back. Liam was standing right there in front of him, one hand raised to bang on the door and the other clutching a plastic bag from the convenience store on the High Street. Jeff took a step back in sheer surprise and Liam walked into the room.

'Here's your stuff. And the receipt. Can I have my money now?' He looked curiously at the howling baby. 'Why's it crying?'

Jeff felt dizzy with shock. It took a tremendous effort to gather his thoughts together. Be a normal father, Jeff. Relax. Act as if this is all in a day's work.

'She's tired. She'll go to sleep in a minute. Okay, here's your money, a bit extra too. Now off you go and leave me to get her to sleep. Thanks.'

Liam was still staring at the baby and Jeff felt the hairs on the back of his neck rise. This boy could ruin everything.

'Never have kids, son,' he said, forcing himself to sound matey. 'They wait till their mum's away at her sister's and then they howl non-stop. We had to leave our place for a few days, um, burst water pipe. We'll be going back soon. Thanks, son. Bye for now.'

To his relief, Liam merely grinned and turned back to the stairway. Jeff closed the door after him and lifted the baby, who stopped crying immediately. He rocked her against him, feeling her warm against his chest. Her forehead was hot.

'It's all right now,' he crooned. 'Daddy's got you, it's all right, all, all right.'

If he said it often enough he might believe it.

Julie

The library was deserted. It was if the inhabitants of Bridgehead were holding their breath, barely venturing out, waiting for the missing baby to be found. The media presence in the town centre made it all too obvious that this was anything but a normal Wednesday. Reporters and TV crews had already been crawling around the High Street when Julie passed that morning, and they'd probably be at Riverside Gardens too. Poor Sharon.

Julie shivered. It was forty-eight hours now since Jael had been taken, and each passing hour meant an increase in the danger to her. According to this morning's news, 'the suspect' had no experience in looking after babies. Sharon must be in hell.

Alongside the worry about the baby, her conversation with Max last night was heavy in Julie's mind. Had she done the right thing, telling him she didn't want to get involved at the moment? Oh, they hadn't fallen out. They'd been quite civilised, in fact; she could see that he really did understand what was going on in her head. If the situation had been different, their relationship would have developed very differently. The attraction was there… and look how well he got on with her kids. It wasn't every bloke who wanted a woman with a baby.

Maybe she should give him a quick call, touch base. Last night had ended with a quick 'See you sometime, then,' as they'd parted outside Julie's building, and that was no way to leave things. She stood for a moment, staring at her mobile, then pressed connect. He picked up almost at once, saying, 'Hi,' in guarded tones.

Julie's thoughts raced back to Jael. 'What's wrong – is there any news?'

'No. Sorry. Are you okay?'

Relief flushed through Julie, to be replaced by resentment. Of course she wasn't okay. She snapped before she had time to think. 'Apart from my friend's child being in mortal danger, I'm fine. Sorry, sorry. I'm on edge. I can't think of anything else.'

'I know. Would you like to meet again, just to talk? I don't like to leave things the way we did last night, Julie. I think we could be good together.'

Julie gripped the phone, angry with him and with herself too. She should never have called him. He liked her, but his police training would mean he was able to detach his working life, including the horror around Sharon and the baby, from this non-relationship the two of them were in.

'Stop. If things had been different I guess we might have been good together but I can't think about that now. There's too much bad stuff going on. I shouldn't have phoned. Bye, Max.'

She rang off as his reply came.

'Bye, love.'

Caro

Caro was stuffing letters into envelopes, the most boring job in the world but one of the few things computers didn't do yet. At least it didn't involve much brain work, because all she could think of was Jeff and that poor baby. She'd arranged to take the day off, but Louise had to organise an emergency dentist appointment, so Caro was holding the fort for a change. She yanked the drawer open and rummaged for stamps, not allowing the tears that were constantly welling in her eyes to escape. Her husband, the man she had chosen to father her children, had *abducted a baby*. How could she have lived with him all those months and not realised he was capable of something like this? He was the man she had laughed with and slept with, and she had never known what was going on inside him. She felt shell-shocked.

How often had she seen the same kind of disbelief in TV interviews and news reports? People talking about their relatives or neighbours who had murdered, stolen, beaten… they all said, *'I never knew,'* and, *'We didn't suspect a thing.'* And in real life you thought, *'Yeah, right. Things like that don't happen out of the blue.'*

But now it had happened to her. Her husband had *planned* this crime, and she had put his strangeness of the past few weeks down to the shock about the no-baby and the breakdown of communication between them. He must have gone mad; there was no other explanation. It didn't bear thinking about. How on earth would Jeff manage to look after a baby? Shit, the past couple of weeks had brought her nothing but grief. The no-baby, no Liam, the worry about the boy and his wretched ecstasy, now Jeff and that poor baby.

Her phone rang in her handbag and Caro's heart began to thump. Dread was filling her life – she felt like a criminal too. She grabbed the phone and held it to her ear, shaking fingers sliding on the black case.

'Morning, Mrs Horne, DS Sanders at Bridgehead Police Station here,' said a man's voice, and Caro recognised the older of the two policemen who'd been to the house on – good grief, it was only yesterday. 'We're finished with your house now, so you can go back whenever you like. We shouldn't need access again.'

'Thanks. Did you find anything?' Was she allowed to ask questions like that?

He answered readily enough, so apparently she was. 'We've sent some hairs off for analysis. And a small amount of white powder that was found on the kitchen table and floor.'

'White powder?' said Caro, realising as she spoke what it would be. 'Oh no. Was it milk powder?'

'It could be, but it's being analysed too,' said the policeman.

His voice was kind, and Caro was grateful, because in a horrible way she felt partly to blame for Jeff's actions. If only she'd realised – but no one could be expected to realise that their husband was going to kidnap a baby. She gave herself a shake.

The policeman was still speaking. 'Mrs Horne, have you heard anything from your husband, or remembered anything that might help us find him?'

'Nothing,' said Caro, aware that Louise had returned and was listening avidly. 'I just hope you find him soon.'

'Yes. We'll be in touch. Goodbye, Mrs Horne.'

'Goodbye,' she managed, and sat staring at her desk.

'Any news?' said Louise greedily, and Caro sighed.

'None. The police called to say they've finished at the house.'

'Are you going to move back in?'

Caro almost jumped. She hadn't considered this option, but – actually, why not? It would be easier than finding a new place or staying on at Rosie's. If and when Jeff was found he'd be kept under arrest or in a psychiatric hospital, so the house would be empty anyway. Wow. She'd be living alone in that big house...

'I might,' she said to Louise. 'I'll get off, then. I hope your tooth's okay?'

'I'll be fine,' said Louise. 'On you go. I know you're having a tough time.'

Caro rushed out, waving to Louise sitting heroically at her desk. She had to run for the bus and sat panting while it wandered towards home. Now she thought about it, what was happening with the car? Couldn't the police track cars – or had Jeff taken it to Ireland, or even abroad? She could certainly use it here... Guilt swept through her. This was beginning to feel like disposing of someone's possessions after they'd died.

Back at the house, she walked through every room, looking for signs of the police search. There was dust everywhere and the drawers and cupboards had all been disturbed. Caro slumped down on the sofa and stared apathetically round the living room. After just three days the place already had a neglected feel to it. Did she really want to live here alone?

Children's voices came in through the open window. There were so many children round about, so no, she didn't want to live here any longer, but it would do until things were organised.

After all, this had been her home as much as Jeff's, and she shouldn't squeeze herself in with Rosie and Gary when this place was standing empty.

Decision made, Caro went through to the kitchen and made herself a coffee. She would watch the news at the top of the hour, catch the latest about the baby. It was a little girl. Those poor parents, what must they be feeling right now?

The missing baby item came first. There was a broad sweep of the camera over the riverside flats where the family lived, then a close-up photo of the baby. A lump came into Caro's throat. What a lovely little girl. And *Jeff* had taken her away… Oh God oh God, they were mentioning him by name now and his photo was shown too. Woodland searches were going on, the river had been dragged, and police dogs taken to sniff round the flats and the park. But the main focus of the report was definitely on Jeff. But where could he be? Caro couldn't think of any place that he might hide.

The appeal came last and tears poured down Caro's cheeks. It was unbearable; here was the same grief she felt about the no-baby, but magnified a hundred, a million times. Those poor people, clutching a big photo of their lost baby. The mother's hands were trembling like an old woman's, and her eyes… A police spokesman came on after the family and said a reward would be given for information leading to the baby's discovery. Telephone numbers were blended in at the end, and Caro switched the TV off. If she'd only known. If she'd told someone Jeff was acting strangely, maybe none of this would have happened. But she hadn't realised it was this serious, and it had been a bad time for her as well, coming to terms with the no-baby. This wasn't her fault.

Miserably, she tidied round the living room and kitchen. She would spend one more night with Rosie, and move back here tomorrow.

Her mobile rang as she was locking the front door behind her. Caro's fingers started to shake as she pulled it from her bag. This was how it was going to be now – shakes and jitters every time her phone or the doorbell rang.

It was Liam. Caro's lips trembled as she pressed connect.

'There's a – a bloke here.' His voice was shaking.

Caro blinked. With everything else going on in her life now, she hadn't given that awful youth and his ecstasy pills a thought for days. But Liam had obviously remembered, and if he'd seen this boy now, then it was a different kid who'd overdosed in the library. Nothing to do with her after all. Thank God, thank God. One small thing had gone right.

Caro took a deep breath. 'Thanks for letting me know. Are you okay, Liam?'

'I'm okay, but there's something I can't say on the phone. Can you come here?'

Caro hesitated. It was enough to know the ecstasy boy was still alive, but maybe Liam wanted a reward for his trouble. That could end up being awkward, if Alfie's mother was around. On the other hand – maybe Liam wasn't as okay as he'd said. Caro compromised guiltily.

'Why don't we meet at the newsagent's near your square, at quarter past six, and you can tell me what's going on.'

'Okay,' said Liam, and rang off.

Caro pulled a face. This could turn difficult, especially if Pete was still around. Hopefully, though, he and his lorry were on the road again. She would go very briefly, and she would make sure Liam understood that this time it really was 'goodbye'. She had no wish to have her brother back in her life.

A thought struck her, and Caro stood still on the front path. She was going to meet Liam, but she might end up meeting the boy with the ecstasy pills too, and that wasn't nearly such a pleasant prospect. He was older. Bigger. Stronger. And after everything that had happened recently, she didn't know if she'd have the guts to stand up to him again if he turned nasty.

Slowly, she opened the front door again and went upstairs. She had a pepper spray in the wardrobe. Her mother had given it to her years ago, when she'd had a job involving late shifts. She would feel much safer with this in her pocket. Better put her phone on silent, too – she didn't want it to ring while she was talking to the youth – he might pinch it.

Liam was waiting outside the newsagent's, jigging up and down on the balls of his feet, his eyes alert. A little twist of concern pulled at Caro's insides. He looked nervous – what was going on?

'Come quick,' he said, trotting off down the High Street.

Caro strode along beside him. 'Where are we going, Liam?'

Liam turned, looking at her with wide, excited eyes. 'Did you see the news? There's a baby missing and there's a new man in a room up here with a baby and he is one funny bloke, I tell you. And there's a reward, too, but I don't know how to get it. Come on – I'll show you where he is.'

He ran off again and Caro had little choice but to follow. Her heart was thudding away under her ribs. Could it really be Jeff, this man with the baby? If it was, she might be able to end the horror for everyone concerned in just a few minutes. Hope flaring inside her, Caro followed Liam along the other side of the square, to the building opposite the one where he lived.

'Didn't you tell your dad?' she asked.

Liam shook his head. 'He's away again.'

A disturbing thought struck Caro as they started up the dirty staircase, and her breath caught. Supposing it wasn't Jeff? It could be another 'funny bloke', and she was about to knock on his door. Only now did she realise how much she was hoping that, somehow, it hadn't been Jeff who'd taken the baby, that he'd just gone off for a few days to think things through. But there was a new man in a room with a baby... She stopped and gripped the greasy bannister with both hands.

'Liam, tell me what he looks like?'

Liam shrugged. 'Bigger'n you but not real big. Short hair, sort of red, blonde. Scary eyes.'

Dread crashed heavily into Caro's gut. It must be Jeff. She would go and check, anyway. She made Liam point out the room, then gripped the pepper spray in her pocket and strode along the short dark corridor.

'Auntie Caro!'

Caro ignored the fear in the boy's voice. She stood for a second at the door, listening. Nothing. Slowly, she raised a hand and knocked.

Was that a baby whimpering? Steps thudded to the door and it was yanked open. And it was Jeff. And there was a baby on the bed behind him.

'Scram, you–' he hissed, then stared at her, the colour draining from his cheeks.

'Jeff–' she began, but a look of utter fury distorted his features and Caro took a step back.

'Where – have – you – been?' He spat the words out, and grabbed her arm. The pepper spray fell from her hand and rolled back along the corridor.

There was nothing Caro could do to stop him pulling her inside and slamming the door. Her legs gave way and she sank to her knees, choking as the stink in the room hit her. Thick, cloying, a mixture of dirty nappies, urine and sweat – it was disgusting. No wonder the baby was crying. And Jeff – she'd never seen him like this, his cheeks mottled red and white, spit shining in the corners of his mouth as he stood there panting, his eyes wide and staring into her face. He was holding her left arm so tightly Caro moaned in pain, pulling away from him. He released his grip on her arm to grab her shoulders and force her upright, then slammed her backwards against the door, jerking her head viciously against a metal hook that was screwed into the door. She hardly noticed this new pain at first, she was so shocked.

'Jeff! What are you–' She couldn't go on; he put his face right up to hers and snarled in her face.

'Shut it!' His breath was rancid, and Caro recoiled, moaning and trying to move away. But he wouldn't let her. He gripped her upper arms again and shook her, slamming her time and again against the rattling wooden door. 'You stupid, stupid cow – where have you been all this time?'

The moment she drew breath to speak he was shaking her again. He was beside himself with rage and it was all directed at her. 'Shut up! This is all your fault – you should have been waiting at home. I've got you a baby and now I'm having to play some stupid cat and mouse game with the police!'

Caro was more afraid than she'd ever been in her life; she was shaking all over. She'd never seen him like this. His eyes were like Liam had said – scary. Remembering Liam was a small comfort – surely he'd have run for help now. If not the police, then Alfie's mother or some other adult. Jeff let go of her arms and she sank to the grimy floor, saying nothing, trying to muffle the whimpers of pain shaking through her.

The room was indescribably dirty. Everything was old and run-down; she was sitting on ancient, cracked linoleum, stained with God knows what. Near the window another door was half open, and the smell wafting out brought burning tears to Caro's eyes. How could Jeff bring a baby to stay in a place like this?

The baby had stopped crying and was moving her arms and legs in that uncoordinated way babies had, uttering odd little mewing sounds. Jeff lifted her and started to walk up and down between the door and the window, singing under his breath and ignoring Caro completely.

Slowly, she lifted a hand to the back of her head and felt the warm stickiness of blood. She had to get out of here. If she played along with Jeff, made him think she was on his side, he might agree to them leaving this place together, and she could get help. When he was walking towards her she stood up unsteadily and reached towards the baby.

'Jeff, she's lovely. Let me–'

'No!' He shoved her towards the bed this time, and she fell awkwardly, banging her head again as she went down, her wrist catching and twisting between the bed and the wall. White-hot pain seared up her arm, but Caro lay still, her eyes closed. Logic was beyond Jeff at the moment. All her hopes were pinned on Liam bringing help.

Chapter Eighteen

Thursday 9th June, morning 7.10 a.m.

Sharon

The sun was tipping round the side of the building opposite when Sharon woke and rolled into a tight ball, the knowledge that her baby was still missing crashing back into her mind as viciously as it had done every morning since Jael was taken. Tuesday, Wednesday, Thursday. Three times she'd woken and been hit by a sledgehammer.

There was nothing to get up for other than to pump off the milk that Jael should have been drinking. A sad little row of jars was waiting in the freezer now and Sharon sobbed every time she saw it. Breast milk, the best for your baby. Except she didn't have a baby any more.

Tears dripped off her chin. *Jael, sweetie, where are you? Is Jeff Horne good to you? Oh baby, I'm so sorry I didn't love you better before you were born.* The misery was unbearable, but she had to bear it, because the only alternative was to go mad. She had to believe what the police told her, that this was like those women you sometimes heard of in the news, the ones who stole babies from maternity hospitals because they'd lost one of their own. Jeff Horne *had* lost one in a way, because he couldn't have any of his own.

Sharon screwed the lid on yet another jar and placed it with the others in the freezer, biting down on her lip to keep the hurt in. Tea. She would make tea, because she had to drink to keep producing milk for her baby.

Craig was still asleep in the spare room, but he should get up too, because the family liaison officer would be round soon with the usual non-progress report, the doctor would come by, there would be a few visitors. But none of it would help.

Sharon spooned sugar into mugs and took the tea through to the spare room where Craig was hunched on the edge of the bed now, dark shadows under his eyes.

'Thanks. Did you sleep much?'

'No,' said Sharon. 'Oh, Craig.'

They sat together, sipping tea, neither with anything to say. It was non-communication for a different reason. Unable to stand the inactivity, Sharon put her half-empty mug on the dressing table and went to open the curtains. The street was deserted; today's media presence hadn't arrived yet. Another beautiful summer's day was dawning – birds were singing and other people were starting their normal Thursday morning. Sharon ducked behind the curtain as Mr Blythe emerged from his house across the road with their two whippets, and began the usual stop-and-go walk.

A dark-haired boy appeared at the end of the road, walking briskly in this direction. Sharon watched him because there was nothing else going on out there now. He looked about nine or ten. What on earth was a child like that doing out so early? He drew level and stood for a long moment looking up at the flats, then sat down on the garden wall. He must be waiting for someone.

Craig stood up and reached for his clothes. 'Anything happening out there?'

His voice couldn't have been duller, but she answered because already, there was too much silence in the day.

'Nothing at all.'

8.30 a.m.

Caro

A thin, plaintive bleat woke Caro. The baby. She started to roll towards the sound, then pain crashed through her head and she froze, eyes still closed. A shudder ran through her as the horrifying reality hit home. She was in this hellish room with Jeff and the baby, and she was in danger of her life. What was he going to do? Her gut cramped with fear and she struggled to stop herself retching. Be quiet, Caro, be still, your life may depend on it. She made herself breathe regularly, calmly, as if she was still asleep, and the pain in her head subsided to a dull ache. But her wrist was still agony – could it be broken? She couldn't move her fingers.

Rustling noises were coming from the other side of the room, and Caro lay motionless, trying to work out what Jeff was doing. He had slept beside her, in fact all three of them had slept on this narrow little bed, the foul stench of Jeff mingling with baby-sick and urine. She had vague, pain-filled memories of the baby crying, and Jeff talking to it, but he'd ignored Caro and she had feigned sleep. Carefully, without moving, she half-opened her eyes.

The baby was beside her, whimpering quietly, and Jeff was over by the cupboard, a packet of digestives in his hand. He crammed one into his mouth. Caro shuddered. Thinking about food made her feel sick, but she needed water; her throat was burning. The air in the room seemed even thicker than yesterday. Jeff, the stench from the toilet, and the collection of dirty nappies in a carrier bag in the corner were all contributing to the miasma in this terrible, airless room. Caro cleared her throat. There was a carton of orange juice on the cupboard – would Jeff share it with her?

'Can I have some juice?' she asked timidly, and he turned to look at her.

'Ah, you're awake. At last. Some mother you make. I had to take care of the baby myself all night. You're as bad as Sharon.'

Caro tried to sound apologetic. 'I'm sorry.'

He held out the carton of orange juice and Caro struggled into a sitting position. Her left arm was blue and puffy halfway up to her elbow, and her fingers were stiff and swollen. Every movement was agony. It must be broken, and dear God, her own husband had done it. She sipped from the carton. The juice was unchilled and too sweet, but at least it was wet.

'Don't drink it all – it's all I have left.' Jeff snatched the carton and shoved her down again.

Darkness rolled over Caro and she sank into it.

When she next came to, Jeff was sitting on the chair, rocking the baby. This time, Caro was careful not to antagonise him. He allowed her to use the dark, smelly toilet, where she cupped her good hand under the tap and drank some water. That helped, though her head was still pounding. She leaned against the wall, fighting nausea. She had to think; she had to get the baby out of here. Why, why hadn't Liam brought help? He must have been too afraid to tell anyone what had happened. She would have to deal with this herself.

Caro put up her good hand and felt the back of her head. There was huge lump and her hair was stiff, so the cut must have stooped bleeding. Moving slowly so that Jeff wouldn't feel threatened, she went back to sit on the bed.

'My head's been bleeding. Can I – can I have the headache pills from my bag?'

He tossed her handbag onto the bed and she rummaged for the pills. Her headache cleared slightly in sheer relief when she saw the pills were still there, and so was her mobile. She would wait until Jeff went into the loo, and then she'd run with the baby, and call nine-nine-nine. But no – shit. With an injured wrist, she only had one hand. She couldn't possibly grab the baby, unlock the door, and then operate her phone, all with one hand. She could maybe get herself out, but she couldn't leave this poor little soul here with Jeff; heaven knows what he'd do. She would have to risk calling nine-nine-nine. Or – brilliant idea – she would text Rosie.

Caro pulled out the packet of pills and swallowed two. Casually, she put the bag on the floor by her feet. He mustn't get suspicious. Good job her phone was on silent.

It was ages before Jeff went into the toilet. Caro sat poised, ready to grab her phone as soon as the door swung shut behind him, but to her dismay he didn't close it properly, and half a minute later he was out again, still doing up his flies. She shuddered. Something had happened to his mind – he wasn't the same person. Had this madness been in there all the time, waiting for the news of the no-baby to let it out? What a horrible thought.

The baby on the bed gave a little whimper, then jerked and started to cry in earnest.

Jeff glared at Caro. 'Pick her up, for Christ's sake. You can hold her while I heat her bottle,' he said belligerently, turning to the electric ring.

With an effort, Caro gathered the baby up. Poor little scrap. She must be missing her mother, and there was nothing to say that Jeff was giving her the right kind of baby milk. In spite of the pain in her wrist Caro rocked the little body and kissed her hot head.

'What's her name?' she asked, watching as he prepared a bottle.

'Sharon called her Jael, but you can change that if you want to. I know you always liked Melanie. Or Miriam.'

He looked at her with those over-bright eyes and Caro's thoughts raced. What would upset him least, a name suggestion he possibly didn't agree with, or an 'it doesn't matter' answer?

'I'll – we'll have to think about that, won't we?' she said at last. 'It's too important to decide quickly. We – we can both have a think and talk about it later.'

This answer seemed to please him. 'All right,' he said, smiling at her. 'You can give her the bottle now.'

He handed over the bottle, and Caro slid to the floor where she could lean against the bed and prop the baby on her legs, almost crying because her wrist hurt so badly. It all seemed so hopeless. But Jeff must sleep sometime. She would wait until then and get out. The baby drank half-heartedly and Caro closed her eyes.

The bed moved behind her as Jeff flung himself down, and Caro inched herself round until he was back in her line of vision. No way could she sit here with Jeff behind her, there was no telling what he'd do. His face was pale as he lay there, eyes closed and one arm stretched above his head, and after several minutes Caro laid the bottle down and stretched her good arm slowly towards her bag. This could be her chance, while he was dozing. The baby howled in protest.

Immediately, Jeff jerked awake and hissed at her. 'Give her the bloody bottle.'

Caro flinched. She would have to be more patient.

She sat there, waves of dizziness sweeping over her. After a while the baby fell asleep and Caro slid her onto the bed beside Jeff, and touched her wrist gingerly. The swelling was getting worse.

Jeff sat up. 'My head's really bad too,' he said, reaching for her handbag. 'Where are those pills?'

He was rummaging in the bag before she could do a thing to stop him. It was like a scene in a film, where you know something horrendous is going to happen but you don't know what exactly, and there's nothing you can do to prevent it. Caro's heart was thumping wildly as Jeff peered into the bag, then glared at her with the most terrifying expression, and drew out her phone. One tap and he could see it was on.

'Have you used this?' he screamed, and Caro flinched, ducking her head as he rose and towered above her.

She could hear a voice moaning in her head, but only a whispered, 'Please, no,' came from her lips.

8.30 a.m.

Julie

'Why do I have to go to After School Club when it's your day off?' Sam kicked the leg of the kitchen table with a trainer-clad foot, his voice aggrieved.

Julie sighed. They'd been through this last night and again during breakfast, but poor Sam was beginning to feel hard-done-by. If she wasn't very careful they would end up with tears and tantrums, the worst possible start to Sam's day. And hers.

'Because it isn't a proper day off,' she said, putting the milk back in the fridge and turning to stroke Sam's hair. 'I should really be at work, but Dee said I could go and help Sharon today, because of all the upset about Jael. Amy's going to Rona's just the same as usual too.' She kissed his cross little face, but Sam wriggled free and stood pouting at the floor.

'I wanted you to come and get me at four o'clock.'

Julie sighed. The uncertainty about Jael was taking its toll on Sam, too. 'I know, sweetie, and I'll come for you as soon as I possibly can,' she said gently. 'But I don't know what's going to happen today, so I can't promise to be there on the dot. Please be good about it, lovey.'

Sam nodded, his lip still trembling, and picked up his schoolbag. Julie watched him, her heart torn in two. Was she right to put Sharon's needs before Sam's? But it wasn't as if she was changing Sam's routine in any way.

She dropped Amy off at the child minder's and walked Sam to school. He ran off with another boy as soon as he entered the playground, and Julie waved, relieved. More parents than usual were here today, and the few snatches of conversation she caught on the way past told her why.

'Poor little soul…'

'Nothing to say that baby's not dead by now, and him waiting to find another kiddy…'

'Hanging's too good for the likes of him…'

Julie hurried away, barely stopping to nod to the mothers she knew. The whole town seemed despondent and grey this morning. Everyone knew about the baby missing from the riverside flats, and they were all was feeling the same kind of shock that such a thing could happen in their community. It was something that belonged on the news on telly, not in your own High Street. Julie rushed on. The internet café was closed. Where *was* Jeff Horne, and where was Jael? It didn't bear thinking about. Still walking quickly, she crossed at the lights at the bottom of the High Street and turned towards the river. It was times like this that she missed having a car. With wheels, she'd have been making coffee in Sharon's kitchen right now.

A crowd of reporters was hanging around the street in front of the flats, armed with cameras and microphones. TV cameras were out as well. Julie stopped in dismay – she would have to go right through the middle of them. Hopefully they would let her pass without asking intrusive questions and taking photos.

She walked on more slowly. Much to her surprise the reporters did allow her to pass without accosting her, although she was aware of a couple of flashes as she walked up the path towards the front door. They were waiting for developments, she realised miserably. For Jael to be brought home, or…

A loud sneeze from a bush a few yards from the building made Julie jump, and she stared into its depths to see a boy squashed up on the ground. He gazed up at her with a startled expression on his face.

'Are you okay?' asked Julie, and he nodded.

'Just waitin' for someone,' he said, rubbing his face with a grubby sleeve.

Julie shrugged. He and 'someone' were probably bunking off school, but it was none of her business. She nodded at the boy and carried on.

As was usual now it was Craig who let her in. Sharon was perched on the edge of the sofa clutching the television remote, her face blank.

'She's zapping through the channels, looking for news items about Jael,' said Craig, both frustration and tears in his voice. 'I couldn't stop her, but it's breaking her heart.'

Sharon turned and Julie saw the numbness on her face. 'It's the only thing I can do to make it seem like she's real,' she said, her lips quivering. 'If she's on TV then she's real, isn't she?'

Julie went to hug her. 'I'll make some coffee. You finish checking, then come through to the kitchen,' she said, relieved when Sharon nodded.

Julie wiped her eyes on a tea towel before starting a pot of coffee. How petty her own problems seemed now. She had two children; she knew exactly where they were and she knew they were safe, warm, fed and above all, alive. She was lucky. She should remember that next time she felt like having a moan about something inconsequential.

A few moments later Sharon and Craig came in.

'See, it's better in here. It's no good watching all those reports – you'll only get more upset,' said Craig, pulling out a chair and almost pushing Sharon down.

She glared at him, and Julie was struck, horribly, by the sheer misery of the other woman's entire posture.

'And you think I don't want to be upset? She's my baby–' Her voice choked into nothing.

'She's *our* baby and I'm just as upset–' Craig was indignant, but Sharon gave him no chance to continue.

'You bloody aren't. You never want–'

Julie knocked on the table, wishing she could bang their heads together. 'Guys. This isn't helping. Craig, Sharon needs support, not criticism. Sharon, Craig needs support too. I'm sure he feels horribly guilty now.'

Craig glanced at Julie, his chin wobbling and she nodded towards Sharon. He reached out his hand and thankfully, Sharon took it. For a few moments, no one spoke.

Julie sat struggling for control. These two had what she'd never had. It was a kind of intimacy, something she'd always longed for but never found. Sharon and Craig's marriage had been good before Sharon's pregnancy, and maybe that would help them now.

Abruptly, Julie stood up and started to tidy round the kitchen. At least she could do something practical to help.

'My parents are coming tomorrow,' said Sharon dully. She stared at the table top.

'Excellent news,' said Julie. 'Isn't it?' Sharon nodded, and Julie went on. 'Are they staying here? Come on, then – I'll help you get their room ready.'

She stayed with the couple until twelve, putting a pie in the oven for them before she left, and promising to return at two with some shopping.

It was a relief to get out of the flat, away from the intensity and despair. Please can Jael come home today? It was years since Julie had prayed, but going down in the lift today she found herself begging for Jael's safety. Craig and Sharon may be intimate, but there was nothing to say their marriage would survive the death of their baby.

Chapter Nineteen

Thursday 9th June, early afternoon 12.00

Caro

His face – it was like something in a horror movie where a skull, thinly covered by skin, and with mad glassy eyes, looms up on the screen. He flung her phone into the corner and reached for her throat. Panicking, Caro made a dash for the door, forgetting all about the baby in her terror, but Jeff bounded after her, bringing her to the floor in a rugby tackle. He was snarling at her, but no-one would hear because he did it all in a whisper, and such obscenities – she'd never heard him use language like that. He pushed her flat onto her back on the cramped floor and held her there with his hands round her throat.

Christ, no; she couldn't breathe, no, no. She didn't want to die here, not in this disgusting place. Unable to scream, Caro struggled and kicked out, managing to get him off-balance when her leg shoved into his inner thigh.

'Bitch!' he hissed, jerking a hand out and grabbing the cupboard by the door. Something clattered to the floor by Caro's head.

'Jeff! Let me help you! We'll work something out, I promise.'

He grabbed the thing on the floor and to Caro's horror she saw it was a knife. She screamed, and the baby on the bed screamed too.

Jeff brandished the knife inches from her face. 'You *promise* – you promised to love and cherish me, didn't you? But now I can do what I want and it isn't enough for madam, oh no, only a bloody baby will do. Now I've got one, and you're still the same ungrateful cow, trying to get away. We are going to wait here, do you understand?

That will be our baby as soon as bloody Sharon comes to her senses. You're not leaving – I won't let you.'

Caro's heart was pounding in her ears, and bile was right there in her mouth. She had never been so afraid. Adrenaline surging through her, she used her good arm to pull at the hand still round her neck.

'Keep still!' He wrenched his hand away and slapped her face, then – Christ, no–

'You will stay – right – here!' he shouted, spit landing on Caro's face.

'Aargh!'

He was slashing at her foot, raising the knife and then hacking downwards, over and over. The pain, oh God the pain, it was the worst yet. After about the fifth stab he dropped the knife and crawled over to the bed.

Caro lay shaking, the room swirling around her. She was losing blood… If she didn't stop the bleeding, she would die in the filth here on the floor. Moaning, she forced herself into a sitting position and pulled out the two tissues she had in her trousers pocket, but they were pitifully inadequate; there was too much blood, and oh, it hurt so much. Jeff made no effort to help her. He was standing at the window with the baby now, his back towards her, staring out at whatever was going on below.

Caro remembered the nappies in the toilet. Could she get there? 'I'm going to get a nappy for my foot.' Her voice was shaky and old. Like someone who was going to die soon, oh please, she didn't want to die.

He ignored her, and Caro shuffled into the toilet on her backside, using her good arm and leg to propel her. The pain of getting there made her vomit, and for a moment she was forced to hang over the unspeakable toilet bowl. She couldn't see what injuries her foot had suffered; she couldn't move it. Praying that Jeff would stay where he was, she gave the toilet door a push, to let some light in. Her foot was bleeding freely from several stab wounds, there was a trail of blood across the floor, it would be a pool soon if she didn't do something. Shivering, Caro pulled a nappy from the bag and opened it, pressing down as hard as she could bear on her foot, seeing stars as the pain intensified tenfold. But it was the only way. She leaned against the wall, pressing down, counting under her breath to prevent herself passing out. If that happened, she was doomed. '…seventeen, eighteen, nineteen…'

'Get back out here.'

All she could do was obey.

12.00

Julie

To her surprise, the boy was still in the bush in front of the building. He blinked at Julie when she peered in at him and she saw traces of tears on his face.

'Didn't your friend come, then?' she said, wondering why he had stayed so long. He shook his head, sniffing, and Julie crouched down until they were eye to eye. This kid was probably supposed to be sitting in a classroom in Sam's school right now.

The boy blinked at her.

'Why don't you come out, and we can walk into town together?' said Julie, holding out a hand.

He grasped it and allowed her to pull him out of the bush. Julie looked at him ruefully. Here was someone else needing help, but oh, Lord, there was only so much she could cope with in one day. The boy brushed grubby hands down his trousers, then stared up at the flats before turning abruptly towards the main road.

Julie hurried after him and together they walked past the crowd of reporters. Several held out microphones and shouted questions, but Julie gripped the boy's arm and half-pushed him along.

'Awful, isn't it?' she said, when they were clear of the crowd.

The boy stopped and looked back, two tears running down his face.

'I don't know what to do,' he said, and Julie fished for tissues. The boy blew his nose vigorously.

'That's better,' said Julie encouragingly, wondering what on earth she was getting involved in now. But this was just a kid – she couldn't leave him crying on the street. 'If you tell me what's wrong maybe I can help.'

The boy sniffed loudly. 'There's this man near where I live, and yesterday my aunt went to see him, and when he opened the door he grabbed her and pulled her into the room. I don't think she got out again.'

He looked at her sideways, and Julie stared. There must be more to the story than that.

'Didn't you tell your parents?'

He shook his head. 'My dad's away with the lorry again.'

'So who's looking after you?'

'Alfie's mum. I didn't tell her. I said I was going to the dentist with Kev and his dad.'

'Then what were you doing in that bush?'

'I tried to call Auntie Caro again this morning, but she's still not answering. So I found her address, and I was going there to see if she'd got back okay, then I saw this is where the missing baby from the telly lives, and this man, he's got a baby, see, and I wanted to ask the missing baby's mum if it was the same baby, but then they all came–' He waved back towards the reporters camped by the flats '–so I hid in the bush.'

Julie could hardly believe her ears. There was no way to tell if this man was Jeff Horne, but someone should check it out. Her hands were shaking as she pulled out her mobile. The easiest thing would be just to call Max, that way she could avoid explanations about who she was and what she was doing.

'Max? Sorry to call you like this but it might be important.' Quickly, she relayed the story the boy had told her, getting him to add names and addresses as far as he knew them. Her heart was doing triple time when she finished. If this baby was Jael, the whole ghastly situation was about to come to an end. But of course, it could still be an innocent man with his baby.

Max remained calm. 'Okay. We'll get right onto that. Can you take the kid back to his home, Julie, and stay with him in the meantime? I don't want him doing a disappearing act until we see what we find in that room. See you.'

Julie ended the call and turned to the boy. 'We've to go back to your place. I'm Julie, what's your name?'

They started along the road, a tiny flame of hope flickering in Julie's breast for the first time in days. Maybe this *was* it, maybe they'd get Jael back now and everything would be all right.

An air of excitement was fizzing through the High Street. People were craning their necks to see what was going on further up, where police cars were doubled parked on both sides of the road. Julie hurried along, one hand on Liam's shoulder. Max was one of several police officers by the entrance to Mortimer Square, which was now taped off. Two officers were busy stretching tape across the High Street, too. Julie's mouth went dry.

Max saw them coming, and strode over to meet them. 'We've confirmed Caroline Horne is missing.' He smiled briefly, but he was obviously worried, keeping eye contact with her to a minimum.

Julie's stomach lurched anew. She'd hurt him, and now that he was standing in front of her again she realised how very much she didn't want to hurt him. When all this was over she would tell him that, but this was neither the time nor the place.

He continued steadily. 'And Jeff Horne's car was found yesterday evening, in the hospital car park.' He turned to the boy beside Julie. 'Is this your man?' He held out a photograph and the boy nodded energetically.

Max went on. 'I need you to tell us exactly which room this man is in.'

Liam launched into an involved explanation.

Max glanced into the square. 'And where do you live, Liam?

'Garner Road.' The boy pointed to the next street along from the square.

Mx turned to Julie. 'Okay. We've cleared the square. Reinforcements are on their way and as soon as they arrive they'll start negotiating. This is serious, Julie, it could be a hostage situation. We've a public order unit on standby. You and Liam go to his place and wait indoors – someone will be in touch.'

'What about Craig and Sharon?'

'Their FLO's on her way to them now.'

Julie nodded. She took Liam's elbow firmly and blinked up at Max. 'Good luck.'

His expression relaxed for a moment and he smiled. A lump rose chokingly at the back of Julie's throat.

Liam led the way up Garner Road, into a doorway, and along the tunnel-like entrance close to the flat door, which he unlocked. His home, a long flat with high ceilings and shabby paintwork, backed onto Mortimer Square. Liam went into the living room, which overlooked the front of the building, and Julie joined him. There was no way to see what was happening on the square.

'Will your dad be home tonight?' said Julie.

A shake was the only answer.

'Is there a window where we can see into the square?' asked Julie, sitting on the arm of a large red armchair.

'You might from the bathroom.'

He ran off, presumably to check, and a door slammed behind him. Julie waited. It was sickening, knowing that Jael was only about fifty metres away, and being powerless to help her.

The toilet flushed, and a moment later Liam reappeared, his cheeks pink. 'There's an ambulance just off the square and loads more police cars,' he said, his voice high and excited.

Julie pressed her hands between her knees. Had the police found Jeff and Jael? And Craig and Sharon – what was going on there? Julie took out her mobile, looked at it, then put it back into her bag. It might not be a good idea to phone now. But oh, please, *please* let Jael be all right.

There was silence in the flat, and Julie sat picturing what might be going on in the square. What was it usually like there at this time? There would be shoppers, hurrying to and from the High Street. Office workers would come and sit on those benches and have lunch, especially on warm days like today. Kids would hang around and talk and flirt, and play with their phones. It wasn't an unattractive little place on a summer's day, Mortimer Square.

The inactivity was agonising. But all she could do was wait.

2.10 p.m.

Jeff

It was all going terribly, horribly wrong and he didn't know what to do. Stupid, stupid Caro. He could give her another hard slap for this; it was all her fault they were in this mess. He'd done more than could be expected of him – he'd searched for and got her a baby, not their own baby, granted, but under the circumstances this baby was pretty near perfect. And it was even an unwanted baby, so he had done a good thing in finding her a loving home.

Jeff sank down on the bed and wiped his face with one hand. He stared helplessly at Caro and the baby. They were in the corner by the door, where Caro was sitting awkwardly on the floor, the baby clutched to her chest. His head began to buzz as he looked at her; it was all wrong, his Caro sitting there like that. He couldn't stand this, he really couldn't take much more and his head was swinging all over the place now, like on one of those tortuous rides at the fairground. Rollercoaster. The floor was no longer steady – was he really here or was he dreaming? Caro looked pale, poor thing, maybe she had the same appalling headache he had. He could hear her breathing. It sounded funny – ragged, shaky breaths that seemed to come all the way up from her boots. Except she wasn't wearing boots, she had a sort of strappy summer shoe on one foot, and on the other she only seemed to be wearing a bloody sock or something, how odd. Why was there blood on Caro's foot?

Clarity flashed and the room rocked. Oh Christ. He had used the knife to stop her leaving, poor stupid thing that she was. She was the mother of his child, so she had to stay here with him.

He stood up and stamped his feet. That was better, the ground felt steadier now. Encouraged, he walked up and down. What was he doing here again? Oh yes, they were waiting until Sharon confirmed she didn't want the baby, and then they could all go home. Home, home. If he'd been able to stay there with the baby in the first place, everything would have been so much better. But that was what the world was like now – idiots like Sharon and Caro were allowed to manipulate things. It wasn't right.

'Jeff, I need another nappy for my foot.'

He could hardly hear her. How stupid she was, whispering like that. But she was shivering, so perhaps she had a fever. He stood up and picked up the knife. She mustn't run off again. 'Give me the baby, then.'

Her eyes were wild. 'No! Jeff, put the knife down. I can't... go... anywhere now.'

She shrank back against the bed, sobbing in a throaty whisper. Her chin was shaking. Ignoring her, Jeff dropped the knife on the bed and grabbed the baby from her, swearing when Caro screamed in a whisper.

He kicked at her backside. 'Quiet! You'll wake her!'

He clutched the baby to his chest, but she was awake already, mewing in a funny little breathless voice. Jeff sat on the bed and shushed her, rocking back and forth until she was still again, all floppy and warm; oh, how perfect she was. Miriam, they would call her Miriam.

Caro struggled up while he watched. She had gone terribly pale; even her lips were white. He lifted the knife to point at her, the baby cradled in his other arm. Oh – Caro's foot. There was blood everywhere.

He put both the baby and knife down while Caro was in the toilet being sick again, and prepared a bottle. You never knew with babies when they'd need the next feed. He was doing so well today, being a real caring Dad, and how frustrating that he wasn't able to do it in his own four walls.

Caro still looked like death when she came out of the toilet. She'd wrapped more nappies round her foot, what a hare-brained idea. She hopped back to the corner by the door and lowered herself to the floor. Why didn't she sit next to him on the bed?

'You can give the baby her bottle,' he said, coldly to show her how despicable she was. But he loved Caro, so why was she despicable? His head was so up and down today. The knife nestling in his hand again, he passed her the baby and handed over the bottle.

'She's not hungry, Jeff.' Caro's eyes were closed. Talk about uncaring.

Jeff wandered back to the window and looked down to the square below. There was nobody at all out there now. They must all be shopping or working or staying at home. Like he and Caro and Miriam should be right this minute. He would sit for a minute and work out the best way for them to leave here. There was some reason they couldn't just go, but he couldn't remember... Maybe it would come back to him if he thought for a moment.

He sat down on the bed again, playing with the knife in his fingers, staring at Caro and the baby.

2.10 p.m.

Caro

Another wave of dizziness washed over Caro, and she tried to breathe deeply, tried to stay awake. The pain in her foot was almost unbearable. It would be so easy to lie down and let unconsciousness take over. But she was holding the baby and the poor creature needed her. It was her fault this baby was in such in danger. Her little eyes were half-closed, and her breathing was shallow. Please, baby, stay alive until we get out of here. If we get out of here.

Weakness swept through Caro. It was no use, she was getting dizzier by the minute. Her foot was still bleeding; it was all congealing and horrible on the floor, on her hands, and oh, no, there was even blood on the baby now. The pink cardigan was wet with blotches, and they were both breathing in the cloying stench of Caro's blood mingling with the other disgusting smells in here.

Jeff was back on the bed, playing with the knife and laughing, sniggering away to himself and pointing the knife first at her, then at his reflection in the cracked fragment of mirror stuck on the wall beside the toilet door. All at once he turned to her, his expression malevolent, and terror clutched icily at her heart before the scream came, straight from her soul. He screamed right back, then seized the baby and dumped it on the bed to grab Caro by the shoulders. She felt herself being dragged across the room but everything was swirling now; she couldn't see, no, no.

Her head crashed against glass. And everything went black.

2.10 p.m.

Julie

Waiting and waiting and waiting. What on earth was going on over there? Julie looked at her watch, startled to see it was after two o'clock. Sharon and Craig would be wondering where she was.

With heart-stopping suddenness far-off screams rang out from the direction of the square, followed by the sound of breaking glass. Julie leapt to her feet. What had that been? She ran into the bathroom – the window was high up and the glass was frosted, but it was open, and by standing on the toilet seat she could see into Mortimer Square. A window on the other side was broken; long, thin shards of glass were all that was left of a pane on the first floor. Her heart leapt. No, no, not the baby, please... She couldn't see the ground below the window, a bench and a tub of flowers was blocking the view. But Jeff Horne had wanted a baby so much; this whole situation had come about because of that – surely he hadn't thrown Jael from the window?

'What's happening?' Liam was almost in tears, and Julie jumped down and hugged the boy.

'I don't know. There's a broken window, that's all.'

Silence reigned again in Mortimer Square and Julie felt sick. Sweet Jael, please be alive. And Sharon. She should be here by now, surely? Julie came to a decision; she couldn't stay here not knowing what was going on.

'You stay here,' she said to Liam. 'I'll find out what's happening. I won't be long, I promise.'

Leaving Liam in his living room, Julie ran down Garner Road, thankful she hadn't been working today and was wearing jeans and trainers. And how could she even *think* that, when Jael was over there with a madman? *What had he thrown from the window?* Julie's blood was pounding inside her head as she arrived at the lane separating Mortimer Square from the High Street. Jael, baby, please be alive, please go back to Sharon and grow up safely.

Police cars and ambulances were strung along the High Street, which had been cordoned off in both directions. A crowd of passers-by were standing on the other side of the cordons, gawping at the scene, but Julie ignored them. She ran up to the group of police officers standing at the entrance to the square, a stitch in her side stabbing cruelly under her ribs.

It was clear who the chief was. He had that kind of look about him, calm and authoritative. He was standing with Max's colleague from before.

The younger man recognised Julie. 'What are you doing here? Where's the boy?'

Julie burst into tears. 'At home. Where's Max? Is the baby–?'

Max's colleague patted her shoulder. 'DCI McKenna here has radio contact with the guys inside. Max is on surveillance round the back somewhere. He's an experienced cop. He'll be okay.'

'Is Sharon–?'

The radio in DCI McKenna's hand buzzed.

2.20 p.m.

Jeff

It had all gone very quiet. He stood at the window, staring down over Mortimer Square. The place was a sun trap, but today no one was sitting down there in the sunshine, and nothing was moving, apart from a couple of sparrows fighting over an abandoned scrap under a bench.

Something was wrong.

Jeff turned back into the room. The baby was lying on the bed, eyes closed and little arms flopped on the mattress beside her body. She wasn't crying, which was good, because someone would have heard, with the window broken. Stupid Caro, breaking the window like that. Now they couldn't stay here. He would have to take Miriam and go somewhere else.

Go home, Jeff. It was as if the words had been spoken aloud – had he said them? But oh, yes, how wonderful – he could go home now. Home where it was safe and he was loved…

Stepping over Caro's legs, he grabbed the sports bag from under the bed. He'd used it for shopping a couple of times, now it would have to be the baby's bed again. In with the nice blanket he'd bought her. And a couple of nappies, just in case. Were there more at home? No matter, he could get them from the corner shop. The packet of baby food, a bottle, some wipes. What a complicated creature his daughter was. He scooped the baby up and kissed her face before inserting her unresisting little body into the bag and covering her with a sweatshirt. Nice and snug.

He zipped up the bag and glanced round the room. Nothing else mattered here.

A sound from downstairs filled the silence in the room for half a second, a bang – or was it a footstep? Were they coming to get him? No, no, he couldn't have that. A pity he didn't have a gun… the police might have guns… But he had the knife, where was it? Ah, on the cupboard. If he held the bag across his front, and the knife pointing at the bag – no one would shoot him now, would they? It was time to go.

He shoved Caro to the side with one foot – the floor was slippery with blood, careful now, don't drop the bag. Out into the pokey corridor… it was almost dark here, but that didn't matter. Keep the knife to the bag, in case they're watching. Through the dimness to the stairwell, down, as quick as you like, now round the back of the building, away from the bloody room on Mortimer Square. No one was here; he'd been clever – they hadn't noticed a thing. But who were *they*? He had to keep going; he'd remember everything when he was safe.

He'd made it – they were outside, the baby all snug in her sports bag, how lovely the world seemed, how fresh and colourful and special. Where was he going? It was getting more and more difficult to plan things; for some reason, he kept forgetting what he was supposed to be doing.

A little bleat came from the sports bag, and Jeff started. That was it – he was taking the baby home to Caro, yes. He ran along the back court of the building. It was walled in, but to an athletic man like him that wasn't going to pose any problems. He swung the bag to the top of the wall and heaved himself up after it, the knife between his teeth. It tasted salty. A quick jump down and he was in a lane. One end led to the High Street, so he wouldn't go that way. Where did the other end lead? He walked along briskly, cradling the bag and knife and enjoying the warm summer sunshine on his face. A movement further along the lane caught his eye and he stopped abruptly – someone was there. Another quick leap over the wall to his left and he was in a different backcourt, where he dodged round someone's washing fluttering in the breeze, then slunk into a dark close and stopped for a moment. Okay – this led out to Cedric Street. Where did he want to go? Home to Caro, yes. The baby was whimpering, she wanted to go home too.

A sound behind him made him spin round. That stupid policeman was here, look at him, mouth half open and arms stretched towards the bag. What an idiot.

'For Christ's sake, give me the baby, Jeff. She can't breathe in there! Come on, man – I'll help you.'

Jeff gripped the knife, holding it out of sight, and stepped towards the policeman in the dimness. No way was he going to hand over his baby. It didn't look as if there were any other policemen waiting to arrest him. He would manage this one.

'Nice and slow, give me the baby, Jeff.' He reached for the bag.

Jeff snatched it back and waved the knife, first at the cop and then at the bag.

The other man stood still. 'Jeff. She's just a baby and I can't let you hurt her. Give her to me and we'll sort things out.'

Jeff inched a step or two back, the sweat of fear drenching his body and stinging in his eyes. He could Not. Lose. The baby. 'Get away from here! Leave us alone!' He slid the bag to the ground behind him and swiped the knife back and forth as the policeman stepped forward.

'Steady now, Jeff.'

He shouldn't be hanging around here. What if more police were coming? Jeff stepped backwards, one, two steps, then lunged forward and stabbed as hard as he could; the knife sliding under the policeman's collarbone. Feeling the throaty breath warm on his face, Jeff twisted the knife round and back.

The policeman slid to the ground, bright red sliding down his neck and into his shirt. Jeff gave him a couple of kicks to make sure he wouldn't get up again, then grabbed the bag and fled.

Outside, he turned left and walked towards the park. It was a pity he didn't have the car – had he left it at home? It was ghastly, not being able to remember things like that. He must be sickening for something. Home, as fast as ever he could.

2.20 p.m.

Caro

Caro struggled to open her eyes. Pain was everywhere and she felt so weak. She moaned.

Something was shaking her shoulder. 'Can you hear me, love?'

The world swam in front of her, then slid into half-focus. It was a policeman, oh thank God.

'My name's Dave. You're safe; we'll get you out of here now. I'll just get the paramedics in.'

He spoke into his radio and Caro closed her eyes again. A moment later she felt someone take her pulse and touch her head and leg, but she couldn't speak, couldn't even open her eyes. The blackness was taking control. They put something round her neck and she was lifted onto a stretcher. She wasn't alone now but she couldn't move; she could hardly breathe. They were taking her out of here and she was alive, but oh, that poor baby... They were going downstairs now and the air was deliciously fresh, and it was lighter, too, she could feel the sun on her face but the rest of her body was going numb; no, no. She didn't want to die.

2.20 p.m.

Julie

Julie clasped her hands under her chin. Sharon. Sharon and Craig should be here. The DCI was still on his radio, but a moment later he clicked it off and stepped towards her.

'Please – where are the baby's parents?' she said, trying to keep her voice steady.

DCI Brian McKenna was beckoning another officer over. 'They'll be here soon. Go around the back, Stevens, and get the boy out.'

Julie's mouth went dry. Something was going on and they weren't telling her.

There was a flurry of activity in the lane as the paramedics manoeuvred a stretcher towards the ambulance, depositing it on a trolley as soon as they were out of the square. Julie clapped her hands over her mouth. This must be Jeff Horne's wife. The woman's eyes were closed, and she was so pale she looked almost green.

'Broken wrist, head wound, and deep wounds to the left ankle, bleeding profusely,' the older paramedic said as they passed Brian McKenna. He and his colleague slid the trolley into the ambulance, and Julie choked back a sob.

'What kind of wounds?' asked the DCI grimly.

The paramedic looked back. 'She's been slashed, but I didn't dig around inside it. We have to get her to A&E ASAP. She's lost a lot of blood.'

He slammed the ambulance doors shut and ran round to the driving seat. The ambulance moved off, siren wailing as soon as it was clear of the scene.

Julie bit her lip. Jeff Horne had done all that.

Liam appeared at her side. 'I can go back to Alfie's now,' he said glumly.

Julie shivered. Had the danger passed, then? What was going on? But she shouldn't show Liam how afraid she was. 'That's best, until things get back to normal here. You did well today, Liam.'

She watched as a tall policeman led him away, then turned back to DCI McKenna.

'Will Sharon and–' she began, but she was interrupted. Footsteps thundered along the lane and the other policeman was back, clutching his radio.

'Horne's stabbed Max.'

2.20 p.m.

Sharon

'Go and lie down, Sharon. A rest will do you good.'

Sharon wiped round the kitchen work surface for the fourth time. Her body was on automatic pilot now. She was clearing the kitchen after dumping the almost untouched chicken and mushroom pie into the bin; the very smell of it made her feel sick. A sob welled up in her throat and she choked it back.

'I don't want to lie down. Julie'll be back soon.' She stared at Anita, wishing the other woman would leave them alone. She never usually stayed this long, and apart from the usual 'the team's investigating everything that comes in', she didn't seem to have anything to tell them.

Sharon went through to the sofa and reached for the remote, then chucked it into the corner of the sofa. With Anita here outstaying her welcome, there would be nothing new on TV, surely. So she, the baby's mother, could do nothing except sit in her luxurious, empty flat, fear twisting inside her. But at least she and Craig were speaking to each other, even if they didn't talk much because ordinary conversation had no place in their lives now.

Craig's mobile buzzed on the table and he grabbed it. Sharon's hands began to shake. Any phone call now could be the start of an even more horrific chapter in their lives, something so black she couldn't begin to think about it. If Jael... No, no, that simply mustn't be – and they would call Anita, first, wouldn't they?

It was Craig's mother, phoning for a progress report. Craig talked for a few minutes then rang off, promising to call back later.

Anita joined her on the sofa and Sharon lifted the remote again. Flipping through the channels meant she didn't have to talk. It occurred to her that Julie was very late. Oh, well, it didn't matter, nothing mattered really, except Jael. Anita's mobile rang while Sharon was still thinking about this, and she took it into the kitchen and closed the door. Sharon's stomach began an even more nauseating dance, and Craig sat staring at his hands, clasped as though he was praying.

The kitchen door opened. 'Sharon, Craig – we have to go. They've found Jael, but Jeff Horne's still got her and–'

'Where?' Sharon's voice was hoarse.

'Just off the High Street, at the entrance to Mortimer Square. They're working to get her back.'

'*Working* to get her back? What do you mean?' Craig's voice was belligerent.

'We'll know more when we get there. Quick, come on.' Anita put a hand under Sharon's elbow and pulled her to her feet.

Sharon stumbled into the hallway. Her baby was found, but she must still be in grave danger, or Anita wouldn't look so serious. She caught sight of herself in the hallway mirror as they passed – a crazy woman with long tousled hair and a white face.

Anita's car was at the side entrance to the flats, and they drove away to flashing cameras and reporters talking into their microphones. Sharon shielded her face with one hand, her stomach churning wildly and her breath coming in short pants. What were they going to find in the High Street?

A million questions were flitting through her mind, but they drove in silence through the traffic lights and past the internet café up to the middle of the High Street, where blue and white plastic tape had been stretched over the entire width of the road. Several police vehicles were behind the cordon, as well as a whole bunch of policemen. An ambulance further up the High Street was pulling away, and Sharon's stomach began to twist even more. What was the ambulance doing?

Anita parked beside a police car and Sharon stumbled out and ran towards DCI McKenna, who was in a huddle with a group of other officers.

'Tell me what's going on! Where's my baby?' A shrill voice that didn't sound like her at all.

Then she saw Julie, hunched on the ground at the side of the lane, her head between her hands. 'Julie, what's going on? Where's Jael?'

Julie lifted a tearstained face and choked back sobs. 'She was in a flat up there with Jeff Horne,' she whispered. 'Now Jeff has left with Jael and oh, Sharon, he stabbed Max. I don't even know if he's alive or not.'

Her head reeling, Sharon sank down beside Julie. For a moment she couldn't speak; her chest was so tight she could hardly breathe. They'd found her baby and lost her again. Black spots danced before her eyes. Craig, his face sheet white, strode over to DCI McKenna, and Sharon was glad he was taking the initiative now because she knew if she moved, if she even stood up, she would be sick. She breathed through pursed lips, concentrating on not passing out.

Craig returned with Anita and crouched to hug Sharon. 'You shouldn't sit on the ground, love.'

The FLO's face was grim. 'Let's wait in a car,' she said. 'Jeff Horne is still being followed. He still has the baby. Max is alive, but I don't know how badly he's hurt. They're taking him to hospital now.'

Julie sagged against Sharon, then pulled herself up. 'I'm going to him,' she said, grim determination in her voice.

Anita pointed to her car. 'Wait in there, Sharon. I'll get someone to take Julie to the hospital, and join you in a second.'

Sharon looked at Craig, lips pressed together and hands clasped under her chin. 'They'll get her back,' she whispered. 'They have to.' She allowed him to pull her to her feet, leaning against him and by some miracle managing not to vomit. Craig put his arms round her. She could feel his body shaking.

'Come on,' he said. 'Let's wait in a car like she said. It'll be more comfortable and more – private.'

Sharon stared at the crowds of people gawping at them from each end of the cordon. Vultures, just waiting for some excitement, wanting a cheap thrill at someone else's expense.

Jael's expense, and hers and Craig's and Julie's. How could people be so thoughtless?

Her baby was alone with Jeff Horne and she didn't know where. Sharon raised a fist to her mouth and bit down on her fingers. Please, let our girl be saved. When was the last time she'd been to church? Years ago. Maybe God didn't think she deserved to have a daughter. Maybe the opinion in heaven was that Jael would be much better off as an angel, and that Jeff Horne was just the person to turn her into one.

2.45 p.m.

Julie

Julie clutched the sides of her seat as the police car sped around the corner of the High Street and on towards the bridge. There was no sign of an ambulance in front of them, and she couldn't hear any other siren apart from their own. What did that mean? She clenched her teeth together to stop them chattering.

The car sped up the hospital driveway and jerked to a halt at the side of A&E. Julie jumped out and ran to the ambulance parked at the doors. Green-clad paramedics were unloading the trolley, it was Max, and his face looked like a shop window dummy. Unreal, plastic,

soulless... He had an oxygen mask over his nose and mouth so he must be breathing, but she couldn't see his chest rise and fall. Julie sobbed. A squad of medical staff were waiting by the door, and she ran beside the trolley as the paramedic listed Max's injuries – a stab wound, broken ribs, soft tissue injuries – what were they? He mentioned blood loss and GCS levels, but all Julie wanted was to touch Max. Then–

'He's arrested!' A doctor bent over the trolley, hands thudding up and down on Max's chest as different hands on Julie's shoulders pulled her to the side.

She stretched an arm out, but she couldn't touch him. 'Max! I'm here. You'll be okay, you will.' The trolley vanished through double doors.

'Wait here, love. I'll see what's happening.' The officer who'd brought her here patted her shoulder, then disappeared after the trolley.

Julie was left alone, realising she'd left her handbag with her phone in Liam's living room. There was no way for Sharon – or anyone else – to contact her now.

2.45 p.m.

Jeff

He'd made it and none of the other stupid policemen had even noticed him. Jeff fled through back courts and closes; they were like a little maze in the centre of town, up and down and in and out. Now all he had to do was get home, and it was a bit of a way from here.

He glanced right and left before crossing the road, his head clearing when he saw the taxi approach. Brilliant – he'd get a cab. He slapped his pocket and sure enough, his wallet was there, but he also noticed his hand was covered in the policeman's blood. He dodged into a doorway, and fished a couple of wipes from under the baby, sleeping peacefully in the bag. There! Clean again, and fortunately, his jacket was black so no bloodstains were noticeable. He could go in a taxi without worrying the driver might get suspicious.

Back at the main road, Jeff flagged down another cab and got into the back, tossing the bag in first. The baby gave a little squawk, and he winced. Mercifully, the taxi driver didn't appear to have heard her.

'19 Alton Gardens,' said Jeff, and the driver swung his cab into the traffic. The baby was silent as they drove, and Jeff relaxed.

He eased the zip of the bag open an inch or two, remembering his brother driving around with his eldest when he was a baby; it was the only way they could get him to sleep, he had said. They could do that with Miriam, too.

It was good to be going home again. He'd be able to relax there, and they would look after their baby and be happy, him and Caro, and... but where *was* Caro? Oh, well, he would take care of the baby until she got back. He rubbed the tightness above his forehead. Caro was hurt, he remembered now. She'd been bleeding, so maybe she was at the doctor. He should have gone with her – they'd gone together last time, hadn't they? Yes, to the hospital. And the doctor had said there would be no babies. That was when the headache had started – had that been his headache or Caro's? But he had a baby now, so the headache should be gone.

'Here you are, mate.' The taxi driver pulled up opposite the house.

Jeff handed over a note and got out. Home. He hadn't been here since... whenever.

'Don't forget your bag,' said the driver, and Jeff turned back. He gripped the sports bag and jogged across the street and up to his own front door.

There was something funny about the house, something not quite right. No Caro for one thing. And it looked all – wrong. As if he was back after being away for a long, long time. But he wasn't – was he? Jeff left the sports bag on the sofa and walked into the kitchen. A double espresso, that was what he needed.

The baby gave a bleat before he could switch on the coffee machine. Jeff turned back. Miriam. He lifted her into his arms and she whimpered, not quite crying but not peaceful either, and he sat down to think. Being at home helped, he could remember things better here.

Everything had gone wrong. Caro had left him; she'd gone away because she didn't want this baby. She wanted her own baby. Well, in that case, this was *his* baby. He would look after her and they'd be together forever. They would, they would.

The positive moment didn't last. Jeff rubbed his face with both hands. It wasn't only him and Miriam – someone else would come and spoil things, they always did. They would try to take the baby away from him, like that stupid policeman he'd stabbed in the close.

Jeff sat still as clarity, accompanied by painful brightness, swept through his mind. Oh no. He had stabbed a policeman. He wouldn't be allowed to keep the baby now. The fog swirled back. She was *his* baby, wasn't she? He wanted to be her daddy, he wanted Caro to be her mummy. A happy family. Yes?

Weariness crept through his head and into his eyes, turning everything black and white with fuzzy edges, like a jerky old film. Jeff ran his fingers through his hair, jumping in fright as a plop from the boiler in the hall cupboard sounded loud in the stillness of the house. He smiled as a wonderful idea struck him. There *was* a way he and Miriam could be together forever. It would be quiet and peaceful and no-one could interfere because no one knew where he was. And it would definitely be forever and ever. Amen.

The pellet gun. You could kill someone with a pellet gun, if you aimed carefully.

He would shoot the baby and then he would shoot himself.

2.55 p.m.

Sharon

There was a flurry of activity amongst the waiting policemen, and Sharon clutched Craig's arm.

'Something's happening. What are they doing?' Sweat ran down the side of her face and she wiped it away.

Several officers drove off in three cars, and another handful ran up the lane towards Mortimer Square. An evil-tasting bile rose in Sharon's throat, and she had to force herself not to hyperventilate. She would be sick if someone didn't tell her what was going on.

But oh, maybe she didn't want to know. Maybe in five seconds someone would come and say, *'I'm so sorry, Sharon. But it was quick. She wouldn't have felt a thing.'* Sharon's body shook with dry, heaving sobs.

'I'll go and ask Anita,' said Craig, opening the car door. His voice was brittle.

Sharon made herself look up. 'Wait, she's coming over.' Sure enough, DCI McKenna and Anita were jogging towards the car. They got in quickly, the FLO in the driving seat. She drove off down the High Street, through the cordon two officers were holding up for then, and down towards the traffic lights.

The DCI turned to Sharon and Craig. 'Jeff Horne has taken a taxi, but don't worry, we won't lose him,' he said grimly. 'By the looks of things, he's heading for his home. The experts in hostage situations are on the way there, and they'll negotiate with Jeff and get the baby out. The first priority is your daughter's safety.'

Sharon nodded, hope flaring inside her. Experts were here, things were being done, and she and Craig were part of it. Jael, baby, Mummy's coming.

A few minutes later they were driving along a pleasant street with red brick detached houses on either side. It was only a mile or so from their flat. Everything was deathly quiet, but Sharon was aware of faces at windows, and curtains twitching as they drove past. People had obviously been warned to stay indoors. How efficient the police were, getting all this organised so quickly.

Brian McKenna was speaking into his radio, but Sharon could barely understand the crackling static that formed half the conversation. Brian answered briefly then turned in his seat.

'So far, so good. Jeff Horne is in his home with the baby. We'll give him a minute or two, then the hostage boys will try to make contact. We're going to wait just around the corner.'

The car drew up behind a police car, and Anita switched off the engine. An uneasy silence fell, and Sharon could feel her heart thumping against her ribs. She took Craig's hand, startled to feel how cold her own was. He was afraid, she could tell, his mouth was a thin slash, and oh God, she was afraid too, she was terrified she wouldn't have the chance to mother this child she hadn't wanted. How crass that sounded, how uncaring. She did want her baby. More than anything in the world.

The DCI was speaking on the crackling radio again, and Sharon looked up and down the street they were parked on. It was a pretty little place, houses with gardens on both sides, and kids' bikes and footballs and other evidence of childhood were lying around. Suburbia.

New dread settled into Sharon's heart. They were back at the waiting game, and it was no easier now they knew where Jael was. Think what Jeff Horne had done to his wife and to Max. What could he do to a tiny baby?

Brian finished his conversation and turned to report to them. 'Everything's in place,' he said, and Sharon could tell he was speaking carefully. 'We've got cameras and police marksmen in various houses on the street so we can see a bit of what's going on in Horne's place. At the moment, Jael is on a sofa and Horne is sitting beside her. He has a gun. They'll wait until he puts it down before attempting to establish contact. Please be assured that our marksmen are ready to act any second *if* it becomes necessary.'

Sharon's mouth went dry. Her baby was in absolute, real danger. Craig was shaking beside her, and Sharon reached for his hand again but he pulled her close. They sat in silence, holding each other. Sharon's eyes were burning, but right at this moment she felt as if she would never cry again. All she was feeling now was ice-cold rage, anger against the man who was trying to destroy her life like this. She had never believed in the death penalty; she had always felt repulsed when a news report came in about yet another execution in America or in the East. But if Jeff Horne killed her baby, Sharon knew she would be capable of murdering him with her bare hands. And when she thought about how she'd felt when she first realised she was pregnant...

An ambulance drew up behind them and sat there, waiting. Sharon looked out of the back window and recognised one of the paramedics. He had taken her to hospital the day Jael was born. He was with a woman today.

Craig had seen them too. 'I could kill that bastard Horne.' He thumped his hand on the seat in front.

Anita turned to him. 'You need to stay calm, Craig,' she said, not unkindly. 'If you can't, I'll take you to wait at home.'

'No!' Sharon and Craig spoke together, and Sharon went on. 'We've had more than enough waiting around at home. At least here we're close to Jael, and as soon as anything happens we can be with her.'

Brian nodded. 'Okay. You must keep calm, though. We could be in for a long wait.'

Sharon leaned back, feeling her blouse stick to the seat. This helplessness was laming. She had waited and waited and waited already, and there was still no knowing when the wait would be over. I can't bear this, she thought to herself, at the same time knowing it was a useless thing to think. She had to bear it. She had no choice.

Chapter Twenty

Julie

The relatives' waiting room was as cheerless a place as Julie had ever been in. All she could see from the window were the high hospital buildings, grey and forbidding. An alien world. She stood there, looking out over the car park. The back of the maternity building was visible; how incredible to think that little more than a week ago she'd visited Sharon and Jael there. She'd sat beside Sharon's bed and joined in the excitement about Jael's birth. There was no sitting with the patient this time – she'd been told very firmly to wait in here. She didn't even know if Max was still alive. They were 'looking after him' somewhere out there.

The door opened and the policeman who had driven her here came in, carrying Julie's bag. 'They brought this. You left it in the boy's home.'

Julie clutched the bag to her chest. She had her phone back now, her lifeline to the outside world. 'Is there any news? They're not telling me anything.'

He shook his head. 'He'll be in theatre for a while yet, that's all I know. He was acting alone, accosting Jeff Horne – he said something to his partner about having to help the baby, and ran away from his post. It was a stupid, brave thing to do, and we're not sure why he did it. By the time his partner had radioed in and gone after him, it was too late.'

Julie wiped her face with one hand. She knew why Max had done it – he was trying to save Jael from the fate of his own unborn baby. 'Has his family – are they…'

'His parents are coming up from Dumfries, so it'll be an hour or two before they arrive. He doesn't have relatives in this area. I'll see you later, probably.'

Left alone, Julie went back to the window. At least there was something to watch outside, people moving about, hospital workers and visitors, going about their lives. If only she had a chance to have a life with Max. But she mustn't think too hard about that or she might break down, and she had to be strong for – shit! Sam!

Julie leapt to her feet, hands shaking as she scrabbled for her phone to see the time. Twenty past four – what a never-ending afternoon this was. Horrified, she opened her contacts, then stopped. Was she allowed to use her phone here? She would take it outside; a breath of fresh air would do her good. She stumbled along the corridor.

The air outside was muggy and hot rather than fresh, but at least it didn't smell of hospitals. Julie called Dee.

'Julie? Is everything okay?'

The sound of her friend's voice brought tears to Julie's eyes. 'No. Jeff Horne kidnapped Jael, practically killed his wife and stabbed Max. I'm at the hospital now and he's in theatre. I'll wait until his parents get here. Dee, can you collect Sam? He's at After School Club and they close at six.'

'No problem,' said Dee immediately. 'Do you want him to stay with me, or should I find someone else for him and come and wait with you?'

Julie closed her eyes. How good, how very good it would be to have Dee here. But could she do that to Sam? On the other hand, he would probably enjoy a play-date, and he didn't need to know anything about all this yet.

'I'll call Ben's mum and let you know,' she said.

Ben's mother was happy to take Sam when Julie told her about 'an injured friend', and offered to keep him overnight, too. Julie called Dee again, and then the childminder, who was less happy.

'I'm sorry about your friend, Julie, I'll keep her another hour or two, but I've had a full house here today and tomorrow's not going to be less busy.'

Frustration burned in Julie's throat. 'I've got no way of getting to her yet. Rona, please, I'm desperate. I'll make sure she's collected by eight at the latest. If I can't make it, my friend Dee-Cee Taylor will come – and I'll keep her at home tomorrow.' No matter what happened tonight, she would be in no fit state to work in the morning.

'OK, but no later than eight, please. See you soon.'

Julie disconnected and leaned against the building. Her legs were trembling, and she slapped them impatiently, regrets in their thousands swirling around in her head. They would be so good together, her and Max. Why hadn't she seen that straightaway? He had. Please, Max, be okay. Julie swallowed painfully, then shivered. Maybe a drink would help.

The main waiting area was busy and noisy. Julie fed coins into the drinks machine and punched a button, not caring what it was. A can of fizzy orange fell into the tray and she popped it open and sipped, the icy liquid soothing its way down her throat. She held the can against her forehead for a moment, feeling marginally better. The kids were sorted and Dee was coming, she could relax a little.

The relatives' room was occupied when she returned. A small, heavily pregnant woman with dyed blonde hair and red eyes was slumped on the baggy sofa, a scrunched-up tissue clutched in one hand. The lump came back into Julie's throat. This was how she felt too, except this woman had obviously had time to have a good cry.

The woman glanced up at Julie, then stared at the soggy tissue in her hand before stuffing it into her pocket. She rummaged in her bag then said, 'Oh, Christ,' in a strangled voice and wiped her face with the palm of one hand. Julie pulled out her own packet; she only had two tissues left.

'Here. One each,' she said, taking one tissue for herself and handing the other to the woman.

'Thanks. It's a real bugger, isn't it,' said the woman. It wasn't so much a question as a statement, and Julie nodded.

'Are you all right?' Julie asked, indicating the woman's bump. The baby must be due any time.

The woman caressed her swollen stomach, and for half a second her expression relaxed. 'Oh, we're fine,' she said bitterly. 'It's my poor sister that's not. She's in theatre because her madman of a husband practically slashed her foot off, as well as breaking her arm and braining her with something. And he's taken a baby – God knows what's going on there.' She scrubbed her face with the tissue.

Julie's throat had gone dry. She opened her mouth but no sound came, and she sipped the orange to give her chance to gather her senses. 'You're Jeff Horne's wife's sister,' she whispered.

The woman nodded, mopping up more tears. 'Rosie Glenn. Who are you – do you know anything about all this?'

'Julie Mayhew,' said Julie, moving to sit beside Rosie on the sofa. 'Jeff Horne stabbed my – Max. He's a policeman. I'm waiting in case he wakes up and needs a friendly face before his folks arrive.' Two tears welled up in her eyes and spilled over on to her cheeks. 'And it's my friend Sharon's baby Jeff's taken, but I don't know what's going on right now either. I left when they brought Max here.'

Rosie held out a hand. Julie took it and they sat in silence for a moment before the other woman spoke again. 'Is your friend hurt bad?'

Julie nodded. 'I don't even know if he's alive. He's up in theatre now.'

'Christ.' Rosie leaned back and massaged her bump. 'Well, love, no news is good news. Just hold on to that for the moment.'

Julie sipped her drink again. It was true, if Max died they would come and tell her. The longer no-one came, the more she could hope. She could be strong, couldn't she? But what, oh what was happening to Jael? Could Sharon still hope too?

'It's such a cruel thing to do, taking a baby,' she said, her voice breaking. 'Why did he do it?'

Rosie shrugged. 'He found out he couldn't have kids of his own,' she said, sniffing. 'But that's no excuse to take other people's babies or half-kill your wife. Or stab anyone. He must have gone nuts, and nobody noticed.'

She started to cry helplessly. Julie patted Rosie's shoulder, suddenly feeling angry. How many lives had Jeff Horne wrecked this week?

Rosie looked up, her face drawn. 'Is there any way to find out what's happening with the baby?' She clutched her own unborn child protectively.

Julie thought. She wanted to know more too, especially if it was good news. But then, if anything at all had happened, Sharon would have got in touch.

'I could text,' she said slowly. 'That wouldn't be so – so intrusive.' She pulled out her phone and typed in a quick message. *'Max in theatre, critical, any news yet?'*

She sent the message and replaced her phone in her bag. They sat in silence for a while, then a nurse appeared at the door. Julie's heart leapt into her throat, but it was Rosie the girl was looking at.

'Your sister's settled on a ward now. The surgery appears to have gone well; she should be fine eventually. You can come and see her, but no excitement.'

She patted Julie's shoulder on the way out. 'They're still in theatre,' she said in a low voice.

Julie nodded. 'Good luck,' she said to Rosie.

The other woman smiled grimly. 'Same to you.'

Silence fell deep and thick when the two women left the room, and Julie rocked back and forwards on the sofa. Max was still in theatre, so he was still alive. And again, there was nothing to do except wait.

4.10 p.m.

Jeff

The pellet gun was heavy in his hand. Funny, how much it weighed. Was it the metal? His hand was shaking too much to shoot at anyone, though, he'd have to rest first. He stumbled over and sank down beside the baby, leaning back in the sofa as an unaccustomed feeling of peace seeped into his head. A short rest and he'd be ready, and it was the right thing for them both. All their worries would be over, and whatever came afterwards couldn't possibly be as painful or confusing as what was happening now. A release, that's what it would be; a merciful release.

The new calmness was enticing, and for several moments he sat still, enjoying the sensation. Everything was going to be all right. He was in control again. Maybe he should leave Caro a note for when she came back from the doctor's? Then the appalled expression on her face the other day slid into his head; he'd opened the door of his and Miriam's room and there was Caro in the corridor, looking at him as if he was the devil himself. How bloody dare she look at him like that. No, no note for Caro, she would see for herself what had happened. Maybe it wouldn't even be Caro who found him. The police would be after him now, watching and waiting, thinking they were in control – but they wouldn't beat him.

Jeff sat up straight, laid the gun on the coffee table and went to the window. The street was deserted, but he could feel the eyes staring at him, taunting him from every direction. Their wait would soon be over.

The baby was grizzling on the sofa and Jeff grimaced. He wouldn't be sorry to get away from those sleepless nights. He circled his aching shoulders, then stretched his arms and legs before moving across to the kitchen doorway where the eyes wouldn't see him, collecting the gun on the way and looking around helplessly. It was time. Where should he sit – or should he stand? Did it matter? The baby was yowling in a thin, little voice now; he should do this quickly and put them both out of their misery.

Eyes fixed on the baby, he gripped the gun.

'Jeff! Can you hear me, Jeff?'

The voice came from outside, but it was speaking to him. Jeff froze, not daring to go back to the window, but after a moment he turned his head and noticed the blue van with the loudspeaker on the roof, parked a few yards down the road.

'Jeff, my name's Will and I want to help you. Don't worry – everything's going to be all right. I'll come a little nearer now, so you'll be able to see me, and then we'll be able to talk better.'

A figure wearing a bulky black jacket emerged from the blue van and walked slowly towards the house. Jolted into action, Jeff ran to check the front door was locked. It was, and he breathed a sigh of relief. No way was he going to let this Will interfere with his plans, because what he'd said was all lies. Nothing would ever be all right in this world, not for him or Miriam. Which was why they were going to depart for the next world. Together forever.

Moving to the side of the room, Jeff could see out to the street. Will was standing in the middle of the road, opposite the living room window. Jeff screwed his face up, trying to remember how much of the inside Will would be able to see. About four metres of grass separated the house and the pavement, so not everything in here would be visible from outside, surely. An idea struck, and he chuckled, then dropped to his front and commando-crawled across the floor to the front wall, where he gripped the hem of the dark brown curtain and pulled it across the window. And the other side. . . There! Now Mr Smarty-Pants-Will couldn't see a thing.

It was time. Gun in hand, Jeff stood sideways in the doorway – from here he could see the living room and the kitchen and the hallway and the stairs up to his bedroom. Home. He'd been happy here, once upon a time.

The baby was still on the sofa and for a long moment Jeff stood gazing down on her. She hadn't been long on this earth. Should he... him or the baby? Or both? If only his hand would stop shaking.

4.10 pm

Sharon

The car was full of thick, sticky silence. Sharon shifted in her seat, feeling the dampness of her cotton top against the backrest. The windows were all open, but there was still no air in here. A hot summer afternoon spent sitting in a police car, in fear of her baby's life – it couldn't get much worse. She leaned forward to see the dashboard clock. It was after four o'clock, hell, how much longer was this going to take? They'd been here for ages.

Anita turned and looked at her and Craig. 'Okay?' Her face was neutral in a grim way, and Sharon's heart began to beat faster again. Anita didn't know if they would get Jael back safe or not. Sharon could see it in her eyes. She and the DCI were being supportive, but neither was saying, *'Don't worry, it'll be all right,'* or any of the other platitudes Sharon was so desperate to hear.

'They'll be making a move any time now,' said the DCI steadily, and Sharon nodded, grateful at least for his honesty.

Craig was motionless in the seat beside Sharon, forearms resting on his thighs and his head drooping low. The set of his shoulders and jaw revealed the tension in his body, and his shirt was sticking to him too. But all they could do was let the experts get on with their job.

A loudspeaker crackled somewhere round the corner and Sharon held her breath. This was it. The start of the negotiations. She listened to Will's speech, and then silence.

'He'll walk to the house now and stand outside where Jeff can see him,' said Brian. 'Then he'll try to get him to talk.' He lifted his radio and spoke into it. 'Status?'

The radio crackled. 'Will's taking up position in front of the house,' said a voice. 'Nothing yet. *Shit*, Horne is pulling the curtains shut. I don't like this, Boss.'

Sharon held her breath, and silence resumed in the car, broken only by a vague hiss from Brian's radio. A wave of faintness broke over her. Jael, baby...

Will's voice came again. 'I'm here to help you, Jeff. Let's talk. We can work this out.'

Brian clicked his radio. 'Anything?'

Sharon held her breath. Her heart was thumping wildly and her fingers and lips were tingling. *You can do this, you're strong, you're in charge.* Except she had never felt so vulnerable.

'They're going in from the back, Boss.'

Sharon's gut cramped in terror but she pushed the pain away and wrenched the car door open. She had to go to her daughter; she couldn't–

'Stay in the car!' Anita spun round in her seat and grabbed Sharon's arm.

'Let them do their job, Sharon,' said Brian, not looking at her.

Craig pulled her back into the middle of the car and Sharon collapsed against him. This was the worst day, the worst time. Nothing would ever hurt her more than this.

Will was still speaking through his loudspeaker, but there was no way to know if Jeff was listening. Would they hear a shot from here?

More static. 'They're in the house, Boss.'

Sharon pushed Craig away and sat straight. An odd kind of stillness came over her, and she felt cold sweat on her back. Any second now...

But minutes passed with nothing but static. Minutes of her baby's life. Please God her baby still had a life. Will's loudspeaker voice spoke comforting sentences, and Sharon raged inside. Jeff Horne deserved no comfort.

More crackling. 'Boss. Horne's gone–'

Sharon's breath caught. Gone? What did 'gone' mean? Gone where? She was out of the car before she had time to think this time, staggering towards the corner, towards her child.

'Sharon! Wait!' Anita's voice was just behind her.

Brian McKenna grabbed her before she turned the corner. 'Stop!' He barked into his radio. 'Report?'

Sharon stood panting, straining to free her arm, but he wouldn't let go. Sobs were tearing from her chest, but the urgency in her head wasn't transmitting itself to her legs now.

'All secure, Boss.'

Still grasping her arm, Brian strode round the corner, and Sharon forced her legs to move. The two ambulances drove past and stopped in the middle of the road, and the paramedics vanished into a house. Jeff Horne's house.

Sharon twisted round to see if Craig was following. He was standing beside the car, leaning on the roof, his head low. Sharon turned to look where she was going; he would have to deal with his faintness alone. Her daughter was the important one now. Brian kept her arm in a tight grasp as they stopped beside a wooden garden gate, preventing her from running hell-for-leather into the house.

The front door was open wide, and moan rose in Sharon's throat as she looked into the hallway and saw the body of a man on the floor, his head covered with a green cloth. And dear God in heaven, was that blood spattered on the wall? *Whose blood?*

'My baby,' said Sharon, but her voice came out so weakly she could scarcely hear it herself.

And then they came. A green-clad paramedic carrying a bundle wrapped in silver foil. A tiny bundle.

'The baby's here. Come on, Mum, we have to go.'

It took a moment for his words to sink into the part of her brain that understood speech. The second paramedic took Sharon's free arm, and Brian let her go. She climbed into the back of the ambulance as the paramedics bent over the bundle, now on the trolley. There was an incubator behind them, too.

And now she could see her child. Sharon gave a cry, her hands hovering over her daughter but not daring to touch. There was dried blood on Jael's front, and her eyes were closed. She was breathing, but she looked as if she might break.

The paramedic was cutting the pink clothes away. 'It's okay – she hasn't been shot. He only shot himself. This blood isn't hers, but she's very shocked and dehydrated. We need to get to hospital quickly.'

'Will she be all right?' Sharon was crying now. Her baby was here, at last, at last, but so pale, and she didn't dare take her child in her arms and comfort her.

'We'll do everything we can. We'll be off as soon as we get this drip up.'

He worked quickly, and Sharon moved to his other side. She stretched out a finger to touch her baby, but oh, how cold the little hand felt.

Craig appeared beside the ambulance. 'Christ. Is she–?'

'Shocked and dehydrated,' said the paramedic briefly. He lifted Jael into the incubator and covered her with the foil.

The second paramedic jumped down beside Craig. 'You can come in the front, sir.'

Two minutes later they were off, Sharon strapped in a seat where she couldn't touch her daughter.

'She's breathing just fine,' said the paramedic as the siren started wailing and the ambulance picked up speed.

Sharon nodded. Her baby was alive, but no one was saying she was going to stay that way.

5.15 p.m.

Julie

'Would you like something to drink? A cup of tea, coffee?'

Julie shook her head. All she wanted was for someone to come and tell her that Max was out of danger. It was after five now, surely news would come soon? He'd been here for ages; they must know something.

Dee gave her shoulder a shake. 'I think you should, lovey. You didn't have any lunch, and you don't want to turn all weak and faint, do you? I'll get you something hot and you can try a few sips.'

Julie shrugged, then nodded. Dee was doing a fantastic job taking care of her, the least she could do was be cooperative about a cup of tea. 'Why didn't I just go out with him like a normal person, Dee? Why didn't I see how much he could mean to me before it was too late?'

Dee sat down again and put an arm round her. 'It was too much, too soon for you, wasn't it? I'm sure Max understood that. Please God you'll get another chance.'

Julie closed her eyes, picturing Max's face as he was wheeled away from her. 'He's really bad, Dee,' she said, her voice breaking.

Dee hugged her again. 'Just – hold on. Don't imagine the worst before it happens. Now let me get that tea.'

She went out into the main A&E area and Julie stood up rubbing her back. If Max made it, she would grab that second chance with both hands. There was nothing like a real horror scenario to show you what was important in your life and–

'Julie! Sharon and Craig Morrison are here and they've got the baby. I don't know if she's hurt.' Dee was standing in the doorway, her eyes bright with tears.

Julie leapt to her feet, but her legs gave way beneath her and she crouched on the floor. Dee rushed to her side and held her shaking body. For a moment, all Julie could do was sob on Dee's shoulder. The older woman patted her back, making no effort to stop the tears.

The A&E sister came in the open door, a mug of tea in each hand. She set the drinks on the table and put a firm hand under Julie's elbow.

'Come on, Mrs Mayhew – Julie. Sit down and drink this. They're examining the baby now, and then Mrs Morrison wants to see you. Drink your tea and calm down; you can't go anywhere like this. I'll go and find out for you how they're getting on up in theatre.'

Julie allowed herself to be settled back on her chair. She sipped the tea, which was stewed and sweet and disgusting, but it helped.

Ten minutes later the door opened again. Julie's heart began to race as the A&E sister sat down beside her. Was this the bad news? The sister took her hand and held it tightly.

'Julie, Max is out of theatre now. He's heavily sedated in ITU and I'm afraid you can't visit him tonight, but you can go up and see him through the window. He's critical but stable and the operation went well. He'll be in ITU until he can breathe himself again. Finish your tea, and someone will take you to see the Morrisons, and then on upstairs.' She patted Julie's shoulder and left.

Julie sat motionless, quite unable to speak. Max was alive. 'Critical but stable'. A piece of real hope.

A young nurse appeared a few minutes later to take them to where Jael was being treated.

Julie, her arm tucked firmly through Dee's, followed the nurse through the waiting area to a doorway with 'Paediatric Trauma' above it, the sign supported by Micky Mouse on one side and Donald Duck on the other.

The nurse held the door open. 'In you go, Julie. I'll come back in ten minutes and take you upstairs.'

'I'll wait for you here,' said Dee, sitting down on a wide window ledge in the corridor.

Julie went into the trauma room. There was space for four patients here, but only one bay was occupied. Craig and Sharon were standing on either side of an incubator, gazing down at the tiny, almost motionless form lying there.

'Julie!' Sharon ran over and hugged Julie, and immediately they were both in tears.

'How is she? What happened?' said Julie, allowing Sharon to lead her to the incubator.

Craig nodded at her. 'She's dehydrated. He didn't feed her properly,' he said soberly. 'She's lucky to be alive. He's dead, did you hear?'

'No,' said Julie, leaning on the incubator. Jael had a drip running into one foot and oxygen prongs looped into her nose.

Her eyes were half-closed and her little face was pale. Julie swallowed. Jeff had done this. But she didn't want to waste her thoughts on him. 'What happens now?'

Sharon sounded much calmer than Julie would have expected. 'They're taking her to a ward for monitoring overnight, but I can stay with her. They said she'll be okay in a day or two.'

Julie nodded. A happy end for Jael. 'How are you holding up, Sharon?'

Sharon dabbed her eyes. 'I've got another chance, Julie. I'll be with her all the way. And so will Craig.' She reached for Craig's hand and smiled at him across the incubator. He nodded, smiling back very faintly, a kind of peace that Julie hadn't seen in them before hovering between them.

Julie took a deep, shaky breath. 'They just told me that Max's operation went well,' she said, looking down on Jael again. Soon, she would be able to go home and sit cuddling her own baby again.

'Are you all right, Julie?' said Sharon, touching her arm.

Julie blinked. Hope was holding her together now, but hope was strong. 'I've got another chance too, haven't I?'

Epilogue

Two years later

Caro limped back to her desk, and turned the fan round to blow the muggy salesroom air towards her. Half an hour to home-time, and thank God for that. This summer was set to be the hottest since records began, according to the weatherman, and heat did her leg no good at all. She eased her left trainer off and sat massaging her ankle.

'Okay?' Louise looked round from the reception, and Caro nodded, grimacing.

She was lucky she still had an ankle to massage; it had been touch and go for a while. Most of the tendons round the joint had been severed, and the wounds Jeff inflicted on her had become infected. She'd had a drain in there for months and they'd operated twice to flush out the bugs. Now she was left with a tight, twisted scar, and nerve damage which meant she barely felt her foot. Some legacy Jeff had left her. She would give up his money in a flash, if it meant getting her health back, but that was an impossible dream. Bitterness rose sourly in Caro's throat – if she'd never gone to find that youth with the drugs, she wouldn't have met Liam and none of this would have happened to her. She knew now that the boy who'd died in the library was a different kid. It had all been for nothing.

Mr Simpson came through to reception with a dark-haired man and a small child, and Caro straightened up and pretended to be working. It wouldn't do for the new boss to catch her with her shoes off. Judging by the fawning expression, though, a sale had just been negotiated, so maybe he'd let them close shop a few minutes early. The little group stopped a few yards away to peer at some documents, and Caro stared blindly at the monitor in front of her – seeing other people with their kids still hurt. Everyone around her was popping babies like it was going out of fashion, but the dream of her own child seemed very far away. Rosie had four kids now, and Pete had remarried and was father to a little girl as well as Liam. And Louise was pregnant again…

The child, who looked about two, wandered towards the door. Her father strode after her and swept her up in his arms.

'Jael, sweetheart, stay with Daddy – we're nearly finished now.'

Caro's scalp prickled, and in spite of the heat, goose bumps rose on her arms. Jael. It wasn't a common name, and the age would be about right… Was this the baby she had clutched to her chest in that terrible room? She stared at the child, who was busy with her father's phone now, suddenly quite sure this must be 'her' Jael. The baby Jeff had stolen for her.

Mr Simpson and the man were shaking hands now, and the little girl waved as they crossed reception.

Louise waved back. 'Are you going home?' she said, in the special voice she used for small children.

The little girl nodded. 'Home. Mummy.' She beamed suddenly. 'Sam!'

Her father laughed. 'That's right – Sam and Amy are coming, and Julie and Max too. That'll be fun, won't it?'

Jael nodded, and Louise and the man grinned at each other while Caro concentrated on not passing out. Max – the policeman Jeff had stabbed was called Max. He'd been transferred to a specialist chest unit in Glasgow the day after her first operation. Rosie had spoken twice to his girlfriend, but Caro couldn't remember the name. What she'd never forget was the relief she'd felt when she heard the baby was going to be all right…

The door swung shut behind the pair, and Caro stood up to see out to the car park.

Jael's father lifted her into a silver Ford, and Caro caught a glimpse of a solemn little face as the car crawled towards the exit and vanished into the traffic.

'You two can get off now,' said Mr Simpson.

Letting Louise's chatter wash over her head, Caro gathered her things and went out into warm summer sunshine. *Her* baby had turned into a beautiful little girl.

For the moment, it was almost enough. Caro limped towards the bus stop.

Acknowledgements

Writing a book is a team effort, and I have an amazing team. Several teams, in fact.

The home team: love and thanks as always to my sons, Matthias and Pascal. Their help, advice and (usually) patience as I negotiate my way through the technological world of today is invaluable; they manage my website and advise me on everything from word documents to storing photographs and making business cards – I couldn't manage without them.

The family and friends teams: My 'teams' in Scotland, England and Switzerland are always there in the background, turning themselves into booksellers, flyer distributors and cheerleaders as required. As time goes on and families grow, I find I have doctors, nurses, teachers, police officers, and experts in many other fields to call upon – and I do! Special mentions here for Dad, Gordon and Calum for going above and beyond, and for everyone who helps with my book cards.

The book teams: huge thanks as always to Debi Alper, whose advice, criticism and encouragement is central to my writing; also to my new team at Bloodhound Books for giving *Baby Dear* such a fantastic cover as well as all the editorial help required. I'm excited to be working with you all!

Last but not least – the social media teams: there are so many people here I couldn't begin to mention you all, but you know who you are and I'm saying the most enormous THANK YOU. Very often it's the online friends, people I've never met in real life, who are first port of call when something goes wrong or advice and encouragement are needed. I hope I can give as much help as I get from you. Online 'friends' are real friends too.

70892935R00145

Made in the USA
Columbia, SC
16 May 2017